WITHOUT

To Janet
Hope you enjoy the book!.
Have a happy retirement!.!
Best wishes
Glenis Stott

WITHOUT

a novel

Glenis Stott

Matador
5 Weir Road
Kibworth Beauchamp
Leicester LE8 0LQ, UK
Tel: (+44) 116 279 2299
Fax: (+44) 116 279 2277
Email: books@troubador.co.uk
Web: www.troubador.co.uk/matador

ISBN 978 1848764 439

British Library Cataloguing in Publication Data.
A catalogue record for this book is available from the British Library.

Typeset in 11pt Sabon MT by Troubador Publishing Ltd, Leicester, UK

Matador is an imprint of Troubador Publishing Ltd

Printed in Great Britain by the MPG Books Group, Bodmin and King's Lynn

For Catherine

1

Here are today's headlines on Radio North West – The Landfill Excavation workforce was honoured by a visit from the Prime Minister today. 'You people are heroes,' he told them ...

I'd only intended to put my feet up for ten minutes but when I looked at the clock it was ten past three. I was going to be late. Again. I slipped on my shoes and left the house, being careful to lock the door behind me. The sun was very bright and I could hear the birds singing. It became noisier when I turned the corner. There was a crowd of women and children heading towards me and it seemed as if all the children were talking at once. Some mothers listened, others were too busy chatting to their friends.

Rose, my next door neighbour, was almost directly in front of me before I saw her. Her hair was all over the place and her face was flushed but at least *she* had been on time to collect Gareth. She was clinging tightly to his hand; he was inclined to run away from her.

1

'Oh God, Celia, you've done it again.'

'Tell me about it.'

When I reached the school, the guard looked at his watch and then back at me. I took my passbook from my bag and held it out towards him. He didn't check it. They never checked in the afternoon. It was only in the mornings when security was tight. He waved me on with his rifle.

The children looked small in the middle of the empty playground. Mrs Kenton was looking out of the classroom window anxiously. She frowned and shook her finger in reprimand when she spotted me, but then relaxed and smiled. It was going to be alright. No report.

Sevvy held up his hand as I approached.

'Mummy, I fell and hurt my finger. Look.'

I looked. Not a mark on it. I smothered it in loud smacking kisses until he giggled. He was three and had been at nursery for three months. He loved it but liked a bit of attention when he came out.

Jasmine pulled at my arm. She had a painting for me to admire. Pointing with her finger, she told me, 'That's Mrs Kenton and this is Gareth and that's me. We're doing sums.'

'That's lovely, sweetheart,' I said but the guard was watching us from his booth and I realised I needed to take the children out of the yard. I held their hands as we walked past him through the gate; I kept my head down so I didn't look directly in his eyes, in the same way you don't challenge a dog.

The streets were quiet. Apart from the mothers already at home with their children, everyone was at work. There was no reason for anyone to be out at that time and I felt as tiny and vulnerable as the children looked in the playground.

'You're hurting, Mummy,' said Jasmine and I loosened my grip slightly.

'Sorry.'

As soon as we closed the front door behind us, Sevvy shouted, 'I'm thirsty,' and dashed into the kitchen.

'Me too,' said Jasmine and followed him, dropping her bag on the floor as she did so.

I picked it up and went into the kitchen. Sevvy had pulled a chair up to the sink and was pouring squash into a glass, too much squash.

'Let me do it.'

Jasmine took the bottle from him and shared the cordial between two glasses.

'I'm doing the water, Jasmine. Let me do the water.'

Sevvy turned on the tap and filled first one and then the other glass with water, right up to the brim.

'Sit down,' I said and emptied some blackcurrant out so it didn't spill. There was the sound of scraping chairs behind me. I handed them their drinks and a biscuit and began preparing the evening's casserole. I suddenly realised Sevvy was standing beside me and looked down into his grinning face. The blackcurrant had extended his smile up his cheeks almost to his eyes.

'Can I play in the garden?'

I nodded and opened the back door for him. Jasmine disappeared up to her room to play with her new doll, the one that had arrived the day before. It was a tatty old thing but she loved it. She'd called her Angela.

I'd had a doll called Angela when I was about Jasmine's age. It was the one they let me keep after the Upheaval. One day a man had arrived at the door with a list of the essentials for a family of two adults and one child: four large plates, four small plates, three egg cups, etc. It said on the list that I was allowed one doll, one story book, one jigsaw puzzle, a box of crayons and a colouring book. I had a lot more things than that and it broke my heart to see this stranger carrying my toy box out of the house and putting it on the back of the cart.

When the casserole was in the oven, I made myself fennel tea and went out to sit on the back door step to drink it. It was the warmest spot in the garden; it could be cool in the rest of the garden because the high walls blocked out most of the sun. There were chopping noises from next door and I smiled at the idea of Rose doing out exactly the same actions as I had. Sometimes I imagined all the mothers doing the same things at the same time, all in a long row. Like in some mirrors I saw in a fairground when I was a child where a row of ever smaller Celias stretched out into infinity.

Sevvy was playing Delivery/Collection Man. Robin had made him a trolley from some old wood from the back of the shed. Sevvy filled the trolley with leaves, stones and some of his toy figures, then pulled it around the garden, depositing various items at certain points. He had a piece of paper covered in his scrawled version of writing to act as his delivery list. Consulting it at each stop, he'd scratch his head and mutter, 'Now, what do these people need?' He left something in each place: a leaf and a large stone at the rhododendrons, a yellow toy bus at the back of the shed, three small stones at my feet. Then he made the return journey, picking everything up and putting it back into the trolley. It was a game he played for hours at a time.

In the distance, I could hear the high pitched whine of the first of the work buses. I watched Sevvy's face. No reaction.

4

It was only at the third noise that he stood still and listened.

'Daddy's coming.'

He was always right, although I don't know how. He instinctively knew that Recycling Bus 3 was about to drop off all the workers in our street. I followed him through the house.

We stood at the front door, watching as the bus pulled up at the end of the block. Rose's husband was first off. He hurried down the street, head down, ignored Sevvy's 'Hello, Uncle Charlie,' and entered his house, slamming the door behind him as soon as he was inside.

Robin was the last. He was a talker and didn't always realise he was home. Like everyone else, he was dressed in green overalls with *Recycling* written across the back. He was very good at his job and liked to fix things at home too. We hardly ever had to send anything back. That was where we met, at the Recycling Centre. I worked in *Allocations* until Jasmine was born. I really liked my job but, unless they changed the regulations, I wouldn't be able to go back until Sevvy was twelve.

Sevvy couldn't wait until Robin reached the house; he was out of the gate and running down the street shouting 'Daddy, Daddy.' Robin picked him up and spun him around before heading towards me, his face grinning as it always did when he arrived home.

Jasmine was still in her bedroom. Robin and Sevvy headed up the stairs to find her while I set the table for tea.

Later, when the children were in bed, Robin and I settled down to listen to the radio. There was a chat show, then the news and, about nine thirty, there was a documentary about a huge water wheel in Birmingham. It wasn't my sort of thing and I headed upstairs to bed.

Some time later I was awoken by a loud knock at the front door. I heard the murmur of voices as Robin let someone in. My heart beat faster. The lack of street lighting after nine meant people rarely ventured out at night. I slipped out onto the landing and shouted Robin's name, as loudly as I could without risking waking the children. He came to the bottom of the stairs.

'Don't worry,' he said, 'It's only Charlie. He wants to talk about a work problem.'

I went back to bed and was soon in a deep sleep.

Robin's, 'Celia, are you asleep?' made me jump. He slid into bed beside me.

'What did Charlie want?' I asked, my voice slurred.

'He's been fired,' he answered.

I sat up straight in bed. 'Oh no, what happened?'

'Do you remember when Jasmine learnt about personal cars at school?'

'Yes, we were days hearing about how wasteful and selfish they were.' I smiled at the thought of Jasmine's lecturing voice.

'Well, that's not how Gareth saw it. He was fascinated. Kept going on about how he wished he could have a car of his own. He drew pictures and stuck them on his bedroom wall. Made a cardboard cut-out and ran it along the floor making engine noises.'

I pushed myself backwards and leant against the headboard, watching Robin's serious face as he talked.

'Anyway,' he said, putting his arm around my shoulder, 'One day a toy personal car came in for recycling. God knows how it had survived so long; I thought they'd destroyed them all in the early days. When Charlie saw it, he knew that Gareth would love it. It was red and had a white stripe painted down the side. Most of the paint was still shiny and there was only one wheel missing. He pushed it into a drawer and over a couple of weeks he buffed up the paintwork and made a new wheel. Then he smuggled it home.'

'I bet Gareth was thrilled.'

'He was. He spent all his time playing with it. Charlie warned and warned him not to tell anyone but one day it slipped out when he was talking to one of the other children. Miss Lewis was listening. She reported Charlie. That's why he was fired. Mr Derwent took him into the office last thing this afternoon and told him not to come back. Stealing is a sackable offence.'

'What are they going to do?'

'That's why he came round tonight. He wanted to know if it was worth going back in tomorrow and pleading for his job.'

'What did you say?'

'I said he could try but I don't think they'll listen. I'm not even sure if they'll let him on the bus in the morning.'

I cried. It wasn't just that I was upset about Charlie, Rose and Gareth but it really hit home how precarious our lives were, how one tiny thing could knock us out of normality and into the unknown. Robin stroked the side of my face.

'Don't get upset, there's nothing we can do about it. We'll just have to hope that Charlie can persuade them to give him his job back or finds another way around it.'

'But what if he doesn't?'

'Then it's out of our hands. We can't help. You're not to get involved. Do you hear me?'

I nodded, knowing he was right.

'Come on, let's get some sleep. It's late.'

He pulled me down under the covers and turned out the

light. We lay like spoons in the dark. I was warm and safe but I kept imagining Rose and Charlie and Gareth out on the street with nothing and I couldn't get to sleep. It was a long night.

2

… and now for the weather. It should be cooler today but there's still no sign of rain …

The following morning I was distracted as I got the children ready for school. Jasmine had to ask me twice to help her find her reading book, *The Wind is my Friend*. It was on the lounge window sill. As I reached to pick it up, I saw the works bus arriving out of the corner of my eye. I turned to watch. The driver checked his list and let everyone on but Charlie. Charlie's posture was dejected as he watched the bus draw away. He waited a couple of minutes then turned and walked in the same direction. It looked as though he was going to walk to the Recycling depot. It was a long way, about three miles. Not the sort of distance people walked back then.

Eventually we were ready and we made our way to school. There was the usual group of mothers around me as the children raced ahead but I didn't join in the conversation. I wasn't in the mood. In the queue at the gate, Jasmine and Sevvy seemed to sense my tension and didn't try to talk to me. Toni Holme and her two children went through the checkpoint before us. Then it was our turn to hand our passbooks over. As the guard carefully compared our photos with our faces, I thought I heard Gareth's voice behind us but I dismissed it; Rose wouldn't risk bringing him into school.

As we went into the school yard to wait for the bell, Jasmine ran off to talk to her friend, Christie. Sevvy stayed by my side; his friends only attended in the afternoon.

Suddenly I heard a commotion at the gate.

'No, it can't be right.'

Rose's voice. I turned to look. She was arguing with the grim-faced guard, one hand waving their passbooks, the other clinging on to Gareth who was signalling eagerly to his friends.

The soldier put his rifle across in front of Gareth to bar his way and said, very loudly, 'This child is no longer entitled to use these school facilities.'

His words made me angry inside. What right did he have to stop a child going into school? I wanted to grab the soldier by the arm, twist it up his back and force him away from the schoolyard. There shouldn't be weapons and children in the same space. I wanted to take the rifle and smash it to pieces. I wanted to make everything right for Rose and Gareth but I knew nothing I could do would make any difference. I stayed where I was.

There was a shout from the Guard. Gareth had pushed his way under the rifle and was running towards the group of children where Jasmine was. Everyone else froze. The guard grappled with his gun to regain a proper hold. I was afraid he was going to point it at Gareth but he held it loosely against him, his hands well away from the trigger.

'Stop,' the Guard yelled, 'stop now.'

'Gareth, stand still,' Rose shouted.

Gareth's abrupt stop made him fall forward onto his face and he let out a huge yell. Several mothers, including me, moved forward towards the crying child.

'Stop,' the Guard yelled again. 'Nobody touch that child.'

Everything seemed to slow down. I turned my eyes away from Gareth to the Guard. He was sliding his hands along the rifle to hold it properly. He seemed to be about to point it in our direction but then he tilted it upwards and fired it in the air.

I was so scared. There was a sharp smell in the air, reminiscent of smoke but with a bitter edge. It was in my nose, it was in my throat, it was in my hair. I put my hand down on top of Sevvy's head to check he was still there and then twisted towards Jasmine to make sure she hadn't been hurt. Her face was white and creased with anxiety but physically she seemed fine. Still, I couldn't hold the children's hands. I couldn't get them away from the danger. I hoped they had the sense to stay still.

'Right. Everyone stay where they are. Now, you,' he swung the rifle towards Rose, 'you go and get your son and take him away from here.'

He followed Rose's progress with the point of his gun as she walked towards Gareth.

Rose knelt and bent over Gareth, her hand on the side of his face. There was a trickle of blood running down from his forehead and both his legs were badly grazed. She lifted him to his feet but when he tried to walk he limped so she picked him up and held him against her, in the same way you hold a baby. After whispering in his ear, she turned and made her way back to the gate. The guard flattened himself against the wall, as if to reassure Rose that she was safe if she did as he had told her. She turned her head towards him for an instant and then left.

As soon as she was gone, one of the teachers came out of the school and called the children inside.

Along with the rest of the mothers, I left the school yard. The Guard was leaning against the wall, looking pale and shaken. It had been more than a decade since they'd placed armed Guards at the entrance to public resources but it was very rare that anything happened. Usually just a word from a Guard was enough to make someone do as they were told but we'd all heard reports on the radio and been told tales about what they could do.

At the corner, out of the sight of the Guard, a group had gathered.

'That's Celia,' I heard Toni say, 'she lives next door to Rose.'

They all turned to look at me.

'What's she done?'

I shook my head. I didn't want to get involved in their gossip and, anyway, I could see Rose turning a corner in the distance and I wanted to catch up with her. See if I could help.

'I don't know anything,' I said and, grabbing Sevvy's hand, began to hurry towards Rose.

'Why was the Guard cross?' he asked, breathlessly.

'I don't know,' I said; I didn't want to explain it all to him.

I was walking too fast for Sevvy and he stumbled so I pulled him up by his arm and carried on; he had to run to keep up. At last I drew level with Rose

'How is he, Rose, how is he?'

'He's all right as far as I can see. Don't like the look of the cut on his forehead though.'

Gareth had been crying; his tears had washed away

patches of the dirt left on his cheek from the playground. There were tiny stones clinging to his chin and to his knees.

Rose's breathing was laboured; the street was steep and we had to slow our pace.

'Do you want me to take him?' I asked.

'He's, huh, never leaving my arms, huh, again.'

I could feel her tension pressing against my arm and wanted to comfort her. I wanted to stroke her back, make her relax. I wanted to say something, anything, that would make it better but there were no words. No words at all.

It was almost silent as we walked. The birds seemed to have stopped singing and all I could hear was the flap of an old *Need not Want* poster against the Community Centre wall. The sun had gone behind a cloud and it seemed completely dark, so dark that I didn't watch where I was going and bumped into Rose as she turned into our street.

At Rose's door, she tried to push down the handle with her elbow but she couldn't. I reached out to open it for her.

'Key,' she muttered, lifting her elbow.

'What?'

'Key, in my pocket. Open the door.'

I fished in her pocket for the key and unlocked the door.

Inside she laid Gareth on the sofa and once more stroked his face.

'Poor baby,' she said, 'my poor little Gareth.'

She looked up at me.

'It's my fault. All my fault. I shouldn't have taken him to school. I should have kept him at home with me. I knew he wouldn't be allowed in. I just hoped ...'

She looked back down at him.

'I'd better clean his wounds up.'

She was turning towards the kitchen as I asked, 'Do you think a doctor should check out that head injury?'

She looked at me with a sadness so deep I could only imagine plumbing its surface.

'They won't help, Celia, I know they won't. If he can't go to school, they won't let him have a doctor.'

'But we have to try,' I replied and, taking Sevvy's hand, I walked outside to the telephone box in the middle of the street. Inside the box, I lifted the receiver and pressed the Medical button.

'Medical. How can I help?'

'This is Celia Travis, Recycling Street 3. I'm calling about my neighbour's child, Gareth Morris.'

There was a pause and I heard the tapping of computer keys.

'Gareth Morris is not entitled to medical help at this time.'

'But he's had a bad fall and he has a head injury.'

'I'm sorry. Gareth Morris is not entitled to medical help.'

I was feeling angry.

'But he's got a head injury. What if he has a concussion? Or brain damage? What are we supposed to do? This isn't right, it isn't fair. He's a little boy and he needs help. How can you refuse to help?'

'Gareth Morris has been removed from the register.' Her voice was angry, 'He has therefore lost his right to any services. There are rules and we have to abide by them. If we don't ...'

'But ...'

'I'm ending this call now.'

There was a click and she was gone, leaving me clenching my fists and feeling like I needed to hit someone.

Back at Rose's, she had dressed the cut on Gareth's forehead with a piece of towel and tape. Some of Gareth's colour was back and he was asking for a drink. I went into the kitchen, filled a cup with water and returned. Rose had taken him on her knee and was rocking him backwards and forwards. She stopped rocking and took the cup from me to hold it to Gareth's lips. Then she looked up at me.

'Celia, you'd better go. You're probably in trouble already. Don't make it any worse.'

'I can't go,' I said, 'I don't want to leave you alone. You must be so worried.'

'It'll be alright, Charlie's gone into work to sort it all out. You know him; he can charm the birds off the trees. I'll get the doctor to look at Gareth tomorrow, just to check there's no permanent damage.'

I wasn't convinced she believed what she was saying. I hesitated but realised she was going to find out soon enough.

'Er, they didn't let Charlie on the bus this morning. It looked like he set off walking.'

She lifted a hand to her face. There was a pale imprint of her hand on Gareth's skin where she'd been holding him. Her eyes filled with tears and her lip trembled. Then she visibly gathered together all her courage and said, 'It'll be okay.'

She nodded, very firmly. 'He'll get there under his own steam. Talk to the boss and sort it out. Everything will be fine. All back to normal tomorrow.'

She pulled Gareth towards her and looked down into his eyes. 'Won't it, sunshine?' He echoed her smile and then closed his eyes.

Rose stood up, still holding Gareth tightly to her.

'He's worn out, poor thing. I'll put him to bed for a nap.'

She turned to me.

'Thanks for all your help, Celia, but I really think you should go now. I'll talk to you tomorrow. In the school yard.'

She walked to the door and I opened it for her. She said goodbye and then made her way up the stairs with a slow but firm step. I went back into the lounge for Sevvy. I hadn't really been paying attention to him and for the first time I realised how distressed he was. He was curled up in a corner sucking his thumb.

'Come on, Sevvy. Let's go back home for a drink and a biscuit. An iced one.'

Sevvy managed a weak smile and came over to take my hand. Out on the street Joe, the Delivery/Collection man, was emptying Rose's locker, the tall grey metal cupboard that stood at the front of every house.

I picked up Sevvy so he could pat the horse. Out of the corner of my eye I watched Joe go over to his cart and put the things in the back. Then, as Sevvy leant forward to put his arms round the horse's neck, Joe checked his list. He shook his head and walked back to Rose's locker to close it. Taking a red sticker from his pocket, he attached it over the lock. I knew what it said without looking; I'd seen them before – *Discontinued*.

'That's a shame,' he said to me, 'They were a lovely family,' and moved on to the next house.

Sevvy helped me empty our locker and, between us, we carried the bags into the kitchen and put them on the table. I put the food in the cold box and fastened that night's recipe, *Home Made Pizza*, on the door with a smiley face magnet. I'd had so many copies of the pizza recipe over the years that I could recognise them. I could have drawn the scribble in the corner of that particular copy in my sleep. Couples who worked were given ready made meals to heat up but we mothers at home were given recipes and ingredients so we could make them ourselves.

I put the vinegar and lemon juice under the sink with the rest of the cleaning materials then made Sevvy his drink and handed him his biscuit. He sat at the table and watched me open the other two packets. The first contained three teaspoons.

'Oh look, Sevvy, spoons.'

I clicked two together, like castanets, to make him laugh. I tried to get him up from the table to dance with me but he stiffened his body and wouldn't move.

'Well, I'm going to dance even if you won't,' I told him and I whirled round the kitchen making music with my new spoons, hitting them against each other and against my thigh. He gave a subdued laugh and, pleased with my success, I pretended they were puppets, waving one in the air.

'Hello, Sevvy, my name's Sammy Spoon.'

Sevvy turned his head away and I put the spoons in the drawer. I was really grateful to have them; we'd got down to one. Central allocation of goods might be resource-efficient but it's no good when you want to make a cup of tea and your only teaspoon has been stolen by Sevvy to dig in the garden.

The other packet held a blue sweater for Sevvy.

'Oh boy, look at this,' I said, 'It's got stripes and everything. Feel how soft it is.' I brushed it against his cheek and he took it from me.

'Come on, let's try it on.'

'No.'

'Come on Sevvy, let's see if it fits.'

I tried to pull off his other sweater but he pinned his arms down by his side.

'No, don't want to,' he said and slid down from his chair.

'Do it later,' he told me and walked out of the kitchen.

It wasn't the day to be strict and I left him to it.

I put the two empty packets together on the worktop ready to take out to the locker on the way to nursery. Then I made myself a cup of fennel tea and followed Sevvy into the lounge. He was curled up in the big armchair, the new sweater held against his cheek, his thumb in his mouth and his eyes closed.

When he heard me sit down, one eye opened and he muttered, 'sleep' before closing the eye again.

Sometimes I wished I could go to sleep like that and make everything go away for a while. But it wouldn't go away. The morning played through my mind on an endless loop. Charlie not being able to go to work. Gareth not being able to go to school. Rose not being able to care for her son in the way she wanted to. What if they lost their home?

Then there was a worse thought. What if it happened to us? What if we did something wrong and we were cut off from everything? I could feel myself beginning to panic and I started to cry. I convinced myself that having a gun pointed at me earlier in the day had unsettled my nerves. I went up to the bathroom to wash my face, taking deep, calming, breaths as I did so.

When I came back down again, it was time for me to make the lunch. They'd sent three eggs and five slices of bread. It would have to be boiled egg and soldiers. I set the eggs to boil and put the bread under the grill. The egg cups always made me smile. We'd built up a very strange selection. One had a picture of a purple dinosaur with *Barney* written underneath. That was Sevvy's favourite. One was head-shaped; it was a woman; *Margaret Thatcher* according to the maker's information. She had a very big nose. The third was a garish orange and purple plastic. Horrible thing. The one I left in the cupboard was fragile and seemed very old; it had delicate flowers painted on it. I tried not to use it because I didn't want to break it. I liked to look at it and think about how it came from a very different time.

When lunch was ready I woke Sevvy. He seemed happier. Perhaps he'd forgotten what happened. He dipped his soldier in the egg and moved it towards his mouth then stopped halfway.

'I've got a new friend at nursery.'

'Eat your lunch properly, Sevvy, you're dripping egg.'

I watched as he shuffled his bottom on the chair so he was nearer to the table.

'She's called Hannah.'

He nodded.

'Her daddy's a jinnier.'

'A jinnier?'

I dipped my toast into the egg.

'Oh, an engineer you mean.'

'A jinnier, that's what I said.'

I'd seen someone new in the playground who must have been Hannah's mother. I'd have to look out for her and say hello.

After lunch I changed Sevvy's sweater, bundled him into his coat and took him to nursery. As we approached, Sevvy let go of my hand and clung on to my leg with both arms. It made it difficult to walk.

'Don't want to go,' he whined, 'let's go back home.'

'It's more fun at school. You can play with Hannah and Watson.'

'Don't want to.'

'Come on, it's Lego day today.' I said, trying to make my

19

voice animated.

He almost fell for it, but then he saw the guard's box and held back again. I dragged him over to the gate. It was a new guard and his rifle wasn't in sight. He checked our passbooks carefully and ran his finger down the list until he found our name. Then he waved us through. Sevvy hesitated and looked up into the guard's face. The guard smiled. A small smile but a real one. Sevvy ran off towards the school door and I followed him to check that Miss Fontaine met him.

Agnes, the Guardian, was just leaving Rose's house as I put the key in the lock of the front door.

'I'd like to talk to you, Celia.'

It crossed my mind that I didn't want to talk to her but there were situations where there was no choice and this was one of them. I led her into the house and took her into the lounge, pointing to the sofa for her to sit down. She stayed standing.

'Fennel or dandelion tea?' I asked.

'Dandelion would be nice.'

She followed me through into the kitchen and I turned the kettle on. The eggcups and plates were still on the table. I picked them up and took them over to the sink.

'Didn't have time to wash them before taking Sevvy to nursery,' I said.

'I understand. Busy mother with a young son. Sometimes things have to wait.'

I didn't like her being in my kitchen and she certainly didn't look like she belonged there. She was too rigid somehow, her grey hair pulled tight back from her face, her white blouse unnaturally white, her black skirt pressed until the life had been taken out of it.

When the tea was ready, we went back into the lounge.

As soon as we sat down, she said, 'I presume you know why I'm here?'

'Because of this morning?'

'That's right. You involved yourself in something that wasn't your business.'

'But Gareth was hurt and I wanted to do something for him. That's why I called the Medical Service. I never thought they'd refuse'

She put down her cup and rested her hands on her knees.

'Of course they refused, Celia. Charlie Morris has acted inappropriately and lost his job. In doing so, he lost his right to all the benefits that working brings for both himself and his family. You know that. We all know that. And neither the decision to refuse help nor its repercussions are anything to do with you.'

She looked at me as though I should nod and agree with her. I was feeling extremely angry; both with the situation and her sanctimonious face. I slid my hands under my knees so I didn't get too carried away.

'All he did was to bring home a toy car for his son to play with.'

'Are you condoning theft now?'

'No, but …'

She leant forward. Her face was angry but it was more than that. Her face was the face of authority and we both knew I couldn't argue with her. Whatever I said, she didn't need to listen. But, whatever she said, I had to hear, or pretend to hear. Everything that dictated our way of life was represented by that woman. With a wave of her hand, she could take away everything I had.

She pointed a finger at me.

21

'Listen. We both know that we live in a world where resources are short. We are lucky. We are given everything we need. Agree?'

I nodded.

'But there's a price to pay. There are rules to follow. Strict rules. And if those rules aren't followed then the transgressors lose their rights.'

I bit my lip.

'But this morning it went too far,' I said, 'this morning a child wasn't allowed to go into school. This morning there was a Guard waving around a rifle in a playground full of children. This morning medical help was refused to an injured child. None of that can be right, surely?'

'The recent events were unfortunate.'

'Unfortunate?' I shouted, 'It's more than unfortunate; it …'

'Steps will be taken to restrict the use of guns around children. But we're straying from the point.'

She picked up her tea and took a sip.

I looked straight in her eyes, 'And the point is?'

'The point is that you need to think before you act in the future. Don't intervene in situations where the authorities have been forced to take action against a particular family. We'll let you off this time but this morning's events have been written on your record and I advise you …'

She took another sip of tea.

'I strongly advise you to take more care in the future.'

3

Preparations are under way for tomorrow's official opening of the new Parliament building in Birmingham ...

Sunday. Robin had gone to work and we had a long, lazy day ahead of us. A day when we didn't *have* to do anything or go anywhere.

It had been a hard week. Both children were very unsettled after Tuesday's events and they were very distressed about what had happened with Gareth. The previous night had been the first night they both slept through without nightmares.

I'd found the week difficult too. Agnes, the Guardian, had returned with two Guards and I'd seen Rose and Charlie, carrying Gareth, walk past the window. I wanted to run out and say goodbye but I didn't dare. Rose had been a good friend to me. We often walked to and from school together and on Sundays we'd spend the day at her house or mine.

I didn't know where they'd gone. I'd heard of rehabilitation centres where you stayed until you were judged ready to rejoin society but I didn't know much about it. It wasn't really discussed. I knew, though, that they wouldn't be back. Once a family was moved from their home, they weren't allowed to return.

I had a great plan for the day. Sitting in the garden while the children played a game of keeping quiet. The sun hadn't reached into our garden yet but it was warm and I'd already smothered myself and the children in sunscreen. I put a cushion on the back doorstep and sat down with a happy sigh.

'Can we go and see Gareth?'

Sevvy was standing by my side; he obviously didn't share in my plan for the day.

'No,' I said, 'we won't be seeing Gareth any more.'

'Never, ever, ever?' asked Sevvy, his eyes full of tears.

'No, Gareth and Rose and Charlie have had to go away and they won't be coming back.'

Sevvy started to cry. I took him by the hand and led him into the kitchen. Jasmine was at the table with her new doll in front of her. She watched hopefully as I pulled the biscuit barrel down from the high shelf which protects it from prying hands.

'Do you want a magic biscuit, Sevvy?'

He nodded his head up and down firmly and I handed him a biscuit.

Jasmine left the doll and came to stand beside me. I gave her a biscuit and she turned it over in her hand.

'Why's it magic?' she whispered.

'Because it stops Sevvy from crying,' I whispered back.

She smiled the smile that meant she was thinking about something else at the same time. She put her hand on the back of my neck and pulled my head down so it was level with her mouth.

'I know something else that's magic,' she told me, 'what about a walk by the canal?'

'That's a good idea, Jasmine,' I said, as I straightened up. 'Sevvy, shall we walk down to the canal? We could take some sandwiches and have a picnic in the park afterwards.'

Sevvy jumped up and down clapping his hands in the air.

'Horses,' he shouted, 'horses.'

'And boats,' said Jasmine. She wasn't keen on horses.

It was supposed to be soup for lunch; not very practical for a picnic with those two. I used the bread that came with it, along with tomatoes from the garden to make tomato sandwiches.

The children rushed off to get ready to go out, which meant deciding what to take with them.

Jasmine, unsurprisingly, said, 'I'm taking my doll.'

Sevvy had brought his trainer from his gym outfit. He held it up in the air.

'It's my boat. I'm going to float it in the canal.'

'Oh no, you're not,' I told him, 'go and put it back. Why don't you bring your blue ball and then we can throw it in the park?'

I was amazed at how quickly he agreed and, two minutes later, we were ready to leave the house. I had a rucksack on my back with the sandwiches, some bottles of water and Sevvy's ball. Jasmine had the doll against her shoulder, like she was burping a baby. I suspected that Sevvy had some stones from the garden because of the tightly clenched fist. I knew what he wanted them for, although I wasn't sure why he had to take his own.

We took a different route to the canal. It was partly because I didn't want to be reminded of the times when we walked the usual way with Rose and Gareth but also because

25

I felt like walking through the area where I was born.

'That's where Mummy lived when she was a little girl,' I told them.

'Where?' asked Sevvy, as usual looking in any direction but the right one.

I crouched down beside him and turned his head in the right direction. 'There. The one on the corner.'

'The one with the big window?'

'That's right.'

'Why is the window so big?'

'It used to be a shop.'

As soon as the words were out of my mouth, I wished I'd made an answer up.

'What's a shop?' asked Sevvy.

'It's a place where they used to sell things a long, long time ago,' Jasmine told him, 'you had to give metal things to do a sort of swap.' Then she looked up at me and shook her head in disgust. 'Why is Sevvy so stupid? He doesn't know anything.'

'I'm not stupid,' he protested, 'I'm not.'

'No you're not stupid, sweetheart. I think Jasmine's learnt about shops at school. Is that right, Jas?'

'Yes,' she nodded.

Sevvy stood still and stamped his foot.

'I go to school. Don't I, Mummy?'

'You go to nursery school, Sevvy. You'll learn about different things as you get older.'

'So I'm not stupid am I? I just haven't had time to learn everything yet.'

'That's right, Sevvy.'

When I was Jasmine's age, I had lots of questions, like

26

Sevvy, but I couldn't get any answers from the people around me.

'What's eco-terrorism?' I kept asking.

'Nothing to worry about,' said Mum.

'It's happening a long way away,' said Dad.

'You can't do anything about it,' said Mr Haworth.

I had some answers. I'd seen the worried faces of people using those words on television, but when they talked about it, they used other words that I couldn't work out. *Strategic* was one. *Nuclear* was another. I didn't get any reassurance from the words I did come to understand; the ones I could deduce from the news reports I watched while Dad was in the kitchen and Mum was in the shop. *Explosion, killed* and *violence* were words that gave me nightmares.

And then, suddenly, the news changed. There was no more talk of terrorism and violence. Instead the words were *shortages*, and *resources* and *the New Way*. Mr Deveraux, the Prime Minister, looking straight into my eyes from the screen, told me, 'Britain stands alone.'

At the canal, we walked down the steps to the bank. As soon as his foot touched the grass, Sevvy put two stones down on the ground and prepared to throw a third.

'Careful,' I warned as he edged too near to the canal.

He stood still and threw. The stone landed *plop* two inches from the bank.

'I can do better than that,' Jasmine boasted.

She reached down for one of Sevvy's stones but his growling, 'No,' made her find her own. Her throw almost reached the middle of the canal.

Sevvy picked up a second stone. His face determined, he pulled back his arm and threw. Something went wrong and

27

the stone dropped down behind him. I was ready for gloating from Jasmine and angry tears from Sevvy but we were interrupted by a noise from the towpath behind us.

Sevvy tugged at my skirt.

'It's a horse, it's a horse.'

A brown and white carthorse was pulling a barge along the canal. The barge was loaded up with timber: obviously heading toward the construction yard on the other side of the park. The ground beneath our feet vibrated from the horse's heavy steps.

We sat on the grass and waited for the horse to pass us. Sevvy was twitching with excitement but I could feel that Jasmine was a little nervous. I put one arm around each of them. As the horse passed, the vibrations in the ground became stronger and I could see how powerful the horse really was. The bargees waved at us and we waved back.

'Oh, smell that,' I said, when the barge had passed, 'That's pine.'

It was a warm smell, one that clung to the inside of my nose and reminded me of a holiday in a log cabin a long time ago when there were holidays. Then the smell changed.

Sevvy pointed and chuckled.

'The horse has done a poo.'

'So I see.'

I wondered if I could get it home to use as fertiliser on the garden but abandoned the idea as impractical. Apart from anything else, what on earth would I have carried it in?

When we reached the steaming pile, Jasmine held her nose and tiptoed past, as though frightened of disturbing it. Sevvy stood still and gazed down in fascination. I took his hand and dragged him away.

The man guiding the horse shouted 'Whoa, Molly.'

The horse stopped and the boatman unclipped the tow rope from Molly's bridle, tossed it into the barge and then led Molly up the towpath and on to the roadway. The tone of the horse's hooves changed from a soft thud to a sharper, clip-clop sound. While we were watching the horse, the boat glided into the tunnel. The two remaining boatmen clambered on to the top of the cabin and lay on their backs, their feet against the wall. They began to propel the boat along by crossing one foot over the other and back, doing a kind of sideways walk.

We followed the horse on to the road and to the other end of the tunnel. It was quite a long way. We watched as the boatman fastened Molly back into her harness and the barge set off again, making the water shine silver as the sun caught the ripples.

'Can we go on a barge some day?' asked Jasmine.

'Maybe,' I answered, although I was fairly certain we couldn't.

We turned away from the canal and set off down Deveraux Avenue.

'Mummy?' said Jasmine.

'Yes?'

'Are you going to send for my party pack soon?'

'It's three weeks off your birthday, Jas.'

'I know but it's best to be ready. Isn't it?'

'Alright, we'll do the form tonight.'

'And my dress. You won't forget my party dress, will you?'

'No, I won't forget your dress.'

We arrived at the park gates. The guard was sitting in his box with his feet up. Pulling our passbooks out of my bag, I held them out towards him but he waved his hand to gesture them away.

'Are you going to feed the ducks?' he asked Jasmine. She looked up at me to answer.

'Probably,' I said, trying to pull Sevvy off my leg where he was clinging tightly.

'Here,' he held out a piece of bread, 'give them this. It's left over from my lunch.'

Again, Jasmine looked at me and I took the bread from him.

'Thanks.'

I tried to keep the surprise out of my voice. It was a strange thing, but the guards at the park were much more relaxed than anywhere else. I suppose it was because a park just *is*. There wasn't a lot anyone could do in there if they went in illegally. They could take the waste bins or maybe one of the ducks, I suppose, but it seemed unlikely that anyone would want to do that.

Once we got away from the guard, Sevvy became excited about the ducks and he started pulling my hand to make me walk faster. Jasmine ran on ahead.

'Oh, Mummy, there's loads,' she shouted back at us.

When she reached the pond, she turned round with her hand over her mouth. 'We've only got one slice of bread.'

When I was a little girl, there was always plenty of spare bread to feed the ducks but this was a time and place when even bread was precious. I fished through my bag and took the top off my sandwich so they could have a slice each. A duck spotted the bread and swam towards us, quacking away. The others followed him. After breaking her bread up into similar sized pieces, Jasmine threw it, bit by bit, towards the ducks, trying to make sure that she distributed it evenly amongst the group. I tore Sevvy's bread up for him and handed him a piece. He was enthusiastic but nervous, holding

30

the bread out towards the ducks but then pulling it back when they came near. I worried he was going to be hurt.

'Come on, Sevvy, do it like this,' I said and crouched down beside him.

When all the bread had gone, the ducks carried on making a lot of noise and staring hungrily at us but, eventually, they realised we had no more bread left, perhaps because of Jasmine's repeated, 'Ducks, it's all gone.'

'Why don't you take the ball and play before we eat our sandwiches,' I told them.

They ran on to the grass and kicked the ball from one to another. There was a bench nearby for me to sit on.

It was sunny but a wind had blown up, ruffling the leaves and making them whisper behind my back. As I watched the children, my mind wandered back to that summer, the one when we began the New Way. It was a time of both happiness and sadness.

Happiness because, suddenly, I could play in the shop. That great big room, once packed full of cans and packages, was now empty. My parents didn't go in the shop. Ever. If I was in there and my Mother wanted me for something, she would shout from the kitchen. If I didn't respond, she'd take two steps, and no more, from the kitchen door and shout again until I answered.

So, since it seemed that no one wanted the shop anymore, I decided it was mine. Occasionally I brought my friends in to play but mostly I was in there on my own. That was the way I wanted it. It was *my* place, somewhere I could act out my fantasy games.

I was a ballerina pirouetting in the spotlight for an enraptured audience. I sailed in a counter-top boat, fighting pirates and chasing dolphins. And, of course, I was both shopkeeper and customer, using the suddenly worthless money from the till to buy and sell the three cans of peaches that had rolled out of sight under the counter.

The sadness? Well, that didn't come from me. Not directly anyway. The sadness was in my father's face when he looked at my mother and said, 'The end of a dream.' It was in the shake of his hand when he took down the key for his Subaru to drive it to the compound for disposal. It was in the droop of his shoulders when he left the house to go to his new job as warehouse man.

When I think about it, there was anger too. I saw it in the news reports; I sensed it out on the streets. With Mum, the anger seemed to be held tight inside her. There was just one time when she let go. It was after the first time we'd been to the Food Distribution Centre for our daily rations. We had to queue outside the old church in the burning sun for a long time. Then into darkness to be handed two carrier bags. Mum had a question to ask: could she be sure there were no nuts in the food. She was worried because of my Dad's allergy.

'No pandering to allergies these days,' said a woman in a yellow flowery hat. She seemed to be in charge.

'But it could kill him,' Mum replied, holding on to my hand much too tightly.

'Then you'll just have to be careful, dear.'

The woman turned to the next person in the queue. Mum took a step forward but two elderly men appeared at either side of her and marched her from the building. I trailed along behind.

She didn't speak on the way home. As she struggled for the key to open the door, I looked up at her. Her face was a deep flushed red and a bead of sweat ran down her cheek, past her ear and on to her shoulder.

'At least I can have a nice cup of tea,' she said when we were in the kitchen.

She switched on the kettle. When the tea was ready, she took the bottle of milk from the carrier and opened it. She lifted it towards her cup but stopped halfway and held the milk bottle to her nose before putting it down on the table. Pressing her left hand against my stomach she pushed me backwards and behind her. Then she curled her right hand around the opposite side of the neck of the bottle and flipped it in the air. Chunks of sour milk dropped down her arm and fell to the floor beside her feet. *Plop, plop, plop*. Like Sevvy's stones dropping in the water. She stood like that for what felt like ages, as I gagged at the smell, then she pulled her arm back and threw the bottle at the wall. It shattered with a crash, launching tiny pieces of glass all over every surface. I cowered against Mum, covering my face.

'Go to your room and play, Celia.'

'But …'

'Go to your room.'

By the time I came back down for tea, the kitchen had been totally cleared of glass and the smell had almost gone. Mum was back to her normal self. When Dad came in from work, he asked for a cuppa.

'No milk today, Steve. Sorry. There wasn't any.'

'Bloody shortages,' he mumbled and found the bottle of whisky he'd hidden behind the washer.

I looked back at the children. Jasmine was kicking the ball to Sevvy and he was rolling it back. It looked like an innocent game but I knew she was being mean to him. She kicked the ball in one direction and he ran to pick it up and send it back to her. Then she kicked it in the opposite direction so it ended up at the furthest point away from him, like she was standing at the point of a triangle and he was running along the base. He was going to be exhausted and I didn't want to carry him home.

'Come on kids, time for lunch.'

4

It has been announced that local security will be reduced to a Level 3, following the annihilation of an underground cell on the outskirts of Manchester …

'Look what I've got here.'

Robin's voice made me jump. I turned to look. He was holding the hand of a little girl, about Sevvy's age.

Sevvy was jumping up and down with excitement. 'It's my friend. From nursery. It's Hannah.'

Hannah looked up at me and smiled. She had a very dirty face and there were tear streaks below her eyes.

'Where did you come from?' I asked.

Robin opened his mouth to speak but Jasmine butted in. 'She got lost. She can't remember where she lives.'

Jasmine wriggled importantly, 'She's from Landun.'

I looked at Robin for a clue about what was going on.

'Apparently, the children were waiting at the gate …'

'Because you were busy and Daddy's bus was coming,' Sevvy explained.

'Right. The children were at the gate waiting for me when this little poppet wandered past. Sevvy asked her in.'

'She was crying because she couldn't find her Mummy,' Sevvy told me, 'So I said she could wait with us for Daddy and then we'd help her go home.'

'Do you know where you live, Hannah?'

She shook her head. The tears were starting again.

'I told you, Mummy, she's from Landun,' Jasmine said crossly.

Robin patted Jasmine on the top of the head.

'That's not a lot of help, Jas. OK, let's think this through logically.'

I looked at Robin. I didn't want the children involved in this conversation.

'Tell you what, why don't you two take Hannah upstairs and show her your toys.'

The three scampered off upstairs leaving me and Robin staring at each other. My mind was whirling.

I spoke first, 'Her Mother's going to be in a lot of trouble if Agnes finds out.'

'But if Hannah doesn't know where she lives, we can't really take her back home, can we?'

I suddenly had an idea.

'How's about we walk her down to the school and then ask her if she remembers which way is home? She's done it every day for at least a week so she might be able to take us there.'

'Good thinking. But if that doesn't work out …'

'Let's not think about that.'

Robin went upstairs and persuaded the children to come down. I could hear Jasmine protesting because she wanted to take Angela with her.

'We've got enough problems without lugging a doll with us,' Robin warned her.

When we left the house, Sevvy and Jasmine walked either side of Hannah, holding her hand. Before long, all three were skipping along. It was a big adventure for my two, being out at that time of day. Suddenly I saw Agnes walking towards us. There was no way of avoiding her.

'Hello,' she said, 'What's going on here?'

Robin thought more quickly than I did.

'Young Hannah here came over to play with Sevvy after nursery school. We're taking her home.'

'That's very irregular. Why isn't Hannah's mother caring for her this afternoon?'

'She wasn't feeling very well when she came to school to pick Hannah up. I said I'd give her a break and bring Hannah home with me for a while.'

'Most irregular. Well, I don't think she's from my patch so it's not up to me to have a word with her Mother. What area is she from?'

My heart pounded and I began to sweat.

'Energy Resources,' Hannah piped up.

I tried to keep my face straight so Agnes didn't realise this was new information to me.

'Oh, that's Nasreen's patch. I'll have to let her know about this. What's Mummy's name?'

Hannah put her finger to her mouth and shook her head. Agnes looked at me.

'I didn't ask. She looked so ill; I didn't want to bother her.'

'Let's hope she's well enough to look after the child when you get her back. Try not to do this too often, we expect mothers to look after their own children.' She looked straight into my eyes. 'That's why they don't have to work.'

'But it's not against the rules,' I said, although it was really a question because I wasn't sure about it.

'No, of course it's not against the *rules*. But, why do you need to ask? Is there more to this than you're telling me?'

'No reason, just checking that's all.'

'Right. I've got to go now. I'm sure we'll talk again soon.'

Agnes turned away. I looked at Robin with relief and we set off for the school again. The children weren't skipping; Agnes had subdued them too. We led Hannah to the school gate.

'Which way home?' I asked.

Over her head, Robin pointed towards the Energy Resources area. Luckily, that was the way that Hannah wanted to go too. We walked down the street to the corner, turned left and carried on for what seemed like ages until we reached the bridge over the canal.

'Can we look for boats?' Sevvy asked. He was obviously determined to make the best of that rare treat.

Robin took charge. 'No, not today, Sevvy, we haven't got time.' He looked down at Hannah. 'Now, Hannah, are we near?'

'That's my house there.'

She pointed to a house that looked very dilapidated. She took my hand and pulled me towards the front door which she opened and ran through. I looked at Robin.

'Should we go in?'

'We'd better. Just in case there's a problem.'

Inside there was a strong smell of damp. The hallway was dark and in a poor state of repair, with no carpet and strips of wallpaper hanging down. Hannah ran in to the front room and we followed her in.

It was a mess. All the cushions had been taken from the sofa and spread around; I could see the crumbs that had fallen down underneath. Toys were scattered on the floor and there was a dirty crumpled rug in front of the fireplace. Then I saw a woman sitting on the floor in the corner. She didn't seem to know we were there. I wasn't sure how to deal with that situation but I knew I had to do something.

'Hello, my name's Celia,' I said, walking towards her.

She didn't look up. I held out my hand.

'Celia,' I repeated.

That seemed to reach her as she held out her own hand towards mine. She didn't quite make it and I had to stretch over to take it.

'I'm Dorey,' she croaked.

'Are you Hannah's mother?' Robin asked.

She nodded.

Behind me, I was aware that Jasmine was putting the cushions back on the sofa.

'Pick the toys up,' she whispered to Sevvy and Hannah, 'Put them in that box over there.'

There was a crash as a toy went in.

'Why don't you come and sit down on a chair,' I said to Dorey, pulling on the hand that I was still holding, 'You'll be much more comfy.'

To my surprise, she accepted the help and stood up. She didn't let go of my hand. I put my other hand under her elbow and guided her to an armchair where she sat down heavily. I loosened my hand from her grasp.

I inclined my head towards the door.

'Robin, can I have a word?'

We went out into the hallway and I tried to close the door behind us. It stuck halfway.

'I think you should take the kids home to eat. This woman needs help.'

'Do you think that's a good idea? Maybe we shouldn't

get involved. I could go and call the local Guardian. The phone box is just outside.'

'No,' I told him firmly, 'Let me find out what it's all about first. It might be something simple. Calling in the Guardian could make it worse.'

'Well, I can't take Hannah back with me in case we meet Agnes again.'

'Just take our kids home and I'll stay here for a little while. At least to give Hannah something to eat and get her to bed and maybe find out what's happening with Dorey. I wonder where the Father is.'

Back in the lounge we found the three children sat in a semicircle at Dorey's feet, quietly staring up at her.

'Come on, you two. Let's get you home.'

'I want to stay with Hannah,' Sevvy moaned.

'Tough. Come on.'

Robin took our children's hands and dragged them to their feet. 'Bye, Hannah,' he said and took the children out before they had a chance to complain.

Hannah watched them leave and then ran back to her Mother. She stroked her arm.

'Poor Mummy, poor, poor Mummy.'

'Come on, Hannah,' I said, 'Let's see if there's anything to eat.'

Hannah walked over to me and took my hand. Dorey didn't even look in our direction.

The kitchen cupboards and cold box were empty but there was a key hanging from a hook on the wall. It looked like it might be the locker key and I took it outside, praying that no one saw me and asked questions.

A curtain twitched as I emptied the locker but no one came out to check. I took the food and hurried back into the house. The food in the locker was the same as I'd taken from our locker that morning. I hoped that Hannah hadn't been sent to nursery hungry.

'Do you like cheese sandwiches, Hannah?'

'Yes.'

I made two sandwiches and sat Hannah at the dining room table to eat hers. I took the other one in to Dorey.

'Nice cheese sandwich here for you, Dorey.'

I waited for her to reach for it but she stayed in the same position. I put the plate in her lap and placed her hand on a sandwich.

'Come on Dorey, eat up. For me.'

She picked up the sandwich and raised it to her mouth. Once it was there, it took her several seconds to open her mouth but eventually she had a bite.

I heard the front door open.

'Damn bus broke down. That's why I'm late.'

I went out into the hallway.

'Who the hell are you and what are you doing in my house?'

'My name's Celia and my son, Sevvy, goes to nursery with Hannah.'

Slightly more calmly, he said, 'That's not an answer.'

'No, I'm sorry, it's not. What happened was that Hannah wandered away. We found her near our house so we brought her home.'

'Wandered away? Oh my God, anything could have happened. Is she okay?'

'She's fine. Eating cheese sandwiches at the table like a good girl.'

He looked through the dining room door at his daughter sat at the table.

'Hi, baby. Are you alright?'

She nodded, her mouth full of sandwich.

The man ran his fingers through his hair. 'And where's Dorey? Is she all right?'

I pointed towards the lounge and he went in. I followed and found him kneeling at Dorey's feet, holding on to her hand.

'Another bad day?'

Dorey nodded. He stood and looked at me, one hand on her head, stroking her hair.

'Sometimes Dorey finds life a little difficult, but she'll be fine now I'm home. Thanks for helping.'

I knew he wanted me to leave but I had to ask.

'Should I ring for a doctor or something?'

His face changed from concern to anger.

'No, no doctors. She'll be fine.'

'But if she's ill, then shouldn't she have help?'

He walked over to me. He was too close; I took a step backwards.

'Just think about what will happen if a doctor sees her like this. They'll take her away. Then they'll take Hannah away and we might never be allowed to be a family again.'

'Daddy?'

Hannah was standing by his side, her hand sliding into his.

'Are you going to send Mummy away?'

He knelt down so his face was level with hers.

'No, sunshine, no-one's going anywhere.'

When he stood up again he looked down at me.

'Thanks for bringing Hannah back but I can manage from here.'

He walked to the door and opened it.

'We'll be fine now.'

'I think, maybe you should …'

His voice was firm and his face was stern.

'We'll be fine. Goodbye.'

'Bye, Hannah, see you tomorrow at nursery.'

'Bye bye, Sevvy's Mummy.'

5

… unless there is a substantial amount of rain, the North West Region will once again be subject to drought restrictions …

'Send it back.'

'I can't, Jas.'

'Send it back. It's horrible.'

'It's not horrible. It's pretty.'

'But why can't you send it back. When that skirt came and it was too small we sent it back. Remember, Mummy? Remember?'

'I remember but we sent it back because it didn't fit. This fits.'

It did fit. The horrible purple thing that was supposed to be a party dress fitted her perfectly.

'Tell them it doesn't fit.'

'But, sweetheart, if we say it doesn't fit then they'll send one that's a different size and then it really won't fit.'

'Don't care if it doesn't fit. If it's tight I'll breathe in. If it's too big then .. then … I'll eat a lot and get fat.'

I would have smiled if it wasn't that she was making me want to cry.

'Ah, Jas, don't do this.'

'Don't care what you say, I'm not wearing it.'

She dragged it up over her head and threw it into the corner. I sighed and picked it up, glad that I could look away and let my face relax its artificial smile. Smoothing the dress over my arm, I headed to the wardrobe to put it away. In the mirror, I could see her reflection. She was slumped on the bed, looking vulnerable in a vest that was too short for her and a pair of knickers that had seen better days.

As I was sliding the dress onto the hanger, she growled, 'Anyway, it looks like an underskirt. I don't even wear underskirts.'

'It doesn't look like an underskirt.'

'It hasn't got any sleeves, it's all straight up and down and it's got itchy lace round the edges. It's an underskirt, Mummy.'

I felt so helpless. I didn't want her to have to wear this purple underskirt that was masquerading as a party dress but what choice did I have? There was no box to tick for *Don't like it* on the returns form. The choice was between *Too big, Too small* or *Damaged*.

'How's about we put it in the wardrobe and think about it tomorrow? Maybe you could wear a pretty t shirt underneath or your sparkly cardigan on top.'

'I'd be too hot.'

'Oh, Jas, for goodness sake. Let's leave it for today, okay? Come on, it's nearly lunch time and then we're going to the gym this afternoon.'

'Don't want to go to the gym. I'm stopping here.'

'Oh no, you're not. Get dressed and come downstairs. That's an order.'

There was a time when it was possible to send something back because you didn't like it. That was in the early days, when there were tons of clothes piled up in stores, in warehouses, on ships that had just come into harbour, on ships about to leave harbour. It must have taken years to even make an indent in the pile. They emptied the ships first, of course. The navy did most of that.

But, even though there was so much, there had to come a time when supplies ran out, even though we had less and what we had we made last or sent for recycling.

I could remember having three party dresses. A pink one that I wore to ordinary parties. A yellow one, with a stiff underskirt underneath that rustled when I walked. I wore that for special friends' parties. And a white one with glittery pink hearts on the skirt, that I wore for my fifth birthday party. But my daughter had to make do with a purple underskirt.

Recycling had the one thirty to three thirty slot at the Sports Centre. The bus arrived at one and it didn't wait so we had to be ready. But, when I looked into the sports bags, one of Sevvy's trainers was missing. He was upstairs in his room.

'Sevvy,' I shout upstairs, 'Where's your trainer?'

I could hear him singing.

'Sevvy.'

Nothing.

'*Sevvy.*'

Still nothing. I chased upstairs, looking at my watch as I went. Twelve fifty.

He had everything out over the floor of his room and was

sitting on a pile of toys waving a green frog in the air.

'… bumped his head.'

'Come on, Sevvy, we're going to be late.'

He looked up at me.

'It turned his smile into a frown,' he sang, contorting his face to match his words.

I grabbed his arm and pulled him to his feet. His left foot was now on the frog and he nearly overbalanced.

He put his arms out to steady himself and sang, 'And turned his nose upside down.'

He pointed to his nose and smiled.

'Sevvy,' I screamed, 'Where's your trainer?'

He put his arm down into the mess on the floor and extracted the trainer.

'It's my boat,' he explained, 'You know it's my boat.'

I picked him and the trainer up and hurried down the stairs. Robin and Jasmine were waiting at the bottom.

Robin pointed at his watch.

'Come on.'

I gave Sevvy the trainer to hold and picked him up. Robin took hold of the bags while Jasmine opened the door. We stepped outside. The bus was just drawing in at the corner. Robin took Jasmine's hand and they ran ahead to delay the bus. After locking the door, I chased after them. Sevvy, clinging tight to the trainer, bumped against my hip at each step.

The driver smiled as we climbed aboard and said, 'Just in time.'

We sat down behind a couple I hadn't seen before. As I was settling Sevvy down on my knee, the woman turned round.

Her voice was soft and musical. 'Hello, I'm Sally and this

47

is Keir. We're your new neighbours.'

I hated her on first sight. Her blonde hair was swept up off her face and held back by a red band. She was wearing a red tracksuit with a dazzling white t shirt underneath. My hair was clinging damply to my forehead and I could feel my cheeks burning scarlet. I wanted to hide. If only I'd been wearing my old but still smart blue raincoat she wouldn't be able to see my yellowed white t shirt. I tried to tell myself it didn't matter what she thought. Everyone wore old clothes. Apart from her, it seemed. What had she got that we hadn't?

'Keir's going to be working in *Salvage* and I'll be in *Allocations*,' she said, smiling and showing her perfect white teeth.

For goodness sake! Not only was she living where Rose should have been and was everything I wasn't: slim, blond and attractive. She also had *my* job, working where I used to work until I had to leave when I had the children. Logically I knew it wasn't my job, at least thirty people worked there and it had been seven years since I'd had to leave to look after Jasmine but that was how it felt.

Robin smiled and turned towards me, obviously expecting me to do the introductions. I wafted my hand over my chest to show I was still too out of breath to speak.

'Hi, I'm Robin and I work in *Optimisation*. This is Celia. She's Mummy to these little scamps,' he pointed at them in turn, 'Sevvy and Jasmine. Celia used to work in *Allocations* too.'

'Really?' said Sally, 'I'm so looking forward to it. We both are. We've just finished our training in Manchester.'

Might have known it. Trained in Manchester! Not learning on the job like I had to. Working during the day and studying at night. Oh no, this one had to have it easy.

Spending all day in a classroom, listening to a teacher. Probably sitting up talking all night long with her friends. She'd start learning properly when she got into the work unit and found how hard it was. That'd teach her.

I didn't want the conversation to go on any longer.

I looked straight in her face and muttered, 'Welcome to the neighbourhood,' and then I turned my head towards the window.

'Look, Sevvy,' I said, 'look at all the flowers in that garden.'

'Where, Mummy?'

I ducked my head till it was on a level with his and pointed again. My view of Sally was blocked.

'There's the Sports Centre,' I said. 'Can you see it, Sevvy?'

It was a big building, built at a time when no one worried about the problems of making one whole wall out of glass. The windows caught the afternoon sun, as did the solar panels on the roof. The whole building looked to be made from gold until we got nearer. Then it was possible to see that some of the windows had been replaced by adobe panels.

The driver carefully positioned the bus alongside a row of identical vehicles and we climb down. I hung back a little, so we didn't have to walk in with Sally and Keir. I felt Sevvy clutch my hand when he saw the Guard in the doorway but we handed over our passbooks and were checked through with no problems.

Inside the centre, it was the usual chaos. I took Jasmine into the Women's Changing Room and Robin took Sevvy with him. I changed into my grey t shirt and baggy grey exercise trousers. Jasmine put on her blue *Muppets* swimming costume underneath her purple *Bob the Builder* t shirt and navy shorts. Our life was full of names that meant nothing to us.

I took her up to the fourth floor for *Gymnastics Stage I*. As I walked back along the corridor, I met up with Robin and Sevvy. We left Sevvy at *Toppling Toddlers* and made our way to the fitness room. The children both went swimming after their fitness classes which gave us a full hour in the gym.

Inside, it was full of treadmills, rowing machines, static bicycles. The shine had worn off the equipment and there were conspicuous signs of mending but it all worked fine. Most of the time.

Message in a Bottle was playing very loudly when we went in. Robin hated that type of music. He preferred the classical music that was on the radio in the evening. He'd made himself some earplugs out of an old blanket so he didn't have to listen while he exercised.

Suddenly I saw Sally on one of the treadmills. Although it looked to be set at quite a high pace, there wasn't a hair out of place nor any sign that she was finding it difficult at all. But that wasn't why I was staring. It was her red and blue-striped leotard. Completely figure-hugging, it looked like it was made for her, fitting perfectly. I've never seen anyone else in a leotard. The only reason I knew the word was from an exercise book I saw once. There was no chance that it had been sent out in the usual way. No chance. To receive something nice was rare. To receive something that fitted was a miracle. To receive something nice that fitted was impossible. Impossible!

I pulled my eyes away and turned to look at Robin. He was frozen to the spot, staring at Sally.

I hit him on the arm and said, 'Stop it.'

He looked at me and mouthed the word, 'What?'

'Stop staring.'

He pulled an earplug out and bent down with his ear next to my mouth. 'What?'

I hit him again.

'I said stop staring.'

'Wasn't staring,' he replied and stepped on to the nearest treadmill. He set it going while he was putting the earplug back in and nearly fell over. Served him right.

I bit my lip as I made my way to the treadmill to start my circuit of the machines. I tried very hard to put Sally out of my mind. Sometimes I succeeded and lost myself in the beat of the music and the rhythm of my exercise but then that stripy leotard intruded and I started to feel angry again.

'Swimming lessons ending in two minutes,' the loudspeaker announced.

I waved at Robin to let him know it was time to go. We collected the children and took them into the changing rooms.

Jasmine gritted her teeth as I worked my way through her wet hair with a comb. When I'd finished dealing with a particularly difficult tangle, she tipped her head back and looked into my eyes.

'I can't have my party with Gareth this year, can I?'

'No, not this year. Sorry, sweetheart.'

'Is he never coming back?'

'I don't think so. No.'

She rested her head against my stomach.

'Gareth was my best friend.'

I patted her cheek. 'I know he was.'

When I tucked the children into bed that night, they both went to sleep as soon as their heads hit the pillow. Richard was engrossed in a quiz on the radio downstairs. As I left Jasmine's bedroom I heard him shout, 'Antediluvian,' much too loudly, at the radio.

I set off downstairs to tell him to be quieter but before I put my foot on the top step, an image flashed into my mind. It was of Jasmine in the purple underskirt which was masquerading as a party dress. She was standing next to *that* woman who was flaunting her fancy clothes. She could only have got them illegally; I didn't know anyone who'd ever had clothes like that. I had to do something; it wasn't fair. She was cheating the system.

I slipped out of the front door and crossed the road to the telephone box. Inside I pressed the *Report* button.

'Hello, this is the report hotline.'

'My name's …'

'No names please, just make your report.'

'There's a new woman. Sally she's called,' I whispered, 'I don't know her last name but she works in recycling. I don't think she's receiving her clothes in the usual way.'

'What makes you think that?'

'They're new and look like they're made for her. I think they're either stolen or black market.'

'Is that the Recycling District?'

'That's right.'

'Thanks for your information. We'll investigate.'

The line clicked off.

I put the receiver back on the hook and suddenly felt dizzy. I'd never reported anyone before. It seemed like the world had tipped sideways. What had I done? I didn't even know the woman and yet I'd told the authorities I suspected her of getting her clothes from the black market.

I thought about ringing back and saying I'd changed my

mind. But there was that image of Jasmine in the purple underskirt again. My only daughter having to wear something like that for her birthday party. I couldn't bear it. I'd done the only thing I had in my power to right an injustice; I was acting like a responsible citizen.

Back home there was a music programme on the radio. I sat down but when the announcer said they were going to play a waltz Robin came over to me, bowed and held out his hand.

'May I have this dance?'

Smiling, I took his hand and stood up beside him. He put one hand on my shoulder and the other on my waist. I did the same to him and together we danced around the room. We might not have known the official steps but we moved like we were one person and it felt so good. At the end of the music he escorted me back to the sofa, watched as I sat down and then bowed again.

'Thank you for the dance.'

He turned and flopped down on to the seat beside me before looking at me with a grin and an exaggerated cough. He wafted his hand in front of his face.

'Raised a bit of dust there, Mrs Travis. Are you sure you've been doing your domestic duties?'

'Don't you be so cheeky,' I said, tapping him on the shoulder.

He put his hands around my waist and tickled me until I was giggling hysterically and begging him to stop. Then he lay down with his head in my lap, gazing up at the ceiling.

We listened to the music for a while in silence then Robin looked up into my face.

'I'm so lucky to have you.'

'And me you.'

6

Recycling levels are down by 5%. A spokesman said, 'A lot of our resources are now past the end of their natural life and it looks as though we're going to have to return to some form of manufacturing …

I put Agnes' cup down on the coffee table and sat down facing her.

'I've had some information about you taking that child, Anna …'

'Hannah.'

She checked her notes.

'Oh yes, Hannah. Anyway, I've been told that you opened their locker while you were there. Is that true?'

'Yes, it is.'

'Why on earth did you need to do that?'

'Well, like I told you, Hannah's mother, Dorey, had been ill all day and so I made them something to eat. I had to get the bread out of the locker.'

'And could this woman not manage to get out to her own

locker? If she was that bad, why didn't she seek medical help?'

'I offered that's all. She looked so pale. Suffers from migraine sometimes. The nurse has told her she should rest when they start.'

'Still, it's not on, going around opening people's lockers. Don't do it again. Do you hear me?'

'Yes.'

I did hear but I couldn't really see what the problem was. I'd had the key; it wasn't like I was breaking into the locker or anything like that.

'Right, that's it for today. Let's hope I don't have to visit again soon. You're gaining a reputation for interfering in other people's business.'

Agnes stood up to leave and I followed her out into the hallway. Sevvy was walking down the stairs.

'It's tidy now,' he shouted, his voice uneven from the effort of carrying his big teddy bear.

'I hope it is.'

He reached the bottom step.

'Hello, Sevlan,' said Agnes, 'Is that your teddy bear? He looks very cuddly.'

'Yes, he is,' he replied and then looked at me. 'Am I in trouble again?'

'Why do you think that?' I asked.

'That's what *you* call me when I'm naughty. That's what you said before, you said, 'Sevlan Stephen Travis, go and tidy your room.''

Agnes sat down on the bottom step beside him. Her face was tense.

'Do you get in trouble a lot?'

'Sometimes. Mummy gets cross when I don't do what I'm

55

told or when my room's a mess or when I hide Jasmine's doll.'

'And what does Mummy do then?'

'She shouts. Really loud.'

'And does Mummy smack you when she's cross?'

Sevvy was as scandalised as I was.

'No! It's naughty to smack. My Mummy wouldn't do that.'

He stepped down off the stairs and came over to me to lean against my leg, staring at the woman who was asking him strange questions. Agnes stood up and moved towards the door.

'I have to ask these questions, you know. Just in case.'

I bit my lip.

'That's OK. I understand.'

Although I didn't. Not really.

Dorey and Hannah arrived at the school for the afternoon session at the same time as we did. Sevvy waved happily at Hannah. We handed the children over into Miss Fontaine's care and left the school building. Walking through the school yard together, I wondered whether I should mention what happened before the weekend.

'Are you feeling better, Dorey?'

She looked towards the guard and then back at me.

'Fine thanks.'

'I'm glad about that.'

There was a moment's silence and then she whispered, 'Thanks for bringing Hannah back. I don't know what I would have done if …' her voice broke, 'anything had happened to her.'

'I know how you feel.'

Dorey went through the gate ahead of me. Since she had left Hannah, her step was slower and her body drooped, like a flower in need of water.

I walked past the Guard. He was staring at a point above my head. I began to turn towards home, in the opposite direction to Dorey but then I had an idea.

'Dorey?'

She turned back.

'Yes?'

'Would you like to come for a cup of tea? Spend the afternoon with me until it's time to collect the children?'

She stood still, a range of emotions playing across her face.

'It's not against the rules although they probably don't like it.'

'There's not much they do like,' Dorey said and then she put her hand over her mouth.

I smiled to reassure her. 'It's up to you. What do you think?'

'Come on then, let's risk it.'

We started walking. I had to slow down my usual pace so Dorey could keep up.

'Sevvy tells me you've only just been transferred up here.'

'Well, Russell's been transferred and, of course, we've come up with him.'

'Did you have to move a long way?'

'Yes, up from London.'

'Oh, that's what the children were saying. I thought I hadn't heard of Landun.'

Dorey smiled. 'Yes, Hannah's accent is strong. It's funny how they pick things up from their friends.'

As soon as Dorey stepped inside the house, she gasped

and said, 'Oh, look at this hallway. You've made a good job of it.'

'This is the last part of the house that we've decorated.'

'Lilac. It's a lovely colour. And those curtains.'

'Yes, I'm proud of those. I loved them when they came but they were too long. I shortened them. Me! Never done any sewing before,' I laughed. 'Don't get too close though. It doesn't look so great when you get close.'

'I used to love sewing. My Mum was a seamstress and made all my clothes. There'd been a textile factory nearby so she could always send for material instead of clothes. She taught me a lot.'

'Brilliant.'

'Yeah, I made some clothes for Hannah when we were in London but since I came up here,' her voice broke, 'like everything else … I can't find the energy. And I lost my sewing machine when … it happened.'

She turned away and I saw her hand go up to her face to brush away a tear. Then she looked back and said, in a stronger voice, 'Can I have a tour? I love looking at people's houses and there's hardly ever opportunity.'

'Course you can.'

We started in the lounge. Lemon walls. Two blue chairs and a green sofa. A greenish carpet; I always told myself it was green, although some would call it grey. Green curtains with a red stripe.

'Oh it's so bright and airy. I'd love this.'

Then the dining room. Lemon walls again; they'd sent a lot of paint. Pine table, teak sideboard, walnut shelves.

'We'll leave the kitchen till last, then we can have tea.'

'Good idea.'

Our bedroom. Soft blue walls; I loved that colour, I would

have liked more. Two wardrobes: one white and one pine. A chest of drawers that I'd painted green because they were scratched. Pine bed with too red bedding. Purple curtains.

'Very colourful,' said Dorey.

'I'm used to it now. Drove me crazy at first.'

Sevvy's bedroom. He hadn't made a good job of tidying and I'd forgotten to check.

'Looks like Hannah's bedroom, except it's decorated better.'

The last-of-the-lemon walls. Battered white wardrobe covered in stickers of a big eared mouse wearing red shorts. Green shelves which should have been full of toys but wasn't. *Mister Men* pillowcase, *Transformers* quilt cover.

Jasmine's room.

'Is she always so tidy?'

'Usually. Likes things to be in the right place.'

Something caught my eye and I went over to the corner of the room to pick it up. It was the purple 'party dress'.

'Apart from this, which she wants me to send back.'

I held it out.

'Supposed to be a party dress. Can't blame her for not wanting it, can you?'

'A party dress? It's an underskirt.'

'That's what she said. She says she won't wear it and, if she hasn't got a party dress, she won't go to the party. It's on Saturday. I can't think what to do about it. Haven't even sent the invitations out yet because she won't take them to school. I've racked my brains but I can't think what to do about it.'

Dorey took it from me and held it up in front of her by the shoulders.

'Tell you what. Have you got any of that curtain material left? From downstairs?'

'A bit. Do you think you could make it look better?'

'I've an idea what could be done but it would depend how much material you have.'

'But you haven't got a machine.'

'No, I'd have to do it by hand but that's alright. If you've got a needle and thread and some decent scissors?'

'I'm not sure where they are but I didn't send the needle and thread back, didn't seem worthwhile. And my scissors are okay.'

Dorey had a sparkle in her eye.

'Let's get going then.'

7

... and it's going to be another scorching day. Keep wearing that sunblock.

'Good morning, birthday girl.'

Jasmine opened one eye.

'Can I put my dress on now?'

'No, wait until this afternoon; you might get breakfast on it.'

The dress was on a hanger on the wardrobe door where she could see it before she went to sleep the night before. It was transformed. Instead of the scratchy lace, there was a narrow edging with the white and purple curtain material. The dress was no longer straight up and down. Dorey had inserted narrow triangles of material into the skirt which now hung in folds until Jasmine spun round to make it flare out.

I sat on the bed next to her and, taking her in my arms, kissed her on the forehead.

'Happy birthday, sweetheart.'

Sevvy peered round the door.

'Come on, Sevvy, give Jas a birthday kiss.'

He jumped on the bed and crawled on his hands and knees to kiss her on the lips. Then he looked at me.

'When's my birthday?'

'It's not for ages yet,' replied Jasmine, 'but who cares. It's *my* birthday today.'

She started singing *Happy Birthday to me* but was interrupted by Robin.

'What's that dreadful noise?'

He came into the bedroom.

'What's going on?'

'It's my birthday, Daddy, my birthday.'

'No, it can't be.'

He looked at me.

'I'd know if it was Jas's birthday. Wouldn't I, Mummy?'

I tried not to laugh.

'It is, Robin, it is her birthday.'

Robin hit himself on the forehead.

'Imagine forgetting my own daughter's birthday.'

He leant over and lifted her out of bed.

'And how old are you?'

'I'm seven.'

'Well, I think that calls for seven spins, don't you?'

He stood her on the floor, slid his arms under her armpits and around her back and then picked her up to spin her around seven times. When he put her back down, they were both looking a little green.

'Bit early in the morning for all that,' he said.

We trooped downstairs and admired the *Happy Birthday* poster that Sevvy and I had made and hung on the lounge wall. Jasmine was starting to look a little nervous.

'Is there presents?'

'I don't know,' said Robin, 'Is there presents?'

'Might be,' I replied, 'Let's look in the kitchen.'

The presents were on the kitchen table, inside my prettiest pillowcase. I was hoping that my present didn't get squashed.

Jasmine settled herself at the table. She took my present out first.

'Oh, Mummy, it's beautiful.'

I'd made her a headband from paper flowers. It had taken me ages curling the petals with the edge of the scissors.

'I'll mix some real flowers in just before the party. They would die if I put them in too early.'

She gave me a quick hug and turned back to the pillowcase to pull out a drawing from Sevvy.

'It's a pussycat,' he volunteered.

'I can tell, Sevvy, I really can.' She looked up at me. 'Can I put it on my bedroom wall?'

'Course you can. We'll do it straight after breakfast.'

Finally, it was Robin's present. It was a doll's living room with a family to live in it, all carved out of the last piece of wood from the shed. The furniture inside was made of various odds and ends: a coffee table from the blunted blade of an old knife, a chair made from papier mâché, a rug from woven grass.

'Oh look, the curtains match my party dress.'

She climbed down from her chair and gave Robin a hug.

'Thanks, Daddy, it's beautiful.'

The birthday breakfast consisted of pancakes, strawberries from the garden and the remainder of the syrup from making biscuits earlier in the week. Jasmine wore her headband as she ate. I worried about the syrup being transferred from her plate to the band but I didn't say anything. I needn't have worried, she didn't get any of the syrup on her; neat as usual. Wish I could say the same thing about Sevvy.

As soon as the breakfast things were washed up, we all became very busy. First there was Sevvy's picture to hang on her bedroom wall and then it was down to the party preparations. I'd already made the flour and water paste and I sent Robin and Sevvy into the kitchen to make the paper chains from the party pack.

Jasmine and I went into the dining room with the rolled up poster to decorate. They'd sent a pink glitter pen and seven stick on gold stars.

'What are we going to write?'

She bit her finger for a minute and then said, 'Jasmine Elizabeth Travis, Seven Years Old Today.'

'OK. Do you want me to write it, or will you?'

'You do the writing, Mummy, and then I'll add some decorations.'

I found a pencil and drew some straight lines across the paper. It was a bit of a struggle, the paper almost covered the dining room table and the glittery ink kept sinking in until I shaded it in underneath with her pencil crayons.

When the pink writing was glittering nicely on the paper, we stuck the gold stars in a semi-circle over her name and Jasmine began to work her way around the edge, drawing flowers and curly shapes in a border. I went to check on Robin and Sevvy.

There was a satisfying pile of paper chains on the floor but it was eleven thirty and Sevvy was covered in paste and bits of coloured paper. The party started at two and we had to have our section of the party hall decorated by then. And have lunch.

We were the last to arrive at the party hall. The other five families had already claimed their spot and we ended up in the corner.

'It's too dark,' Jasmine moaned.

There was a heavy velvet curtain at a window nearby. I heaved it back as far as I could to let more light in.

'Is that better?'

'S'pose so.'

We fixed the poster to the wall and attached paper chains to every possible surface. The caretaker brought in the party chairs and Jasmine raced over to choose hers. She picked the most garish one. It was covered in brightly coloured rainbows and had golden crowns along the back.

'It's beautiful,' Jasmine said when Robin had eventually positioned it to her satisfaction.

Sarah, the Party Organiser, clapped her hands.

'Right, everybody to their seats then we can let the guests in.'

Jasmine walked importantly to her chair and sat down. She gave a little wriggle of excitement then adjusted her skirt so that it hung evenly around her. Finally she settled herself, head held high and hands in her lap.

We took our places in the rows of chairs at the back of the hall.

'Are we ready?' Helen asked, looking round to check as six excited children shouted, 'Yes.'

Sarah opened the door and a horde of children poured in. She sat the guests in a semi-circle facing the birthday children then led them in six rounds of *Happy Birthday to You*. Thankfully it was in alphabetical order so Jasmine wasn't last; the performance was a little lacklustre towards the end.

Then there were games and songs and food. I watched in admiration as Sarah organised forty children with an ease that I couldn't achieve with two. At the end Jasmine, eyes sparkling, told me it was the best party ever.

8

A report out today identifies the need for the country to return to manufacturing. A spokesman said, 'We can no longer rely on supplies from the past. The warehouses are almost empty ...

'Mummy, are you all right?'

I lifted my head away from the toilet bowl.

'Yes, Jas, I'm fine. Just go downstairs. I'll be down to make breakfast in a minute.'

'Has something made you sick?'

'I've probably eaten something, that's all.'

'Was it from the party?'

'Jas, just go downstairs. OK?'

I started retching again but there was nothing left in my stomach. I stood up and, ignoring the threads of blackness that floated across my eyes, walked down into the kitchen.

'Right, toast and cereal for breakfast.'

'I want pancakes,' said Jasmine.

'I want eggs,' said Sevvy.

'You'll have what we've got. I want you to get yourselves ready while I'm making it. Jasmine, don't forget your reading book. Sevvy, find your shoes because I don't know where they are.'

I was trying to count backwards over the past few weeks but couldn't work it out. I'd have to wait until Robin comes home so I could use his diary. Or maybe Dorey had a calendar or something.

As we neared the school, I saw Dorey waiting on the corner.

'Hello, Dorey, is everything all right?'

'Yes, fine.'

'Bit of a surprise seeing you here in the morning.'

'Well, I was wondering if you'd like to come to my house, when you've dropped Jasmine in to school.'

'Yes I would. I was going to look out for you this afternoon. Have you got a calendar?'

'Yes. Sort of. It's called a perpetual calendar and it's an ancient thing. Found it in a drawer. We should be able to work it out between us. Why?'

I put my finger to my lips and whispered, 'Little ears,' and Dorey nodded.

We walked along the street, past the water tower, towards school.

'Jasmine, say thank you to Dorey for your dress.'

Jasmine flung her arms open wide and hugged Dorey, nearly knocking her over.

'Thank you so much for my dress. It's the prettiest dress in the whole world.'

'I don't think I'd go that far, but I'm glad you like it.'

I sent Jasmine into the yard and we waited outside the gate until the bell rang and Jasmine went in. Then we set off for Dorey's house with Sevvy and Hannah skipping along in front of us.

'Are you late?' Dorey whispered.

'Not sure but I was sick this morning.'

'Is that good or bad news?'

'I'm trying not to think about it.'

At the house, Dorey fitted the key in the lock and twisted it backwards and forwards, muttering, 'Stupid lock.' Then the door opened and she almost fell in.

Inside the house, it was just as I remembered it. Dark and musty smelling.

'Come on into the kitchen and I'll make some tea.'

My stomach rebelled at the thought of tea but I managed to hold on.

'Just water please, cold water.'

I leant against the worktop as Dorey sorted out drinks for the four of us. The smell of her dandelion tea made me feel queasy but sipping on water took the feeling away. We went into the lounge. Hannah and Sevvy pulled a whistle and a drum out of the toy box and began to play but thankfully, they disappeared into the hallway after a couple of minutes; the noise was almost too much for me. I wanted Dorey to find the calendar but couldn't pluck up the nerve to rush her. Then she started talking and it almost took my mind off my fears.

'I bet you think I'm pathetic,' Dorey said.

'Why would I think that?'

'You've seen how we live. The state of the house. The state of me. What else would you think?'

'I'm not thinking anything of the sort. I do think you're unhappy though.'

She brushed the back of her hand over her cheek.

'You're right. I am unhappy and I can't seem to do anything to make it better. I try to make myself believe I'm happy. I have Hannah and Russell. There's a roof over our heads and food to eat. What more could I want?'

I knew there were things she could want, that I could want, but I couldn't name them. They slipped through my mind like ghosts; shapeless and intangible.

'But there are things we don't have these days, things …'

My voice broke. What was I doing? Talking like that to someone who was almost a stranger. How did I know she wouldn't report me?

Dorey was quiet for a moment and then she looked straight into my face.

'I do know what I want. I want to go home. I want to go back to London.'

'Couldn't Russell apply for another transfer?'

Her hands were over her face now, covering her mouth so she seemed to be mumbling.

'There's nothing to go back to. Not where we were. It's under water. We only just got out.'

'That's dreadful. What happened?'

'It was so unexpected. It was a Saturday. Hannah had been ill in the night and we were having a lie in. That's what saved us. The weather had been really bad for a couple of days, torrential rain. Some areas had been evacuated but it seemed like we were going to be all right.'

I was nodding, as if I knew what it was like but I didn't.

'So what happened?'

'A wave swept up the Thames. Broke the barriers. Flooded the entire area.'

'God, that's awful.'

'Well, like I said, we were in bed. Upstairs. Then we hear

this roar and Russell goes to look out of the window. 'Look at this,' he says and pulls the curtains back. Water's gushing down the road, knocking over everything in its way. I run for Hannah and bring her to be with us, holding her tight in my arms.'

'That's terrible. I can't imagine …'

'And then the water's coming in downstairs. Pushing the door in, crashing through the windows and up the stairs, into our room. We climbed on to the bed, then on to the dressing table and then it didn't get any higher. But all those other people, the ones who had been up eating breakfast, were trapped. Couldn't get out. Were drowned. In their own kitchens.'

'How did you get out?'

'The emergency service came some time later. Sailed down in rowboats, collecting those who survived. We were rescued through the bedroom window. I'll never forget how grateful I was when they came but now, sometimes, I think, maybe we would have been better off, if, you know, we'd been downstairs eating breakfast.'

'No, Dorey, no, that wouldn't have been better. Not for you, not for Hannah, not for Russell.'

'I suppose not. But nothing's the same anymore. This house is horrible and it's not home. I'd always lived down in London, in the same area. Grew up there. I knew every street, every building. I don't know anything or anyone here.'

'You know me.'

'I do feel I know you. That's why I asked you to come round this morning.'

I sipped on my water and nodded. The music from the hallway had ended and I could hear Sevvy talking.

'And Jasmine sat in a golden chair …'

'Do you think I can help make things better? I'm not sure what I could do.'

'Well, I was thinking, maybe you could help me get the house sorted. Help me with some of the decorating. If someone else got involved, I think I could make this house into a home.'

'What about Russell?'

'Russell? He'd help if he could, but he's so busy, works long hours and,' tears suddenly ran down her face, 'we're not living in the right area for his job. That means he has to leave home early and gets home late because it's a long walk to the bus. Then he takes over from me looking after Hannah because I can't always cope with looking after her all day.'

'But, if you're struggling now, are you going to be able to cope with doing the extra work on the house?'

'Part of the problem is that I tend to sit in the chair all day doing nothing. It makes me worse but somehow I can't stop doing it. I thought, if you were willing, you could help gee me up a little bit. After all, if you were here helping I couldn't just sit in the chair, could I?'

'No, I suppose not.'

'So, what do you think? I know it's a lot to ask but …'

'I think I'd like to help, Dorey.'

I didn't say anything but I thought it might help me too. Give me something to focus on. Then I remembered something else.

'Have you got that calendar?'

In the afternoon, we went to the local Loans Centre. It was in the church that had acted as Distribution Centre when I was a child. When I was waiting for Mum I used to wander around reading all the gravestones; I loved that.

We opened the creaky door and stepped inside, our feet echoing on the stone floor. I hadn't been in there for years; Robin usually dealt with borrowing equipment. All the original furniture had gone: I think the pews and lectern had gone to the school.

'Yes?' a voice said from our left. It was an elderly man. His hair was long and white and he was wearing an enormous knitted blue and white sweater; it was cold in there.

'We're going to do some decorating,' Dorey says, her voice shaking a little, 'and we need some equipment.'

'Decorating, eh? Just you two?'

'That's right. My husband's a bit too busy at work to be able to help much.'

'Have you ordered your paint and such like? '

'Not yet.'

'That's good because I can't get a decorating kit to you this week because my delivery man's off sick. I'll mark you down for a kit and we should be able to get the kit to you by,' he ran his finger down a list, 'next Thursday. Is that okay?'

'Fine,' we said together.

Dorey showed her ID and filled in the forms then we went back to her house for the rest of the afternoon. Her step was lighter already.

9

A spokesman from the Ministry of Work said, 'A return to manufacturing will require a larger workforce and it may be that we can no longer afford to have our children cared for in the home until they are twelve.'

'Sevvy, stop it. You're going to leave dirty fingerprints on the glass.'

He had been chasing raindrops down the window with his finger. He took his finger off the glass but still held it in the air, like it was a temporary break.

'When's Daddy coming home?'

'Soon, Sevvy, soon.'

'I'm bored. I want to play in the garden.'

'Well, you can't. It's raining hard and there's too many puddles out there. I don't want you getting in a mess. Why don't you draw me a picture?'

'I've been drawing all afternoon at nursery. I'm tired of drawing.'

'Well, look at a book or something. I'm too busy to play with you.'

I went back to my pile of ironing. I was very behind with the housework. I'd spent every afternoon with Dorey stripping the walls in her house plus I'd been sick every morning. Not only that, I was feeling so tired. Dorey's calendar hadn't been much help but I was definitely late. I knew I should see the nurse and tell Robin but I couldn't face it.

Sevvy was wiping his whole hand over the window as the raindrops ran down.

'Sevvy, stop that this instant or you'll go to your room.'

He slammed his hand down on the windowsill and climbed down from his chair, making as much noise as he could.

'You're no fun anymore,' he muttered and then flung himself down behind the sofa.

I could hear him banging his feet on the floor in a slow rhythm, with a pause before each beat, as though he was listening for a reaction. I ignored him.

Jasmine came in, clutching Angela by the hair and swinging her backwards and forwards.

'What's up with him?'

'He's sulking.'

'Not sulking. Not.'

The foot banging increased in rhythm and intensity. I banged the iron down on to the ironing board in time with the noise. It felt quite satisfying.

Jasmine stretched out on the sofa and placed Angela face down on her chest.

'I'm hot. It's too hot.'

'We're all hot, Jas. You'll just have to put up with it.'

She tutted loudly and flung herself on her side. Angela fell to the floor. There was a rumble of thunder in the distance. Sevvy crawled out from behind the sofa and peered up at me.

'What's that noise?'

'It's just thunder.'

Jasmine sat up and put her hands on either side of her face.

'Will there be lightning? Will there?'

'There could be, but it's nothing to worry about.'

'I don't like lightning, I don't. It's scary. Kirsty says there's a thing called a fireball and it rolls right through your house when it's lightning and it sets fire to everything and ...'

'Kirsty's just being silly. There's no such thing.'

'She's not being silly. She's not. Amanda said it happened in her house and it set fire to her doll's house and the kitchen table and ...'

Sometimes the ironing has to wait.

'Tell you what. Why don't the two of you come and help me tidy out the pantry.'

The pantry was under the stairs. I was hoping we wouldn't be able to hear the thunder from there. It didn't have much in it, mainly things that didn't seem worth sending back. That didn't mean it stayed tidy.

I unplugged the iron, made the children a drink and we went into the pantry armed with dusters and a waste bin.

'Close the door,' says Jasmine, 'then the fireball can't get in.'

'There's no such thing as a fireball and, anyway, it's too hot.'

'I'll close it then,' she said and did so.

I took a sip of my drink.

Like I said, there wasn't much in there. First thing we found was an old sandwich, covered in green mould.

'Oh, that's where it went,' said Sevvy

I picked it up with one of the dusters and slid it into the waste bin. I covered it with a baby book that belonged to both Sevvy and Jasmine. It was called *1, 2, 3* and all the pages were loose which is why I didn't bother to send it back. I didn't think anyone would have any use for it but it was serving a useful purpose that day; covering up the sandwich so I didn't have to rush for the bathroom.

We found two old t-shirts and a towel. I put them near the door, ready to take out to the locker. There were a couple of baby's dummies which we put away when Sevvy became a 'big boy' and didn't need them any more. I should have sent those back; they were in good condition. Sevvy immediately put one in his mouth and I had to wrestle it from him.

'It's dirty, Sevvy, it's been in here for ages.'

I put them both back on the shelf, not trying to think about why I was keeping them.

On the top shelf were two empty cardboard boxes which I'd obviously never got round to putting in the locker for recycling. That was about it and I gave each child a duster to do the lower shelves while I dusted the higher ones.

'What's this,' asking Jasmine.

I was hoping it wasn't a spider. That wouldn't have been a good day to find a spider. It wasn't. Something was down the back of one of the shelves.

'It's stuck,' she said, going red in the face from pulling. I was red in the face from the heat.

'Let me have a go.'

I leant over the top of her. I tugged and tugged. Eventually it came loose, sending me staggering backwards against the far wall and almost standing on Sevvy.

'It's an old newspaper.'

It had to be fairly old; they'd decided newspapers were a waste of money before Robin and I married.

'Let's look, let's look.'

I sat down on the floor with the children either side of me, their hot bodies leaning against me.

Jasmine read out the front page headline, *The New Way*, and started on the article.

'Today, the Prime Minister, Mr Devoy, Devor, Devway …'

'Deveraux.'

'Said that the … oh, it's too difficult, Mummy, you read it.'

She pushed the newspaper into my hands and I stared at the article. The letters were blurred and unintelligible.

'Come on, Mummy, hurry up. I want to know what it says.'

At almost the same moment, or so it felt, Robin opened the pantry door and the shreds of blackness that had been floating in front of me suddenly become an all-enveloping darkness.

When I came to, I was propped up against the kitchen wall with a damp cloth across my forehead. Robin was hovering over me.

'Are you all right?'

'Yeah, I'm fine. Where are the kids?'

'I've sent them up to Jasmine's room to play. What's wrong, Celia? What happened?'

'I took the kids in the pantry so they couldn't hear the storm. Jasmine insisted on keeping the door closed and it was so hot. I must have fainted.'

77

'It's more than that, isn't it? You haven't been well for days.'

'No, no, it was just the heat.'

'Celia, I've heard you throwing up in the bathroom. I've been waiting for you to talk to me. Are you pregnant?'

'Well, I am about six weeks late but it's probably the upset over Gareth, not pregnancy.'

'And the sickness and the fainting, is that from the upset?'

'It could be.'

'What about talking to the nurse? Have you thought about that?'

'No, it's too early.'

I tried to push myself upwards but the dizziness came back and I slid down against the wall.

'I'm going to ring her. I'm going to ring her right now.'

'No, don't do that. She'll be eating her dinner or cooking or something. Don't bother her. I'll do it tomorrow. I promise.'

'You'd better. Now, I'm going to carry you upstairs to bed and I want you to stay there till tomorrow morning. Do you understand?'

'I suppose so.'

'No suppose about it.'

10

… First we had too little rain and now there's too much. Over in Clitheroe, the River Ribble has reached a dangerous level and sandbags are being distributed.

Robin had forbidden me to help Dorey although I hadn't had chance to tell her. I rang Parveen, the nurse and she promised to come round, when she could. It was nearly time to pick up the children from school and she still hadn't arrived.

There was a knock at the front door. When I opened it, I was surprised to see Agnes instead of Parveen.

'Is everything all right?' I asked.

'Can I have a word, Celia?'

'Yes, of course you can. Come in. Do you want tea?'

I was racking my brains trying to think what I'd done but the only thing I could come up with was helping Dorey and I'd already discussed that with Agnes. She wasn't happy about it but couldn't find any regulation which said I couldn't do it.

'No, no tea today. Is it all right if we sit down?'

I took her into the lounge and she settled down in the easy chair. I perched on the edge of the sofa, too worried to relax.

'We've had a message from Blackpool.'

That was where Robin's parents lived.

'Yes?'

'It's Mr Travis. Sevlan.'

Robin's father. I'd never met either his father or mother although we exchanged messages in the monthly postal delivery.

'Is he ill?'

'Yes, gravely ill. They don't think he has long to live.'

'Oh no!'

'Well, yes, under the circumstances, the Compassionate Board has granted a week's leave for Robin and passes for the all the family to go for a visit. It's not far as the crow flies but with public transport it's going to be quite a difficult journey and need an overnight stay.'

She handed me a folder.

'Everything's in there. The itinerary, travel passes, and accommodation vouchers.'

'What about Robin's work and the children's school?'

'It's all taken care of. Someone should be talking to Robin about now explaining what's happening. And the school has been informed. The teacher will probably give Jasmine some work to take with her so she doesn't get behind. Sevvy, of course, being so young, hasn't such an onerous timetable and so it won't make any difference if he's out of nursery for a week or so.'

There was another knock at the front door.

'Excuse me,' I said and went to let Parveen in.

'Is everything all right?' Agnes asked

I looked at Parveen warningly. I wasn't ready to discuss it with Agnes.

'Just a routine check-up,' said Parveen. 'Nothing to worry about.'

'Well, I'd better go. I've said everything I want to say. I'll let myself out.'

Parveen and I waited until we heard the door closing.

'Thanks for that, I don't want anyone to know just yet. Until I've got it confirmed and Robin knows.'

'That's fine. Do you want to go upstairs for me to check you over?'

'Yes please. It won't take long will it? I have to pick the children up soon.'

'No, twenty minutes at the most.'

Upstairs I provided a urine sample for Parveen to test.

'Let's have a look at you while we're waiting.'

She took my blood pressure and pulse.

'They seem to be up. Are you worried about the pregnancy?'

I told her about Sevlan and the long journey I was about to undertake. She didn't think the journey would be a problem. When the test was ready it was positive. It was still a shock, even though that was what I was expecting. I was trembling and sat down heavily on the bed.

'There's something else,' Parveen said, looking worried.

'What?'

'I'm going to have to fill in a form. You ... you need permission to carry this baby to term.'

'No, that can't be right. There aren't any regulations about how many children we can have.'

'There are now. It's all very new. Only got the notification last week.'

'But when I had Sevvy, they were saying we need more babies. Get the population up again.'

'That would be,' she checks her notes, 'about three years ago. Right?'

'Yes.'

'Things have changed since then. The population numbers are up, resources are down and there's been a huge influx of people from the south because of the floods. But don't worry yet. It's being done on a local level and no decision has been reached on how many children should be in a family. It might be two, it might be three. Best thing is to do the form and then forget about it until you see me again.'

'That's not going to be easy.'

'I know. But there are other things going on in your life which are much more important at the moment. So let's get this form over then you can forget about it.'

She worked her way through the form, mainly finding the answers from her notes and asking me the odd question. I sat next to her, watching her write but unable to read what the words said. My mind was spinning.

'Okay, that's done.' She put the form in her bag and patted my hand. 'When are you travelling?'

'I think it's tomorrow.'

'Well, I suggest you let your husband do the heavy carrying, suitcase and all that, while you take it as easy as possible. You'll be fine if you relax.'

'Oh God, we haven't even got a suitcase.'

'Leave that to your husband to worry about and everything else. All you have to do is pick the children up from school and leave the rest to Robin. Are you listening to me?'

Poor Robin. He arrived home upset after having heard that his father hadn't got long to live and he had to deal with the children, the cooking, the packing for next day and the news that he was going to be a father again.

'One thing at a time,' he kept saying, 'one thing at a time.'

I didn't tell him about the form.

11

A further two thousand young people in the North West are to be conscripted into the medical service, the Prime Minister announced today. 'Not enough people are declaring an interest in medicine …'

Arrangements had been made for us to travel on Robin's work bus to get to the bus station for the first leg of our journey. The bus had to take a slight detour to reach Burnley bus station but we arrived in plenty of time for the 8.30 to Rochdale. It was going to be a long and complicated journey but, like Agnes had told me, we were lucky we didn't have to stay overnight in Rochdale too, the buses only went to Manchester from there once a week.

The bus dropped us off at the bus station checkpoint. The children were very quiet and their eyes were round as they stood by my side at the checkpoint counter.

'Purpose of journey?'

'Compassionate,' said Robin.

'A relative?' asked the Guard.

'Yes, my father.'

'I'm sorry to hear that. And you're going to?'

'Blackpool.'

'No buses to Blackpool from here. Where will you be transferring?'

'Rochdale and Manchester.'

'Let's see your passes.'

Robin handed them over.

'And your passbooks.'

He gave him the passbooks. The guard looked from the passbooks to us and back again.

'Could you lift the little boy up so I can see his face properly?'

Sevvy hung his head in shyness but, at a sign from the guard, Robin put a finger under his chin and tilted his face upwards. The guard took his rubber stamp, touched it on the ink pad and stamped our passes.

'Right. Stand 6. Bus should be along in about ten minutes.'

Sevvy kept running off to explore while we waited and Robin had to chase him. Jasmine gazed around her taking it all in. At long last the bus arrived. Sevvy sat next to me and Jasmine sat next to Robin so they could both have a window seat. They'd never been out of the town before. When we reached the outskirts of town, Sevvy stared through the window in fascination.

'Look at the sheep,' he shouted.

'Oh look, there's cows.'

'I can see a pig.'

Jasmine said, 'He's so childish,' in a voice intended to be heard by Sevvy but she was staring hard out of the window too.

Next we came to the solar farms. Rows and rows of solar panels, seeming to go on for ever.

'Boring,' said Sevvy but he became interested again when we reach the wind farms.

'Windmills,' he said, 'Like Jasmine made at school.'

Jasmine turned round to talk to me, her face alight.

'There's so many, Mummy. I never thought there'd be so many.'

It was when we left the power sector behind that I became interested. I'd thought that the countryside would be totally empty but it wasn't. There were still some rows of cottages and houses with the occasional farm. Most of them looked abandoned but, occasionally, I spotted someone at a window or in a garden.

There were other people about too. Riding horses or walking. Quite often they changed direction when they saw us coming, disappearing down dirt tracks or taking cover in the bushes. A horse driven cart passed, going in the opposite direction. The cart held six adults and a child, about Sevvy's age, sitting on someone's lap. The child raised a hand to wave to us but someone took hold of the hand and pulled it down.

Sevvy went to sleep, his thumb in his mouth. He was warm against my side and I soon drifted off too. I only woke up when we drew in to Rochdale. Luckily I only felt slightly sick.

We had a three hour wait in Rochdale. We took our travel passes to the Canteen and they provided us with cheese sandwiches, apples and a drink of water. We sat at a metal table to eat.

'This chair's cold on my bottom,' complained Sevvy. He'd been bad tempered ever since we had to wake him to get him off the bus. 'And my sandwich's not very nice, it's all curly.'

'Don't eat it then.' I was feeling irritable too.

Jasmine, a peacemaker for once, offered to swap her sandwich for Sevvy's because hers wasn't as 'curly'.

I looked at Robin. He was very quiet.

'Are you all right, love?'

'Yes, I suppose so. I'm just worried about what we're going to find when we get there.'

He hadn't seen his parents for over ten years.

'It's going to be hard. Did they tell you what's wrong with him?'

'Not really. I know he's never been right since he worked on the sea defences.'

'Yes, I know.'

'It was bad, Celia, you wouldn't believe how bad it was.'

'Can I have my apple now?'

'Have you eaten all your sandwich, Sevvy?' asked Robin.

I was surprised. Robin wasn't usually the strict one.

'There's just a bit of curly crust left. Just a tiny bit.'

'Well, eat that and then you can have the apple.'

We wandered around the bus station for ages trying to amuse the children. Then we sat down and took turns at reading them stories and playing *I Spy*. We had to alternate letters with colours so Sevvy could join in.

'I spy something beginning with blue'.

'A bus?'

'No.'

'Your coat?'

'No.'

'Jasmine's t shirt?'

'No. Shall I tell you?'

'Go on then.'

'The sky, silly.'

The bus to Manchester arrived on time but it needed recharging so we had to wait again. Robin talked to the guard at the checkpoint and he let us take the children outside for a break. We found a patch of sunlight to sit in.

'This wall's cold on my bottom now,' grumbled Sevvy.

'Stand up then.'

He jumped down, rubbed his bottom and then wandered off. Jasmine followed.

'Don't go too far,' I shouted after them.

'It was the smell,' Robin said, 'the smell from the sea. When the wind was in the wrong direction, we had to keep all the windows closed all the time. And Dad worked in that. Every day.'

'I suppose I was lucky, living inland.'

'They had to leave their clothes at the Sea Defence Depot to be decontaminated. And go through special showers before they were allowed to dress again.'

'They did a good job, Robin, they helped to protect us all.'

'I suppose so.'

'Mummy, Sevvy's climbing.'

I turned to look. He was scrambling up a wall that didn't look very safe. I shouted his name but he ignored me. I rushed off to pull him down. Robin followed but more slowly. Then he stopped.

'They're announcing our bus will be ready in five minutes.'

'Come on, Sevvy, let's go and get back on the bus. We should be able to see some more sheep.'

We passed through whole areas that looked like they'd been abandoned. Places where the roofs had caved in and where pavements were almost entirely grass.

It was about five years into the New Way that the re-allocations began. They'd realised that the most resource effective arrangement was to have people who worked in the same place living in the same area. It would only take a few buses to transport them in, even if their workplace was a long way away. I'd never really thought about it before but I realised there'd be areas which were just too inconvenient to use.

As we neared Manchester there were all the usual provision, solar and wind farms on the outskirts. Miles and miles of them. Boring, as Jasmine kept telling us. But when we got past those, it was a different world. Full of young people. Everywhere. Talking and laughing. Walking along in huge groups. Leaning against walls in couples, in their own private world. Sitting in the middle of the road, so the driver had to beep his horn to make them move. Just occasionally there was an older person, a tutor perhaps, walking through the crowds alone.

'Daddy was a student here,' I heard him saying to Jasmine, 'A long time ago.'

That reminded me of Sally and Keir. They'd moved away from next door suddenly. I had a sinking feeling when I thought about it. I reassured myself it probably wasn't anything to do with me, but, even if it had something to do with me, Sally deserved it.

Sevvy was staring out of the window but clearly not interested.

'Do you see that building there?' I asked.

He nodded.

'Well, when I was a little girl, my Mummy used to take me there to see a man in a red suit. He had a long white beard. He was called Father Christmas and every year, in December, he used to give children toys. I got a really pretty doll one year. And another year I got roller skates.'

'Why?'

'Why what?'

'Why did he give children toys? Why didn't the Delivery/Collection man bring them?'

'We didn't have a Delivery/Collection man in those days.'

'Oh, I wouldn't like that.'

He went back to looking out of the window.

The hostel where we were to stay the night was near to Chorlton Street Bus Station. It was a place of contrasts. Some bits of it were elegant, chandeliers and fancy ironwork on the staircases but then other areas looked totally neglected. Like our room. It had two sets of bunk beds with threadbare sheets and there was a bathroom that made Jasmine say, 'That's disgusting.'

It took ages to have all our documentation checked and, almost before we realised it, it was six o'clock and the children were 'staaaaarving.' The man on the desk had suggested we go to the hostel canteen but, when we peered round the door, it was dark and smelt strongly of cabbage.

'I don't want to go in there. It's scary,' said Jasmine.

The children had never stayed anywhere overnight nor eaten more than one meal in a day away from home. They were finding the whole experience overwhelming.

'Tell you what,' said Robin, 'there's a place I used to go when I was a student. It might still be there.'

He took us out of the hotel and down on to Oxford Road. We passed quite a few eating places full of young people; they looked fine to me but Robin was determined to revisit the place he went to when he was younger. Then he stood still and stared.

'That was my college.'

It was a big building with an adobe repaired glass frontage.

'Daddy, I'm hungry. When are we going to eat?' Jasmine said, hopping from foot to foot impatiently.

'Oh yes, sorry. If I remember rightly, it's just around this … oh look there it is.

More glass, more adobe but it looked clean and there were several older people inside, mixed in with the students. The children hesitated on the doorstep and I had to give Sevvy a push to get him inside. At the counter, we handed over our vouchers.

'Spaghetti tonight,' the woman said, 'Got some blackcurrant squash for the children if they want it, otherwise we've only water to drink. Supplies are low just now.'

'That's fine,' I said.

'Go on, sit down, I'll bring it over to you.'

There was only one table but it was covered in dirty plates. Robin carried them over to the counter.

'Thanks, love, been a bit pushed today, my helper's off sick.'

Sevvy filled in the time counting tables, 'one, two, five, three,' and Jasmine kept correcting him. I felt I should intervene but was suddenly exhausted and couldn't be bothered.

The woman arrived with the food.

'Sit down now, Sevvy, so you can eat your spaghetti.'

I was busy chopping up the children's spaghetti when Robin spoke and had to ask him to repeat what he'd said.

'Two years I spent here. It's a long time.'

Then his face clouded over.

'I haven't seen Mum and Dad since the day I left

91

Blackpool to come to Manchester. It's such a long time and now,' his voice breaks, 'now I'm going back to see my Dad because he hasn't long to live.'

He pushed his plate away and buried his face in his hands.

'Don't cry, Daddy, don't cry,' said Jasmine, patting his leg.

Robin shook his shoulders and sat up straighter before blowing his nose and pulling the plate back towards him.

'Come on children, eat up your spaghetti.'

12

Deveraux Medical School is to expand by two thousand places it was reported today, in order to keep up with the increased demand for doctors and nurses in the North West ...

I woke about five thirty. We'd gone to bed at the same time as the children; we were both tired and it was easier than risk disturbing them by our conversation. The children woke at six thirty; I was worried they were going to get noisy and wake the other people in the hostel. Robin had taken the top bunk so I climbed out of bed to reach up to shake him.

'Robin, wake up.'

'Is it time for work?' he asked, his eyes still closed.

'We're not at home, Robin, remember?'

He half pushed himself upwards and opened his eyes.

'Oh no,' he said, throwing himself down again. He rolled on to his back and covered his face with his hands. 'I can't face it. I can't bear going to see Mum and Dad. Not after all this time with Dad being so ill and about to …'

'Sh, don't let the kids hear.'

I turned to look at them. They were at the window with the closed curtain draped over their heads, looking at a world that was new to them.

I put my arms around Robin and he rested his head on my breast.

'It's hard, Celia, it's so hard.'

'I know, love, I know.'

I stroked his forehead. Jasmine turned towards us. The curtain had pulled her hair off her forehead and she looked especially pretty.

'The sun's shining, can we go out?'

Sevvy twisted round, the curtain covering one eye.

'When can we have breakfast? Can we go to that place we went yesterday?'

'Probably,' said Robin, 'but they won't open for a while.'

'Will there be spaghetti for breakfast? I like spaghetti.'

'You don't have spaghetti for breakfast, stupid.'

Next minute they were rolling on the floor. He was pulling her hair; she was hitting him in the stomach.

Robin slapped his hand down on the bed.

'Stop it!'

They carried on.

'Stop it now.'

They slid apart and sat with resentful expressions, facing towards us. Sevvy reached out a hand towards Jasmine's hair.

'Sevvy!'

Jasmine started giggling.

'It's not funny, Jasmine,' I said, making a move towards her.

She put out a hand to stop me.

'I know, Mummy, I know. It's just, I was thinking,' she giggled again, 'you can't send us to our rooms.'

Sevvy thought for a moment and then, understanding the joke, started to laugh. Suddenly, they were both rocking with laughter.

I was beginning to laugh myself but managed to say, 'It's not that funny.'

Robin was not amused.

'It's not funny at all. And we can still stop you having breakfast.'

That sobered them and the room became silent. I climbed out of bed and began to sort out clothes so we could get dressed.

'How's about we go for a walk before breakfast?'

Sevvy smiled, obviously comforted by the clue that he would be able to eat at some point in the future.

When we were all ready, we left the room and went downstairs. The hostel was almost silent, apart from the echoing of our footsteps and the sound of one door slamming.

Downstairs, there was a sleepy looking young girl on the reception desk. She gave us a half smile. The canteen was open but there was an offensive fatty smell wafting out of the door; even Sevvy wasn't that hungry.

Our first stop was the place where we'd eaten the day before but the notice on the door said it didn't open until seven thirty. We wandered down Oxford Road until we found an open grassed space with a bench nearby. Robin and I sat down while the children played. They found an old punctured ball and began to experiment to find out what it would, and wouldn't, do.

When Sevvy was running around wearing the punctured ball as a hat and Jasmine was trying to knock it off his head, we decided it was time to eat.

'Come on, kids. Let's go.'

At the eating place the woman from the night before said, 'Nice to see you back again. There's just enough squash left for the children if they want it.'

Jasmine nodded her head and Sevvy smiled.

The breakfast was laid out down one side of the room. There was a good choice. Cereals, yogurt, ham, cheese and bread rolls.

'I'll make you some toast.'

We filled our trays and sat down at the nearest table. The place was almost empty, just an old man sitting by the door.

'It's a shame, it's a bloody shame,' the old man shouted. 'What they've done to us, it's a fucking shame.'

Jasmine wriggled in her seat so she was sitting closer to me. Sevvy stared, open mouthed.

The woman arrived with our toast.

'Don't mind him. There's no harm in him. He was living in a home somewhere but couldn't stand being cooped up like that. Now he sleeps in an alleyway nearby. Should report him really but I don't like to. So I feed him instead. Just hope the Guardian doesn't turn up when he's here.'

She turned and went back to the counter. Two students came in and distracted Sevvy. It was a girl and a boy with identical haircuts, fringes cut in a zigzag pattern and the backs of their heads shaved. The girl was wearing a thick woolly jumper with a ripped white t shirt on top. The boy wore a corduroy shirt open to show his bare chest which had a dragon drawn on it in what looked like red marker pen. A patch of coarse black hair sat on top of the dragon's head. Both of them wore jeans with slashes cut in them.

'Those people should put their clothes out for the Delivery/Collection man so they can get some new ones.'

'Eat your cereal, Sevvy,' said Robin.

We finished our breakfast and prepared to leave.

'Jasmine, where are you going?'

She ignored me and made her way to the counter.

'Thanks for breakfast,' she said to the woman behind the counter.

The woman smiled down at her and then looked around behind the counter.

'Here you are.' She handed Jasmine two biscuits. 'One for you and one for your brother.' She looked up at me. 'Don't get to see many children around here. It's all students.'

Jasmine said 'thank you' again and walked towards me, holding the biscuits up for me to see.

'Bloody students,' the woman mouthed at me, 'they're a pain.'

As we were leaving the old man reached over and put a hand on Jasmine's arm making her jump. Then she stood totally still, obviously too scared to move and gazing up at Robin for help.

'Don't let the buggers grind you down,' the old man said.

Robin said, 'Come on, Jas,' and pulled her out of the door by her other arm.

She was visibly shaken.

'Come on, I've got something to show you,' said Robin.

He took us across Oxford Road to a big building. There was a lot of glass on the front, all of it intact, and through the glass, it was possible to see that the building had been split into two. Half looked to be part of a college because the rooms were full of tables and chairs.

On the wall, in big white letters, it said *BC*. There was a lighter patch in front of the two letters, as though something was missing.

'You see this building?'

The children nodded.

'This is the building that the radio comes from. I went in there once to take part in a college quiz. Recycling against Education. We won. Mum was so proud. Got all the neighbours in to listen.'

'You were on the radio, Daddy?'

'Certainly was.'

'I wish I could have heard that.'

On the way back to the hostel, Robin stopped again.

'Oh look, that's where I used to live.'

It had a big window with *Giorgio's* written on it in peeling paint.

'It had been a restaurant before the Upheaval. It still smelled of garlic, like it had seeped into the walls. All my clothes reeked of it. I remember I asked a girl for a date once. She sniffed and said, 'No thanks, not when you smell like that.''

I laughed but Jasmine patted his hand and said, 'Poor Daddy.'

My last image of the centre of Manchester was of the old man from the eating place, slumped against the wall of the bus station with his coat rolled up behind his head and his eyes closed. People passing by made an obvious detour around him. I suspected it wouldn't be long before he was sent back to the home and that made me feel sad.

Robin's parents' house was within walking distance of the bus station and we'd been given a map because they'd moved since he was last there. As we drew nearer, he swapped the suitcase over to the other side and took hold of my hand.

Jenny, his Mother, must have been watching for us as she hurried out of the house as soon as we turned the corner that had a dilapidated sign saying *Applegate Avenue*. Robin dropped the suitcase and then stood still, watching her hurry towards us. As she approached, he opened his arms and, when she ran into them, he lifted her in the air and spun her round.

She was a tiny woman, with short grey hair. Her skin was pale and she seemed very delicate, as though she would break easily. I soon found out that wasn't true. When Robin put her on the ground, she wiped her eyes on the sleeve of her green cardigan and turned towards the children.

'Sevvy and Jasmine,' she said, 'come and give Nana a hug.'

She scooped them both into her arms at the same time and told them, 'You're such beautiful children.'

Sevvy wriggled, trying to escape but she was having none of it. When she was finally finished with them, she turned to me.

Holding out her hand, she said, 'Hello, Celia, it's lovely to meet you at last.'

'And you,' I muttered, feeling confused about what I should call this woman who was so closely related to me but I'd never met before.

'Call me Jenny,' she said, 'that's what everyone calls me.'

The handshake didn't feel to be enough and I hugged her gently. She returned the hug with a stronger hold and I felt like struggling to escape as Sevvy did.

'Come on, let's get you settled and then we'll go and see Dad.'

The house was a semi-detached and looked fairly new from the outside but when we got inside, it had the feeling of a much older house. The air was musty and the furniture was dark. The place needed decorating and through the window

I could see that the back garden was overgrown, although the front garden was immaculate.

'You'll have to excuse the state of the place. The last few years have been hard, with Sevlan being ill.'

'I haven't been ill,' said Sevvy, in surprise.

'Sevlan is Grandpa's name as well,' I said, 'remember?'

'Grandpa Sevlan in Blackpool?'

'That's right,' said Jenny, 'and we're going to see him soon.' Then she put her hand to her mouth. 'That's if you don't mind the children seeing him. His face is a bit of a mess. But he really wants to see these two.'

'Let's see how it goes, Mum,' said Robin.

We went up to our room and unpacked while Jenny made the children sandwiches. I was worried there wouldn't be enough food but apparently the Delivery/Collection man had been given food for us too.

The hospital was only a five minute walk away from the house. Robin didn't know that area of town at all and he walked alongside his Mother. They held hands and talked quietly all the way. The children were with me.

'What did Nana mean about Grandpa's face?' Jasmine asked.

'It's part of his illness, that's all. Nothing to worry about.'

'I don't think I want to see him if there's something wrong with his face.'

'Grandpa really wants to see you because he hasn't met you before. You'll have to just take a deep breath and be a brave girl. If it helps, don't look at his face, look at the wall.'

I felt nervous too. I'd never been good with illness but I was going to do this for Robin.

The hospital was a big modern building, more modern

than the one in Burnley where both my parents were when they were ill. Robin had explained that this was a hospital that dealt with the health problems created at the time of the Upheaval. We showed our passbooks and signed in at the door. The Guard told us we could stay with Sevlan for two hours.

Sevvy walked between Jenny and Robin holding both their hands. For some reason he was singing *I'm a little teapot.*

'Sevvy, this isn't the place to sing,' I whispered but Jenny told me it was making her feel better so I didn't push the matter.

The hospital seemed to be all individual rooms rather than wards. In Sevlan's room, the curtains were closed halfway, so that most of the room, including the bed, was in shadow. He was asleep when we entered and his face looked to be fine but when Jenny woke him he turned towards us and I gasped. The left side of his face was distorted totally out of shape. The cheek was twice the size of the other one and his forehead was distended, hanging down over his left eye so that it was almost totally obscured. Jasmine took a sharp breath in and clung tightly to my hand but Sevvy went up to the bed to take a closer look.

'Oh my goodness,' said Sevlan, 'is this little Sevvy?'

Robin went and stood by the bed. He swallowed loudly.

'Yes, Dad, that's right.'

'Oh and Robin too.'

Sevlan held out his hand and Robin took it in both of his, up close to his chest. Sevlan put his other hand on the top of Sevvy's head.

'Hello, Sevvy. It's good to meet you.'

'Are you my Grandpa? My Grandpa Sevlan from Blackpool?'

'That's me.'

Sevvy looked up at Robin. 'It's Grandpa Sevlan.'

'Where's Jasmine? Is she here?'

Jasmine took a deep breath and went to stand behind Sevvy.

'I'm here, Grandpa Sevlan.'

He moved slightly forward to get a closer look at Jasmine. She took a step backward.

'There's nothing to worry about, Jasmine. It's just that my face's poorly that's all. It's not catching or anything.'

He moved his hand from Sevvy's head to stroke the side of Jasmine's face. She visibly relaxed as though his touch had stopped her feeling afraid.

'What a pretty little thing you are. I always wanted a daughter.'

'And this is Celia,' Robin said and I moved to stand with the rest of my family.

'Hello, Sevlan. It's good to meet you at last.'

Sevlan looked at the four of us and smiled, then he rested his head against the pillow. In an instant, Jenny was by his side.

'Are you tired, Sevlan? Do you want us to go?'

'No, don't go yet. Don't go.'

Robin found some chairs and we sat close to the bed; Jenny on one side, Robin and myself on the other. Robin had Sevvy on his knee and I had Jasmine.

'Did you have a good journey, son?' Sevlan kept his eyes closed as he spoke.

'It was all right but we had to stay the night in Manchester.'

Sevlan made a rasping noise. It worried me until I realised it was a chuckle. 'Manchester? Don't they have shortcuts these days?'

'No. Only longcuts, Dad.'

Sevvy suddenly said, 'Grandpa Sevlan, can I touch your face?'

'Sevvy, I don't think Grandpa's going to want you to touch his face. It's probably sore.'

'No, it's not sore. Let the lad touch it if he wants.'

Sevvy slipped down from Robin's knee and walked round to the other side of the bed. Jenny slid her arm around his waist as he softly stroked the side of his grandfather's ravaged cheek.

'It's all bumpy. Does it hurt?'

'No, it doesn't hurt. Not any more.'

Jenny brushed a tear away and held Sevvy tighter.

'Why don't we go and get a drink?' she asked. 'Leave Robin and his Dad alone for a while to talk.'

When we arrived back at the house, Jenny suggested that we take the children out while she prepared the meal. I offered to help.

'No, I'll be fine. Be fun cooking for a family again. It's only been me and Sevlan for such a long time.'

'Where should we go, Mum? Is there a park nearby?'

'Why don't you take them along the sands?'

'Is it all right to go down there?'

'Yes, it's fine. They declared it safe a few years ago. Me and your Dad have been down there lots of times since. Don't go in the sea though, just in case.'

We left the house and walked toward the beach. I could tell by the smell that we were going towards the sea. It was a smell I remembered from being a child when we went on holiday. I could remember the golden sand and sparkling blue seas of Spain but there were also trips to places like

Scarborough and Morecambe. The sand was darker and the sea was greyer but the sky was just as blue and the sun was bright in the sky. Then there came a time when we couldn't go on holiday any more; Dad worked all the time and only essential travel was allowed.

When we reached the promenade, we were confronted by rolls of rusting barbed wire but there were places where gaps had been broken through and signs put up saying *Entrance to beach.*

'Do we want to risk it?' I asked Robin, suddenly remembering Sevlan's face.

'If Mum and Dad have been down there, then it's fine. Dad wouldn't ever put Mum in danger. Anyway, look at that.'

There was a blue sign saying, *Department of the Environment. This area is now safe to use for recreational purposes.*

Sevvy stood in the opening between the barbed wire and looked out to sea.

'What is it?'

'See the blue in the distance? That's the sea. And this yellow stuff, that's sand.'

'Like in the sandpit at nursery?'

'Yes, that's right.'

He stepped on to the sand and put his hand down towards it. My heart twisted about in my chest.

'Don't touch it, Sevvy, there's a good boy.'

He pulled his hand back and turned towards us, his face disappointed.

'Come on, let's race,' I said, and the four of us ran down the beach. We ran until I couldn't breathe anymore. The children stopped beside me, laughing. Robin carried on running.

We followed him, slowly. Eventually he stopped and, as I neared, I saw his shoulders were shaking and he had his hands over his face. As soon as I reached him, I slid my arms around his waist and pressed my face against his chest. His heart was pounding and the movement of his chest wall told me he was sobbing rather than gasping for breath. Jasmine put her arm around both of us.

'Family hug.'

Sevvy grabbed on to my thigh and rested his face against it. The wind was suddenly chilly around us and I moved even closer to Robin.

'Come on,' Robin said, his voice uneven, 'let's go back to Mum.

13

Despite the recent storms, The Regional Water Authority has issued a region wide ban on hosepipes and it may be necessary to go on to water rationing …

'Don't like this shirt, it's itchy. I want to wear my blue t shirt, the one with the footballer on.'

'I want you to wear this one. It's smart for Grandpa Sevlan's funeral.'

Sevlan had died in his sleep three days after we arrived.

'I don't want to go to his fural. I want to stay here and play in the garden. Like yesterday.'

'Tough.'

I heard a knock on the front door and the sound of Jenny letting Dorothy, the Guardian in.

'Come on, Sevvy, get this shirt on now before I'm really cross.'

He slid his arms in and I fastened the buttons, pulling at the material a little too hard, making his head bob up and down.

Downstairs, Dorothy was handing out black armbands.

We put them on but Sevvy's was too big and slid down to his wrist. He gave his hand a shake and the band fell to the floor.

'I'll get a safety pin,' said Jenny.

She knelt down beside him and fastened the pin at the back of the band so that it clung to his arm. Then she pushed herself up slowly.

'Everyone ready?' she asked.

We all nodded and headed to the door. Each clutching a flower from the garden, we stood on the pavement waiting for the funeral float.

'I'll have to leave now,' said Dorothy, 'I have somewhere else to go. The float should be along any minute and, if there are any problems, the funeral director will sort you out.'

Almost before she'd disappeared around the corner, we heard a high pitched whine.

'Is it a bus?' asked Sevvy, 'it sounds like a bus.'

'No, it's the funeral float. Now, no more questions until we get back home, do you understand?'

'Yes.'

The float stopped at the front door and a tall man stepped down from the passenger seat. He was wearing a dark suit like Dad used to wear when he went into Manchester on business.

'Hello, my name's Bernard and I'm the funeral director. Any problems, please let me know. Now, I presume this is Jenny?'

Jenny stepped forward and held out her hand.

Bernard took it.

'I'm sorry for your loss.'

'Thank you,' she whispered, for the first time looking as though she might cry. Then she straightened her shoulders and composed her face.

'Right, Jenny, I'd like you at the front of the group behind the float. Is that okay?'

'Can I have my son with me?'

'If that's what you want, that's fine.'

He took her by the hand and led her to stand at the back of the float facing towards it. Robin stood beside her, looking tall against her tiny frame.

'Is that Grandpa Sevlan?' whispered Jasmine.

'You're not supposed to ask questions,' said Sevvy.

I put my finger up against my lips to silence him but then whispered, 'Yes, it is Grandpa Sevlan.'

Of course it was Grandpa Sevlan, that's why we were there. He was almost totally covered by a white shroud apart from the undamaged side of his face which looked calm and serene. His body was slotted into a niche created by black cushions and, overhead, a black canopy protected him from the drops of rain that had just started falling.

'Now, the rest of you.'

I stood between Sevvy and Jasmine behind Robin and Jenny

'Will the children be all right walking?' asked Bernard, 'it's not too far.'

'Think so,' I said.

'Well, if they're struggling, just call me and we'll put them in the front. It's not a problem.'

The float set off and we followed. Several neighbours had come to stand at their front gates and all bowed their heads respectfully as we passed.

The children seemed to understand the solemnity of the occasion and they walked purposefully, their heads held high, their faces serious. The rain fell a little harder, leaving dark spots on our clothing and I was glad that Sevlan had the canopy. It felt strange to be at the funeral of a man who was so important to my family but whom I'd only just met.

Although it was a walk that seemed to go on forever, it was still a surprise when I saw the sign that said *Daisy Field Burial Ground*. We passed through the gates and into an enormous green space. Robin had told me it used to be an industrial estate when he lived in Blackpool but there was no sign of that now.

When the float stopped, the driver and Bernard climbed down and produced, as if from nowhere, a trolley. As they slid Sevlan on to it, his shroud fell from his face and, just for a moment, I saw the damaged side before Bernard adjusted the sheet. He took the front end of the trolley and the driver took the back. Together the two moved the trolley along while we followed.

A complex series of paths led through acres of lawn with the occasional tree dotted around. At each intersection was a board inscribed with names. Sevvy pointed his finger and I could feel a question building up inside him but he swallowed audibly and looked straight ahead.

We reached the spot where Sevlan was to be buried. The hole had already been dug and two men, presumably gravediggers, stood respectfully by. We gathered around the edge; I had to pull Sevvy back a little because he was leaning forward to look down into the hole and I was afraid he was going to fall in. Bernard began to speak.

'Friends, we have gathered here today to say goodbye to Sevlan Robin Travis. He was a special man. Special because in the days when this country was at risk, he stepped forward and volunteered his services in helping to protect us all from the contamination of the sea. That was a brave act because we didn't know what risks there were and, indeed, it was the exposure to those elements that led to the illness which has taken him from us.

'But we have cause to be thankful because his family were granted a period of twenty five years between that time and this. A period he spent mostly with his wife, Jenny, because, as we know, the needs of this country often dictate that we have to leave the ones we love behind and so his son, Robin, had to make a new life elsewhere. It was only in the past week that the family have been able to be together and, I'm sure, they are all grateful that Sevlan had the opportunity to meet his daughter in law and his two grandchildren.'

While Bernard was speaking, the clouds had dispersed and the sky was blue above us although there was a soft wind moving through my hair.

'Now, I believe that his son would like to speak. Robin?'

Robin took a step forward and turned to look at Jenny.

'Daddy,' escaped from Sevvy's mouth and he clamped his hand over it.

'I wish I could have spent more time with Dad. There were times when he was working on the sea defences that he would leave the house before I got up and only return after I was asleep. But I'm glad that I've had chance to talk to him this week. I'm going to miss him but I'll never forget those talks we've had. He was a very special man.'

Bernard took charge again.

'Now, we're going to spend a quiet minute saying our own goodbyes to Sevlan.'

I listened to the peace around me. I thought about Sevlan and the changes he must have seen in his life. I felt sad that I was only able to be with him for a short time and, in my silent goodbye, I promised to keep his memory in my heart and in my head.

After a minute, Bernard spoke, 'Here ends the life of Sevlan Robin Travis,' and then he set off down the path.

We hesitated, not sure what to do then, one by one, we followed him. Out of the corner of my eye I could see the gravediggers move forward. We left the burial ground, Bernard and the funeral float behind us and walked along the streets together as a family group. All the way home I tried to rid my mind of the image of the earth falling on to Sevlan's damaged face.

14

Postal deliveries are to be reduced to once every two months. The Minister for Communication said, 'Too much time is wasted dealing with inconsequential letters ...

At long last we arrived home after hours spent fielding 'are we there yet?' questions. Robin had tried to persuade his mother to come back and live with us but she refused. She said she was settled where she was and didn't want to leave. Robin was worried about her and so was I, in a way, but at the same time I was grateful that we wouldn't have her living with us.

Inside the house the children raced off to reacquaint themselves with their toys while Robin and I took a much needed nap on the sofa. When I awoke I was lying with my head in Robin's lap. He was looking down into my face and I could tell he'd been crying again.

'Oh, Robin, I wish I could do something to make it better.'

'I wish you could too but it's one of those things that

can't be made better. I just have to get used to the fact that Dad's no longer there.'

'He was a good man and you can be very proud of the things he did.'

'I know. I wish I could have spent more time with him though.'

Sevvy rushed into the room.

'Look what I've drawn. It's Grandpa Sevlan from Blackpool.'

The picture was of a stick man (a skill Sevvy had only just mastered). The left side of the face was even more out of shape than the rest of the head but there was a big smile on the face.

'That's the sea,' Sevvy pointed, 'and the sun and the sand.'

'That's lovely,' I said, rubbing my hand against the side of his face.

Robin didn't say anything as he picked up Sevvy and held him tight on his knee.

Next day life should have been back to normal but it didn't feel normal. Everything in the house suddenly seemed new or different. The table in the dining room looked small and it felt significant that we only had four chairs; I keep expecting Jenny to come in the room. And Sevvy's picture of Sevlan caught my eye every time I went into the kitchen.

When I'd dropped Jasmine off at school, I took Sevvy down to Dorey's house. Her face lit up when she saw me.

'I've missed you so much. Where have you been? I asked around but no one knew. I was worried you'd been moved but I walked past your house yesterday and there was no sticker on the locker.'

'We've been up to Blackpool. Robin's Dad was ill and then he died.'

'Oh, I'm sorry to hear that.'

'Thanks.'

'Anyway, come on in.'

I stepped into the hallway and then stopped.

'Goodness, you've done a lot of work in here.'

The hallway was fresh and bright. The paintwork was white and the walls had been painted a lemon colour.

'Well, you got me started and now I've got the bug. Russell's helped as well when he's had time. And come and look at this.'

The front room had all the wallpaper stripped off. The furniture was in the centre of the room, covered with an old sheet and there was a stepladder against the far wall. Hannah was standing next to a can of paint with her finger outstretched, about to dip it in.

'Oh no you don't, young lady.'

Dorey picked her up and carried her to the door.

'Why don't you and Sevvy go and play in the dining room while I talk to Celia?'

The two children ran off into the dining room. I heard Sevvy say, 'And there was an enormous sandpit as big as the sky.'

'Have you got another brush?' I asked.

'Are you sure you want to help? I can always put the lid on and do it another day. Then we can have some tea and a chat.'

'We can talk while we work.'

She found me a brush and pointed me to the door. I began to cover it in white paint. The regular movement of the brush soothed me and made me feel better. The smell was a bit much, but my nausea seemed to have almost gone.

'So, how's things?' says Dorey, her voice distorted from the effort of reaching into the corner.

'Not good,' I replied.

'It's going to take a while to get over losing Robin's Dad. Were you close?'

'I hadn't met him before and Robin hasn't seen him for a long time. But he was there, do you know what I mean?'

'Yes, I felt like that about my Mum. Now she's gone there's an empty space in my life where she should be.'

'But it's not just that. You remember me checking your calendar?'

'Oh, God, yeah. I was so worried about you going away that I'd forgotten. Did you see the nurse?'

'I did. She said I was pregnant.'

Dorey jumped down off the ladder and held out her arms.

'Come and give us a hug. That's brilliant.'

I stayed where I was.

'It might not be so brilliant. Parveen says I might need to have an abortion.'

Dorey dropped her arms down by her side and then lifted them up again.

'I think you need a hug anyway.'

I stepped into her arms and she held me for a moment. Then she pulled away.

'Come on, let's sit down and talk about it. Is there something wrong with the baby?'

I told her what Parveen had said.

'Oh God, that's terrible. When will they let you know?'

'I don't know. That's the worst bit really. Apparently they're just setting up committees and things so no one knows how long it will take.'

'Well, with a bit of luck, it will be too late and then …'

There was a crash from the back of the house. We looked at each other for an instant and then hurried off to the kitchen. There was a chair lying on its side and a purple puddle on the floor with an orange beaker in its centre; a purple puddle that had splashed all over the newly painted wall.

'We were just making a drink, Mummy,' Sevvy said, 'just making some blackcurrant and it all went wrong.' He turned to look at Hannah. 'Didn't it, Hannah?'

Hannah didn't say anything. She was cowering in the corner; her big eyes looking to my left where Dorey was standing beside me, her body drooping, her face dead.

'Just when I think things are going okay for once, something happens to spoil it. It's not worth trying.'

She turned and went into the dining room where she sat down, put her forearms on the table and rested her head on them. For a moment I considered joining her but there were children there and I'd never do that in front of children.

'Right you two. Let's think what we need to do.'

'We need to clean this mess up,' said Sevvy, 'with a cloth.'

'What do you think, Hannah?'

Hannah looked through the doorway at Dorey and then back at me. She nodded. 'A cloth. That will make it better. And we need to look after Mummy.'

'I think Mummy needs to be alone for a little while. Let's make it look good in here first and then we'll see to Mummy.'

There were some old rags lying on the worktop. I ripped one in three, soaked them in water, wrung them out and gave the two smaller pieces to the children.

'OK. I want you to clean off all those splashes so the wall looks nice and new again.'

The worried look left Hannah's face when she had something to do. The two children worked hard on the surface while I put the beaker in the sink, mopped up the puddle, and took the chair back into the dining room. Dorey didn't move.

'We've finished, Mummy.'

'Oh, that's perfect, Sevvy, just perfect. Tell you what. The sun's come out again, how's about I make you both another drink and you can have it outside. Is that a good idea?'

The children both nodded. While I was busy at the sink I heard whispering and, when I turned round, the children had their sunhats on.

'Got to be careful in the sun, that's what Miss Fontaine says,' Hannah told me.

'That's right. What clever children you are.'

When they were both outside, I returned and wiped away all the splashes they'd missed and then cleared away the painting things from the front room; all the while thinking that I had enough problems of my own without taking on someone else's. Finally I made two cups of dandelion tea and sat down beside Dorey. She stayed in the same position. I put my arm around her, in the same way that she had put her arm around me.

'Come on, Dorey, drink your tea and talk to me.'

She lifted her head slowly. Her hair was over her face and, in places it clung to her damp cheeks.

'I try so hard, Celia, I try so hard but nothing ever goes right. Not since we came up from London. We had a lovely home there and now it's gone.'

'But you're making good progress in this house. It's only been a couple of weeks and you've done more than I managed in six months.'

'But it's only cosmetic. There's so much needs to be done, a lot of it more than we have the skills to do. After the rain the other day, Hannah's room was so damp we had to move her in with us. One of the window frames is rotten and I'm frightened it will fall out if we go anywhere near it. A bit of paint's not going to cure that.'

'Have you asked about having it fixed?'

'We've asked but Parveen says there isn't the manpower at the moment. They're all working on some building project.'

'Makes me wonder why they put you in here in the first place.'

'There wasn't anywhere else for us to go. Mrs Sewell next door told me this house had been condemned as unfit for human habitation. Been blocked up for years before they put us in here.'

I sipped on my tea. It tasted bitter and, as my stomach was already unsettled from the paint fumes, I felt a wave of nausea rise up. I put the cup down and concentrated on finding a solution for Dorey.

'What about asking to move in next to us? The house is empty again.'

There was that guilt again.

'But it's in a different area to us. They're not going to let us move to a new sector.'

'You're already living in the wrong area. It wouldn't be any further for Russell to walk for the work bus. In fact, I think it might be a bit nearer.'

I made the last part up. I had absolutely no idea whether it was nearer or not.

'Do you think we've a chance?'

'It's certainly worth trying.'

When Robin came home from work he went straight upstairs. I followed. He was lying on the bed, his arm over his face.

'Are you all right, love?'

'Had a bad day. Thought I could fix a cooker and spent all day working on it but it was knackered. Then I got bollocked by Bruce for wasting my time. He said it was obvious the thing had no life left in it and it was only sheer stubbornness that made me try. I'm sick of it, Celia, I'm sick of the whole thing. What is the point of keep re-using the same old stuff? What is the point?'

He pressed his elbows down into the bed and pushed himself up so he was lying at an angle.

'Do you remember, Celia, when we were children? How, if you wanted something you'd pop down to the shops to get it. Do you remember?'

'Yes I remember but …'

'Nobody does any popping these days, do they? No, you fill in a bloody form, send it off and then wait to see if it comes. And when it does come, it's some tatty old knackered thing that some idiot like me has tarted up to make it last a bit longer. I'm sick of it.'

'Oh, Robin, what's making you talk like this? You love your job, love it. Mending things, improving things, making sure they're the best they possibly can be before they go out.'

'Well, I didn't love it today. Not at all. Bloody waste of time.'

'Come downstairs and have something to eat. That will make you feel better.'

'No, I'm not hungry. I'll stay up here thanks.'

Downstairs I dished up three plates of soya casserole but when I looked at mine I found I wasn't hungry either. I tried to scrape my plate into the compost bin but the smell when I opened the lid led to me running upstairs to the bathroom to rid my stomach of what was left from lunch.

Back in the kitchen, the children had finished eating. I filled the sink with hot water and approached the table to clear away. The nausea rose up in my throat and I couldn't get near enough to the table to pick the plates up.

'Jasmine, can you empty what's left into the bin please, then put the plates in the sink to soak.'

'Okay, Mummy.'

She had to pass me on the way to the bin and the sight of a carrot clinging to the sauce on the plate made me rush from the kitchen. I grabbed Sevvy on my way.

'Come on, Sevvy, it's time for bed.'

'No it's not, it's too early.'

'Well, go into your room, put on your pyjamas and play for a while before you get into bed.'

'But I haven't had my bath.'

'You're clean enough. Now go.'

Jasmine walked out of the kitchen licking her fingers. My stomach heaved.

'You go up to bed too, Jasmine.'

'But it's early and ...'

'Yes, I know, I've had it all from Sevvy. Now go. Find something to do in your room until it's time to go to sleep.'

I followed her up the stairs. Luckily the power cut waited until I was at the top of the stairs and Jasmine was in her room. Both children wailed that they were scared of the dark but I couldn't do anything about it. I went into each room, persuaded them into bed and told them to go to sleep.

In our bedroom, Robin was fast asleep and snoring

loudly, still fully dressed. I lay down beside him and it didn't take long before the noise turned into the sound of Sevlan, in his Blackpool grave, choking on the earth that dropped down from above.

15

A virulent virus is spreading rapidly throughout the area. Doctors advise scrupulous hygiene and suggest all those affected avoid contact with others as much as possible.

I woke and looked at the clock. Five thirty. It had been a long and restless night and Robin wasn't beside me. I was worried; it wasn't like him to be up before he had to. I decided to go and find him but when I lifted my head, I began to retch.

I raced for the bathroom but the door was locked and there was no answer when I tried to call, 'Robin?'

My voice was weak and I realised he probably couldn't hear me. I ran downstairs to the kitchen sink but it was full of the previous night's dishes and made me retch even more. I went out to the grate beside the back door but my heaving stomach seemed to be completely empty and eventually I returned to the kitchen. My skin was cold and clammy and there was blackness around the edges of my vision. I sat at the kitchen table and rested my head on my arms, in the same way that Dorey had the day before.

When Robin came downstairs, he looked very flushed and his crumpled t shirt was covered in dark sweat patches.

'I think I've got the flu,' he told me, 'I'm not well enough to go to work.'

'You need to be in bed then.'

'I know that! I've come downstairs for a drink of water. There's no glass in the bathroom.'

I knew where the glass was, in Sevvy's bedroom where he kept it to throw at any witches that might come in the night. Jasmine would insist on telling him scary stories.

Robin had reached the sink.

'My God, Celia, what's all this mess?'

'It's last night's washing up. I didn't feel well enough.'

'Do you think you've got the flu too? That's all we need. Who's going to look after the kids if we're ill?'

'No, I think it's the baby that's making me sick.'

'And that's another thing.'

He stopped to drink his water, rocking slightly on his feet, as though he wasn't safe to be standing.

'Whose idea was it for us to have another baby? I don't remember being consulted.'

'No one consulted me either, Robin. It just happened.'

'Well, it doesn't seem right to me.' Another sip. 'Bringing another child into this world to wear second hand shoes. No, I take that back. Third hand shoes. Fourth hand shoes. Fifth …'

His words were overtaken by a bout of coughing that was so strong he had to hold on to the table to keep himself upright.

'You need to be in bed.'

'I know. I don't think I can make it back upstairs on my own. Can you give me a hand?'

As we made our way upstairs, his arm around my shoulders, mine around his waist, I thought about the poor baby who seemed to be very unwelcome. I hoped it was just the illness that was making Robin talk that way; I needed him to be on my side if we were told we couldn't have it so that we could fight back.

I tucked him up in bed and tackled the mess in the kitchen sink by turning my face away and washing the dishes by feel alone. It still wasn't pleasant; the water was cold and greasy and it was a battle to keep my stomach under control.

I called Robin's work on my way to school with Jasmine. Back home I spent the morning playing with Sevvy and dashing upstairs when Robin called: *I'm too hot; I'm thirsty; I'm too cold; bring me a blanket.*

'Have you had a busy day? I have.'

It was Dorey, waiting for Hannah in the school yard.

'Not really. What about you?'

'I've finished painting the walls in the front room. I'm really proud of myself.'

'So you should be.'

'It's funny but the more I do the better I feel. It's just getting going that's the problem.'

'Did you talk to Nasreen?'

'She's coming round in the morning. She sounded a bit doubtful on the phone, until I told her what you said about us not living in the right area anyway.'

There was a sudden outburst of noise as the children ran out of the school door, all full of energy and things to say after a day of sitting still and listening. Jasmine came out slowly looking tearful and upset.

'I don't feel well and I think I'm going to be …'

She threw up all over my feet and I had to suppress the urge to follow by reminding myself that I hadn't eaten for over twenty four hours.

Sevvy talked all the way home in a high pitched excited voice, something about dinosaurs but I was worried about Jasmine and didn't join in the conversation. Her hand was trembling in mine and I was glad when we got home.

As soon as we were inside I picked Jasmine up and carried her upstairs. Robin came out of the bedroom and stood by the door, then followed us into the bedroom.

'Looks like we've got another invalid,' I told him, pulling her t shirt over her head and replacing it with her nightie. Robin pulled the covers back and I slid her into bed. I put my hand on her forehead. It was hot and clammy.

'Do you think I should call the nurse,' I asked Robin.

'Yes, I think so. She's not big and tough like me.'

He followed his last statement with a bout of coughing that left him gasping for breath. I heard his footsteps behind me as I walked down the stairs. Sevvy was standing at the bottom looking as though he daren't move in case he got into trouble.

'Sevvy, be a good boy and play quietly, will you? Daddy and Jasmine aren't very well and I need to look after them.'

'Yes, Mummy.'

Robin wandered into the kitchen and Sevvy went into the front room. I went to call Parveen. I pressed the Medical button and the service put me straight through to her.

'Hello, it's Celia Travis. My little girl, Jasmine, isn't well. Could you come round?'

'I'm just about to eat. Haven't had anything all day. Can it wait until after that?'

'Yes, that's fine.'

'Be about an hour and a half.'

Back home, Robin was on his way upstairs.

'Sorry, love, not as well as I thought I was. Going back to bed.'

'OK. Parveen's coming. Do you want her to have a look at you too?'

'Can't do any harm, can it?'

16

A recent report from the Institute of Dieticians suggests that ready made meals are not as nutritious as home cooked food. Further studies are necessary before a solution can be found.

The next few days were terrible. Parveen had said that bed rest and plenty of fluids should do it for the two of them. She also gave Robin a herbal medicine to help with the cough. It didn't seem to be working because he kept me awake all night.

I was so tired I couldn't focus on anything. I didn't know whether I had what Robin and Jasmine had or if it was the pregnancy but I didn't seem to want to eat either. I had a word with Parveen and she seemed to think it was exhaustion and the after effects of the trip up to Blackpool. She said I should take it easy but how could I with two invalids in the house?

Luckily, Jasmine recovered quickly and I took her back to school after a couple of days. She really wanted to go and it was going to be easier on me while she was there. Robin had improved a lot too but he'd lost his voice and was very bad tempered. The loss of his father had had a bigger impact on Robin than he would admit. It was bound to. I could remember when my parents died, eighteen months apart, I found it so hard. It was around the time I met Robin and he had given me a lot of support but, even so, I could remember mornings when I didn't want to get out of bed and face the world. It knew it took time to get over things like that but if I tried to talk to Robin he became angry and I didn't have the energy to cope with that.

Everyone ate breakfast that morning, first time in days and I'd managed to keep a piece of toast down too. I realised I hadn't been sick at all when we were in Blackpool; I must have forced myself to keep going. When I came back from the school, Robin, Sevvy and I played a game of *The Delivery/Collection man came and brought …* which seemed to go on for ever. Then Robin went for a nap and I planned to put my feet up for half an hour before taking Sevvy to nursery. He promised to play with his Lego in his room and not make any noise.

A knock at the door awakened me. When I opened the door, Dorey, Hannah and Jasmine were standing on the doorstep. Jasmine spoke first. She looked pale and worried.

'Mummy, you never picked me up from school. I waited and waited. Dorey waited with me because she wanted to talk to you.'

'That's right. I was worried when you didn't turn up so I told Jasmine I'd bring her home.'

'But, but …'

My brain was like cotton wool and I couldn't seem to get a grip on the situation.

'Did school finish early?' I finally managed to ask.

'No.'

Dorey looked at her watch.

'It's three forty five.'

'I must have gone to sleep. I know I was tired but …' I said and then remembered something.

'Sevvy. Why didn't Sevvy wake me?'

I dashed upstairs and into Sevvy's room. He was curled up on the floor with a huge Lego tower beside him.

'Sevvy, are you all right?'

He opened one eye.

'Yes,' he said sleepily, 'I'm all right.'

He sat up. His cheek was pitted from the pile on the carpet.

'I made a big tower. See.'

He pointed and then asked, 'Is it nursery time yet?'

'No, Sevvy, we missed it.'

Robin came into the room looking even sleepier than Sevvy.

'Missed what?'

'Nursery. I went to sleep and didn't take Sevvy to nursery.'

'Oh, for God's sake, Celia, can't you do one simple thing?'

'You were asleep too.'

'That's not the point, Celia. It was your job to take Sevvy to nursery. And you, Sevvy, should have made sure she took you. You're a very naughty boy.'

Sevvy started to cry.

'Oh for goodness sake, Robin, grow up. He's a young child, almost still a baby. He went to sleep, that's all. Like me.'

I picked Sevvy up and carried him downstairs. Jasmine was still cross at me but was cheered up by a drink and a biscuit. All the children went off to play. As soon as they left the kitchen, Dorey told me that they were going to be considered for the house next door.

'That's great news. Great news.'

Then Robin came into the kitchen. Dorey took one look at his face and decided it was time for her to leave.

After I'd waved Dorey and Hannah off, I went back into the kitchen. Robin was at the table with his bottle of medicine in front of him.

'I'm sorry, Celia, I didn't mean to talk to you the way I did. It's just that everything seems to be upside down at the moment and I don't know where I am.'

'I know. We've had a tough couple of weeks. Maybe things will get better now.'

I began to get the evening meal ready. Robin peeled the potatoes for me while sitting at the table. Then there was a knock at the front door.

'I'll go,' shouted Jasmine.

I heard the door opening and then Jasmine peered into the kitchen.

'It's Agnes, should I let her in?'

'That's all we need,' said Robin, throwing down his potato peeler.

At the door, Agnes looked more serious than I had ever seen her. I led her into the front room and told the children to go up into their bedrooms. Robin came in to join us. I signalled to him to fasten his dressing gown more tightly.

'I'll get right to the point,' said Agnes.

'Please do,' Robin said, 'we're hoping to eat soon.'

Agnes glared at him and then turned to me.

'Celia, you failed to pick Jasmine up from school today. Could you explain why?'

'I went to sleep.'

'It's not much to ask is it, to pick your children up on time?'

'No but I didn't do it on purpose, I ...'

'You were asleep. You told me that. Can you tell me why you felt it necessary to sleep during the afternoon? Most people manage to go the whole day without having to take mid-afternoon naps. Why can't you?'

'Like I said, I ...'

'It's not good enough, Celia. What if Jasmine had decided to come home on her own? What about that? Anything could have happened to her.'

'But it didn't. Dorey brought her home.'

'Yes. Dorey, that's another matter. Didn't I say to you I don't approve of cross-area friendships?'

'I, I,' I couldn't think of anything to say to make the situation better and the change of subject had confused me.

Then Robin spoke.

'Show more respect to my wife. She's admitted she made a mistake this afternoon and you yourself told us that cross-sector friendships aren't against the rules. Just leave us alone. We're doing all right.'

'I'm only doing my job, Mr Travis.'

'Well, we don't need you doing your job in our home. Go and do your busybodying somewhere else.'

'If you think about it, Mr Travis, it's not *your* home. It belongs to the community. It belongs to all of us. And you have certain obligations in order to deserve this home. This afternoon Celia didn't fulfil her obligations. And, may I add, there have been occasions lately when you too have stepped outside the bounds of acceptable behaviour at work.'

Robin leant forward in his seat. 'How dare you talk to me like that?'

131

'Like I said before, Mr Travis, it's my job. I have to make sure that everyone toes the line. That's what I do.'

'Well, I don't want you making sure I toe the line in *my* home at *this* time.'

'Robin, don't! She's right. This is what she has to do.'

Robin slammed his hand down on the arm of the chair. 'Rubbish! Absolute rubbish. I work hard to be entitled to this home. And in return I'm entitled to object to some old biddy coming here and telling us what to do.'

He stood up, dressing gown agape, purple underpants on show, and went over to the lounge door.

'Mr Travis, that's enough. I'm going to have to report …'

'I want you to leave,' he said, 'I want you to leave right now.'

'Robin, no,' I said, 'Stop it.'

'Now, Mr Travis, you need to calm down. You're going to get yourself into a lot of trouble if you carry on with your attitude. What about sitting down and talking about this calmly?'

'I said I want you to leave and I mean it. Now get out.'

He opened the door wider and, when Agnes didn't look to be moving, he went round to the other side of the sofa and pulled her up by the hand, then slid his arm under her armpit and marched her to the door.

'Mr Travis, I'm warning you. You're already in trouble but if you don't stop this right now …'

'Out,' he said, pushing her over the doorstep, 'and don't come back.'

He slammed the door shut behind her but I could still hear her shouting.

'I'll be back, Mr Travis. Don't you worry, I'll be back. And then you'll be sorry.'

Robin leant with his back against the door and then slid downwards, until he was sitting on the floor.

'Stupid old cow. That showed her. Didn't it?'

'Oh, Robin. What have you done?'

17

The number of people living in the London area is down to twenty five percent of what it was ten years ago while Manchester's population has risen by sixty percent.

Robin woke at six thirty. Another night when I hadn't slept. We sat, side by side, talking about what had happened the previous evening. Robin was convinced he was in the right.

'Celia, stop worrying. It's going to be all right. What are they going to do? Throw us out on the street? I don't think so. They're not going to get rid of a good worker like me, are they? They might send a letter of reprimand, something like that. It will probably go on our record but nothing more serious.'

'But remember what happened with Rose and Charlie? They had to leave, didn't they?'

'Charlie had been stealing. That's serious stuff. I only lost my temper, that's all.'

'Agnes isn't going to see it like that. She's not. And what did she mean by you stepping out of the bounds of acceptable behaviour.'

'Just an argument at work, that's all. Look. I'll tell you what. I'm going to ring work, say I'm taking another day sick. At the same time, I'll call Agnes and apologise. Say it was my illness or something. How's about that?'

He looked at me anxiously and held out his arms for a hug. I scooted over and buried my face in his chest as he patted my back. Maybe he was right.

Sevvy wandered in. 'Mummy, I wet my bed. I'm sorry.'

'Don't worry about it, Sevvy. I'll come and change your bed and then we'll get you out of those smelly pyjamas.'

Sevvy bent over and sniffed loudly.

'Oh no, I am smelly. Smelly Sevvy, that's me.'

While I sorted Sevvy out, Robin dressed and went out to the phone box. He was gone quite a while. By the time he came back, I was in the kitchen making breakfast.

'Well?' I said

Robin hesitated

'I rang work first. That went okay. They said they've got a lot of people off sick with this bug but they've been advised that it's better if staff stay off until they are totally well. In that way it might not spread so far and we won't have to go off sick again in the near future.'

'And Agnes?'

He rubbed the back of his neck.

'That didn't go so well.'

'What did she say?'

'Firstly, she was angry because I rang so early. She was having her breakfast apparently.'

'But if you'd rung later, she'd be out on her rounds.'

'That's what I said. But it's what she said after that's important.'

'What was that?'

'She said …'

'What?'

My heart was beating fast and everything seemed darker somehow, as though someone had closed the curtains to keep the sun out.

'She said she'll be round later with some guards. Celia … they're going to take us to an Assessment Centre.'

There was a brief period of darkness, a time when I could feel Robin sitting me down and pushing my head down between my knees but I couldn't see anything nor think clearly.

I heard Sevvy say, 'What's wrong with Mummy?' and Robin's reply, 'Go upstairs and play until breakfast, Sevvy. Mummy's going to be okay.'

'Are you feeling better now?' Robin asked.

I nodded and he moved his hand from the back of my neck. I pulled my head up slowly and rested it against Robin's chest. The room seemed to swing slowly from side to side and then settled down. Everything looked different, like the furniture had been moved around by a stranger. My tongue felt huge inside my mouth.

Eventually I managed to say, 'When?' but it didn't sound like my voice.

'Later this morning. We've to keep the children off school and be ready to go as soon as they get here.'

'Can we run away? Before they get here?'

'I've thought about that. But where would we go, what would we do?'

'You're right. Running's not the answer.'

I tried to stand but didn't make it.

'Surely it's not that serious, Robin?

'It's not just last night. She told me there have been various things lately and it's all added up to us being seen as a problem. We can't take anything back so we'll just have to see how it goes.'

I forced myself upwards.

'Come on, we'll have to get ready. Have to pack.'

'No, Celia. We don't have to pack. We can't take anything with us. Agnes made it very clear to me. None of this is ours.'

I looked around my strange kitchen. Maybe they were right. It certainly didn't look like the place I'd lived in for so long.

'What about the children's toys? Jasmine's not going to want to leave Angela.'

Robin stroked my back.

'No, not even them.'

'Oh God!' I said.

I pushed my head further against him and slid my arms around his back, squeezing him as tightly as I could.

'Is it breakfast time now?' asks Sevvy.

He'd dressed himself after I'd changed him. I hadn't noticed before but he'd chosen his oldest t shirt, the one that was torn and I'd been meaning to send back and a pair of jeans that were much too short for him.

'In a minute, sweetheart, let's go and find you some better clothes first.'

'But I like these. I ...'

'Don't argue, Sevvy, I'm not in the mood.'

We arrived at the top of the stairs just as Jasmine was leaving the bathroom. She looked so frail in her pink *Barbie* nightdress. I wanted to grab her and hold her tight, protect her from whatever might be to come. But I couldn't. There wasn't time. I wanted to be ready for when they came. I wanted to be able to hold my head up, face what had to be with a strength I wasn't feeling. Maybe, when they saw that we were good people, decent, honest, hard-working people, they'd realise it was all a big mistake and they'd let us back home. The home with the view of the hills from the bedroom, the home with lavender in the garden.

'Jasmine, get dressed as soon as you can. Okay? Then go downstairs and eat your breakfast. I want you to be quick. Are you listening?'

'Are we late for school?'

'No school today.'

Jasmine tutted and Sevvy made a sad sighing sound.

'But it's a school day.'

'Don't argue, Jas, there isn't time.'

I found Sevvy some better clothes and left him to struggle to put them on himself. I went into our bedroom and took a clean t shirt from the drawer and my best skirt from the wardrobe. As I was dressing, I had an idea. I waited until I heard the children clattering down the stairs then I went into Jasmine's bedroom. She'd left Angela lying on the bed. I picked it up and, lifting my skirt, slid the doll down into the front of my knickers where it pressed against my baby, the one they might want to take from me. I was worried about the bump showing under my skirt so I pulled a pillowcase from the drawer and, ripping off a strip, stretched it around my middle and tied as flat a knot as I could at the back. It pulled the doll closer to my stomach and there was a light fluttering feeling, as though the baby was adjusting to its new neighbour. I didn't think about why the doll had to come with us, I only knew I had to take her.

When I walked into the kitchen, Jasmine looked up at me with a confused face.

138

'Daddy says we're going away. Again.'

'That's right. Some people are coming to collect us soon.'

'We're going away?' asked Sevvy. 'On a bus?'

Robin patted Sevvy on the head.

'We don't know how we're going this time.'

'Who are these people? Is it Grandma Jenny?'

I looked at Robin over the children's heads. He seemed ready to cry and so I was the one who answered.

'No. I don't think there'll be anyone we know apart from Agnes.'

'Daddy shouted at Agnes. I heard him. It's rude to shout at people.'

'That's enough, Sevvy. Now eat your breakfast.'

I scraped my breakfast into the bin and collected Robin's plate from the table. I washed the plates and then began to wipe the oven over. Holding the damp cloth, I started to work my way around the kitchen, wiping different surfaces over. Robin had taken the children into the front room to play games. He asked me to join them and I said I would but I was too worried about people thinking my house was dirty.

Sevvy came into the kitchen.

'Come on, Mummy, we're having a lovely game.'

'Be there in a minute.'

I opened the cold box, took everything out and lined it up on the table. I pulled the cloth from the edge of the sink and wiped inside the cold box, then I smelt everything before I put it back.

'I spy, with my little eye, something beginning with purple,' I heard Sevvy say.

'Daddy's underpants,' said Jasmine.

'You can't see my underpants!'

There was a knock at the door. I stood still, holding onto the cold box. The house felt big and still around me. It was one of those moments when time stood still and yet moved past in a flash of memories. Seeing the house for the first time. Climbing into bed beside my new husband in our very own bedroom. Jasmine taking her first steps in the hallway into Robin's waiting arms. Tiptoeing into Sevvy's room to gaze at his sleeping face in the night. Robin throwing it all away with his careless words to Agnes.

Agnes walked into the kitchen.

'It's time to go, Celia.'

I didn't move.

'Come on, Celia. We don't want any trouble.'

If I blinked my eyes, she wouldn't be there. She'd turn into a dinosaur or one of Sevvy's monstrouses. Or even disappear. I blinked several times.

She was still there. I closed the cold box door and followed Agnes. Nothing was real. I rubbed my left hand up my right forearm and I was amazed that I could feel it. My feet were moving on their own. I knew that if I told my entire body to stand still, I'd carry on moving forward, through the hallway, down the garden footpath and onto the street.

Robin and the children were waiting for us. There were two guards beside them. Big men with serious faces. One balding and the other with red hair. I noticed that Toni Holme was standing on her doorstep watching us. I wanted her to go inside. This was nothing to do with her.

'Right, let's go,' Agnes says.

'Can I take Angela?' Jasmine whispered.

'No,' I whispered back.

'But she'll be lonely.'

Agnes stood at the side of the red-haired guard.

'Robin, take one of the children's hands and stand behind us. Celia, you hold on to the other child and follow Robin.'

18

The Meteorological Office has reported that the weather has become even more unpredictable and it is feared that we have lost the battle against global warming ...

When we arrived at the Assessment Centre. Agnes handed over our passbooks to the guard at the door and he put them into a box behind him. Then she led us out of the sunshine into a reception area. The guards stayed outside. It took me a while for my eyes to adjust to the dim light.

'This is the Travis family: Robin, Celia, Jasmine and Sevlan,' Agnes announced to the receptionist

'Sit them over there,' the receptionist said coldly, 'I'll deal with them in a moment.'

Agnes pointed to where we had to sit and then left by the door we came through. The door slammed heavily behind her and I felt, rather than heard, the locking of the bolts that would keep us enclosed within those four walls. My heart fluttered in my tight chest and I longed for the sunshine that a few moments ago had been too hot for me.

'That Agnes lady didn't say goodbye. And she called me Sevlan.'

'That's your name,' Robin told him.

'No, that's Grandpa's name. I want people to call me Sevvy.'

'We call you Sevvy,' I said to him, 'that's all that matters. Remember that.'

It felt like forever waiting there.

Eventually the receptionist bustled over and sat down facing us. She had a handful of paperwork.

'Right. Travis, Recycling Street 3. Correct?'

'Yes,' says Robin.

'You're here for,' she looked down at her papers, 'Robin Travis: insubordinate and threatening behaviour towards both a Manager and a Guardian. Is that correct?'

Robin shifted in his chair.

'I suppose you could see it like that but …'

'We do see it like that. Celia Travis: dereliction of duty towards a minor. Is that correct?'

It took me a moment to answer. I was still reeling from the fact that Robin had threatened a Manager at work.

'Not intentionally, no.'

'Yes, dereliction of duty. Previous offences. Robin Travis: none. Celia Travis: interference in the due process of the state, i.e. involvement with a family subject to a discontinuation order.'

'Mummy, I want to wee.'

The receptionist turned to look towards him. He shuffled backwards until her view of him was blocked by me.

'Someone will be down in a minute to take the children away. They can deal with the little boy then.'

'No,' I said, 'you're not taking the children away from us. I won't let you.'

'I'm afraid you have no choice. They'll be taken up to the children's wing and you can see them during the evening recreation period for one hour.'

There was the echoing noise of a door slammed somewhere off to our left and then three people appeared in the reception area; a man and two women. I thought I'd reached the point where I couldn't be surprised any more but I was. It was Sally. The woman who used to live next door in our other life, the life where everything seemed safe and secure. The woman who'd made me so angry that I'd reported her.

'Martina, these are the two children for the children's wing, Jasmine and Sevlan.'

Martina smiled at the children and held out her hands.

'Come on, you two, let's see what we have upstairs for you.'

Both children looked at me. I nodded reluctantly and Jasmine climbed down off her chair and took Martina's hand.

'I don't want to go,' said Sevvy, 'I want to stay here with you.'

'Little boys should do as they're told,' said the receptionist, 'now hurry up and get down off that chair.'

'Don't want to,' he said again, his voice trembling this time.

'Go on, Sevvy,' Robin told him, 'Martina will take you to wee. Won't you, Martina?'

'Course I will. Hurry up, we've got loads of toys upstairs and there'll be lunch soon. I think it's burgers today.'

'All right,' said Sevvy and went to stand at the other side of Martina.

The three of them left through the double doors. Just

before they closed, Jasmine turned and gave us a little wave. Sevvy didn't give us a backward glance and I was hurt at how easily he was persuaded to leave me.

'Right,' said Sally. 'Henry, you take Robin and I'll take Celia.' She spat my name out of her mouth and I felt like saying, 'Don't want to,' as Sevvy did.

I followed her through several locked doors, down a long corridor and into a tiny office. The windows were high up and the light didn't reach the bottom half of the room, merely caused striped patterns on the walls. Sally sat down at the desk and motioned for me to sit down too. As soon as I did so, her face lost any pretence of professionalism and when she spoke her voice was full of venom.

'Was it you?'

I was confused. She knew it was me, she had the paperwork.

'I didn't pick Jasmine up …'

'No, not that. Was it you who reported me?'

'Yes. It was me. I'm so sorry. I don't know why I did it. I've never done anything like that bef…'

'Do you know what happened as a result of your meddling, your busybodying?'

'I know you moved away but I didn't know what had happened …'

'We were taken away and interrogated. They didn't find any evidence of wrongdoing because there was no wrongdoing. I got those clothes in the normal way. The only difference was they'd found a warehouse that had been forgotten somehow and that's why the clothes were new.'

'I'm sorry, I …'

'No good being sorry. By the time the investigation was over, our jobs had gone. Recycling couldn't manage without

145

staff for all that time so they'd replaced us. There were no similar jobs around so, do you know what happened?'

'No, I don't know what ...'

'They kept me here. Doing something I didn't train for. Locked up in this building eight hours a day. Sleeping in the Rehabilitation Centre every night. But what's worse is that they sent Keir away. Found him a job in Preston. I've put in an application to be with him but I may never see him again. And it's all your fault.'

There was a silence. A silence that pressed down on me, that made me want to slide to the floor and curl up into a ball, with my spine on the outside to protect me and my baby; keep at least some of my vulnerabilities on the inside where they were safe. But I stayed in my chair.

'Let's get on with this,' she said, 'and then I can get you out of my sight.'

She picked up the paperwork and we went through a series of interminable questions. Did I understand why I was there? Did I understand my responsibility to the state? To my family? To my neighbours? She paused and glared at me after that one.

'Right. I think that's all of it. You'll be seeing the psychiatrist tomorrow. He'll make a full assessment and set up a training programme.'

'Do you know how long that will take?'

'No. I have no idea. Oh, and we might have to arrange a termination. You'll have to go to the hospital for that.'

'A termination? You're not going to let me keep my baby?'

'Probably not.' A brief smile flickered across her face. 'Shame.'

She stood up and went towards the door.

'Come on.'

I followed her through a maze of corridors and up some stairs until we came to a locked double door. She opened it with one of the keys hanging from her waist and took me into a long dark passage with doors opening off it. There was a buzz of voices from somewhere near the end of the corridor but she took me through the third door on the left.

It was a long dormitory with ten beds in it. The windows were barred, like the others, but they were large and let in a lot of light. The whole room felt bright and airy and I was grateful for that.

She pointed to a bed in the middle. It had a pile of bedding on the mattress.

'That's yours. Make it up and then take yourself down to the Day Room at the bottom. Meet your fellow inmates.'

She turned on her heel and left.

I walked over to the bed which was to be mine and sat on it. Through the bars I could see the blue sky. There was a tree just outside the window. The leaves were perfectly still as though there wasn't a breath of air outside to disturb them. Maybe all the disturbance was inside me. I was in turmoil. They'd taken Robin and the children away from me and I was so alone. I really couldn't believe that I'd ended up in that place.

I stood up and spread the bottom sheet over the plastic cover on the mattress and smoothed it out, walking around the bed to tuck it in. Next I did the pillows. I slid them into the cases but when I reached over to put them on the bed, I felt the doll pressing against my stomach. I lifted up my skirt and took Angela out from her binding. The strip of pillow case hung loose and empty under my clothing but I didn't know how I could dispose of it so I left it.

I held the doll against my breast. It made me think of home and comforted me; I patted her back before placing her on the bed and sliding her up towards the pillows, so I could hide her underneath. Before she got there the door flung open. It was Sally.

'I need you to sign … what have you got there?'

'Nothing,' I said, hurriedly pushing Angela fully under the pillow.

'You're lying to me.'

She marched over and lifted the pillows. The doll lay there, exposed.

'Where did you get this from?'

'I brought it from home. It's Jasmine's'

'Why did you bring it with you? You were told not to bring anything.'

'It's Jasmine's and …'

'It's not Jasmine's. Nothing is Jasmine's. Or yours.'

She waved the doll in the air.

'I have to report this and it's not going to look good.'

'Couldn't you just forget about it? Throw it away or something?'

'What do you think?'

She held out the paper for me to sign and then left, Angela clutched in her right hand with her hair swinging in rhythm with the clattering of Sally's heels. After the door slammed, I lay down on the half-made bed and cried so hard that my nose blocked up and my cheeks stung. The pillow became cold and wet beneath my face. Outside the birds sang and the sound of laughter floated in. I tried to imagine that Robin was spooned behind me and Sevvy was curled up into my stomach, with Jasmine just in front of him but I couldn't and, for a brief instant, I couldn't even

148

remember their faces. How could so much be taken from me?

Suddenly someone was standing before me. A tall thin woman with a broad smile on her face.

'Hello, you're new. Finding it hard?'

I managed a snuffly, 'yes.'

'Come on down and join the others. It's easier when we're all together.'

'I don't want anyone to see me like this.'

It was partly true but I was panicked about what those strangers might be like. How they might treat me.

'Don't worry about that. We've all been the same. Now go and wash your face. There's a sink down there.'

I took my time and, eventually, I heard the woman's footsteps behind me.

'Okay, you're beautiful enough.'

She handed me a towel, watched me wipe my face then took the towel from me. She put it back on the rack, took hold of my arm and walked me towards the door. I noticed she'd made up my bed for me.

'Thanks for doing my bed.'

'No problem. My name's Libby by the way.'

'Celia.'

'Hello, Celia. Nice to meet you.'

We reached the door. She pulled it open and ushered me through.

'What's your crime then?'

'Crime?'

'What got you in here?'

'I didn't pick my daughter up from school. We've had some problems and I haven't been sleeping. I went to sleep on the sofa and didn't wake up in time.'

Libby stood still.

'The teachers would have kept an eye on her surely. Was she all right?'

'Yes, fine but when the Guardian came round my husband threw her out.'

Libby laughed out loud. A raucous laugh that made me look round to see if anyone was listening.

'Good for him.'

I swallowed before asking, 'What did you do?'

'Moonshine.'

'Moonshine?'

'Yeah, you know. Illicit alcohol. Had had too much when the Guardian came round. Got a bit insulting. Boy, was she mad.'

We'd reached the door of the Day Room. Libby pushed me through into a room filled with armchairs. I didn't see anyone at first.

'Come on,' said Libby, 'the gang's over here.'

The gang turned out to be another three women. Libby did the introductions.

'Gemma, stockpiling.'

Gemma looked to be about ten years older than me. She had long brown hair which almost covered her face. As I looked at her, she pressed her arms against herself, as though trying to hide the row of scars marching up her forearms.

'Alice, murder.'

Alice and I both gasped.

'Libby, you horror.'

Alice was an older woman. In her sixties I would guess. Quite plump, she had a soft round face that reminded me of rising bread dough.

Alice looked at me.

'She's joking. I threw some stuff away that should have gone for recycling. The rubbish man reported me. Bastard.'

'Marie, identity theft.'

Marie was about my age. She had bright red hair and a scar down the side of her face. She smiled at me.

'It's all a mistake. I'll be out of here before you know it.'

'This is Celia. Got a stroppy husband.'

By the time I met Robin and the children at Recreation Hour later that afternoon, I was totally institutionalised. I waited in the corridor outside the Social Room until I had permission to enter, even though, through the doorway, I could see Sevvy and Jasmine waiting for us. Jasmine was curled up in a big squashy armchair sucking her thumb. Sevvy was perched on a pouffe smiling and singing.

'In you go,' said Dot, the guard from my wing.

As soon as they saw me, the children's faces lit up and they hurried towards me. I picked one up in each arm and they rested their heads in my neck. I found a sofa and we sat down.

Sevvy was bursting with news. 'Mummy, there's Lego and we had burgers and I've got a new friend called Leo.'

'That's good, Sev.'

Jasmine was quieter.

'What about you, Jas?'

'I had burgers too and there was a doll's house that I played with. But there's no girls.'

'Yes, there is,' said Sevvy, 'there's Atlanta.'

'She's only a baby like you. I can't play with her. I want to go home, Mummy. I want Angela and my bedroom.'

'I know, Jas, I know.'

'We didn't bring my nightie. They've given me another

one for tonight but it's green. I don't like green. When can we go home?'

'I don't know, Jas. We have to do as we're told and then maybe they'll let us go home soon.'

'Hi, guys.'

It was Robin. He looked pale and his voice was harsh. He pulled the pouffe over and sat facing us. I took my arm from around Jasmine and stroked his face.

'Have you been coughing a lot?'

He nodded.

'Maybe you should ask for some medicine.'

Jasmine grabbed my arm back and put it around her shoulders. Robin made a visible effort and a smile appeared on his face.

'How are my favourite people doing?'

'I've got a new friend called Leo,' said Sevvy. He looked round. 'He's over there.'

The two children looked at each other and waved. Sevvy looked back at Robin proudly.

'He's nice. I like my new friend.'

'What about you, Jas?'

'I want to go home.'

'Yeah, me too but we can't just yet. And how's my Celia?'

'Surviving.'

'That's all we've got to do. Survive.'

Our time together. There was a lot of silence because ... what could we say? But then Sevvy filled the silence with chatter about different colours of Lego and the things he built. I couldn't believe how time could go so slowly and yet so quickly simultaneously. All too soon Dot came in and blew a whistle.

'Women, back to your wing.'

Robin knelt down and put his arms around me. On either side the children wriggled under his arms so that it turned into a family hug.

'Be brave,' Robin whispered in my ear.

'I will.'

'Come on, Celia.'

Robin moved back and I stood, then turned to kiss my children.

'Celia!'

When I reached the doorway I turned back.

'Ask for some medicine, Robin. Ask for some medicine.'

19

Hailstones as big as tennis balls have fallen on the area. Luckily no one was seriously hurt but one Guard received a blow to his head. He told us, 'The first one appeared out of nowhere ...'

The psychiatrist was in his forties, balding and wearing gold rimmed glasses. He asked me to call him Frank. He was wearing a dark suit; it didn't fit him, the sleeves came down over his hands and, when he sat down, the collar went up near his ears. After a minute he stood up, removed the jacket and hung it on the back of his chair.

'That's better. Now, let's get started.'

He reached into a drawer and took out Angela. He placed her on the desk in front of him.

'Now, tell me about this.'

'It's Jasmine's doll.'

'Where did you get it from?'

'The Delivery/Collection Man.'

'Like everything else?'

'Yes.'

'So why did you bring it with you when you were told not to take anything from the house?'

'It was sudden impulse. Jasmine loves her and, I don't know, it sort of symbolised everything that was happy in our home.'

'But you knew it wasn't yours to take?'

'I suppose so.'

He leant back in his chair and clasped his hands across his chest.

'Celia, do you remember the time of the Upheaval?'

'Pretty much. I was only six but a lot of it stands out in my mind because it was such a big change from what we had before.'

'It was a big change. We went from a situation where those who had money were able to have anything they wanted to a situation where everyone was given everything they need. Do you know the reason for that?'

I had to think for a minute because it was jumbled up in my mind.

'It wasn't just one reason, it was lots of reasons. Global warming meant we had to reduce the amount of power we were using so we couldn't keep producing lots and lots of things. We couldn't trade with other countries anymore because there was no one left to trade with. There weren't as many people here so we had to prioritise what was important. We …'

'I'd agree with all those but I think we can sum it up more concisely. We had the chance to make a fresh start and we wanted life to be fairer than it had been. Would you agree with that?'

I nodded and whispered, 'Yes.'

He leant forward so his waist rested against the desk.

'Celia, do you think it's fair that you took something you weren't entitled to?'

'No, I suppose not, but … it's only a doll.'

'Let's think about it only being a doll. What if there'd been two dolls? Would that have been all right?'

He stared hard at me and I couldn't think what to say.

'What if you'd taken three dolls? Ten dolls? Thirty dolls? What if the dolls had been fire extinguishers or hospital supplies?'

'That wouldn't be right.'

'That wouldn't be right. That wouldn't be *fair*. So, where do we draw the line, Celia?'

'I don't know.'

'That's why it's so important. That's why we don't have our own possessions. Because thinking it's all right to take a doll is the first step to thinking we can take two dolls. To thinking we can own a toy warehouse.'

He leant back in his chair again and stared into my eyes.

I hadn't really thought about it like that before but it seemed to make sense.

'I knew I shouldn't bring the doll with us.'

'Perhaps you've learnt a lesson here today. I hope so, Celia, I really do because you thinking that you could bring this doll away with you when you were told not to will have a big effect on the recommendations made for your future. That's a fact, Celia, and you're going to have to face up to it. When Robin is working, you are entitled to keep what the Delivery/Collection man brings to the house until you are asked for it back. At the moment, as Robin is not working, you are not automatically entitled to anything. And, having taken something you were not entitled to has affected how we look at your case.'

He sighed and picked up the paperwork that was lying on his desk and then went over all the information that the receptionist and Sally had discussed; names, dates, accusations.

'Right, Celia, that's what they say. Now you tell me your version.'

I explained what happened. I told him about Sevlan dying, about Robin and Jasmine being ill, about the baby.

'Oh yes. I see you're scheduled for a termination.'

'Is it definite then?

'Yes, it's definite. When they added the doll to the list of the things that have happened, they didn't believe that you and Robin should be allowed to have another baby at this time. Or probably any time in the future. In an overcrowded population we have to ensure that babies are born to responsible parents. You and Robin have shown that you aren't responsible and so the baby will be terminated. How do you feel about that?'

I was crying.

'I don't want a termination. I want this baby. I've got two children who I love more than life itself. How can I let them take Sevvy and Jasmine's brother or sister away?'

'What will Robin say? About the termination?'

'He has no idea that it's a possibility. Well, I don't think he knows, unless they've told him.'

'What do you think he'd say? If you told him?'

I hesitated. I knew I'd cry if I talked about it and I didn't want to show any weakness to the man who held my future in his hands.

'Go on, Celia. I need to know all about you and your family in order to make an assessment.'

'He doesn't want it.' Now I'd started, I couldn't stop.

The words tumbled out. 'He doesn't want it. He doesn't want to bring another child into this world. He went on about shoes …'

'Shoes?'

'Yes. Second hand shoes. He doesn't like his children wearing second hand shoes and he doesn't want it to happen to another child.'

'Sometimes we focus on small matters because we can't face up to the *real* issues, they're too big to contemplate. Do you think that might be it?'

I nodded.

'Is that why you haven't told him about the possibility of a termination.'

'Can they really make me abort this baby?'

'I'm afraid they can. I think you need to tell Robin before it happens. It might be, of course, that someone else tells him before you get chance.'

'Are you seeing him? Don't tell him if you do. I'd like to tell him myself.'

Frank looked at me for a moment.

'Tell you what. I'm seeing him after you. I'll let you have a short crossover period together. It's not strictly allowed and I'll have to stay in the room with you but I think it will be best for all concerned.'

'Is it my fault there has to be a termination? Because of the doll?'

'Yes. It had been decided that you could keep the baby but, that was before this latest transgression. It's the straw that broke the camel's back.'

'I'll never forgive myself.'

He went on to ask me lots of other questions but I wasn't really focussing.

'Okay, I think that's it.'

He looked at his watch.

'I think Robin should be outside. I'll go and get him.'

When he left the room, I stared at the doll on the desk. Such a tiny thing to have caused us so much trouble.

Robin looked tired when he came in. Frank put another chair next to mine, sat down at his desk and began to sort through some papers.

Robin put his hand on my arm.

'Are you all right,' he whispered.

'No, not really. I have something to tell you.'

'What?'

'I have to have a termination.'

'Because of what I said to Agnes? They want to get rid of our baby because of that?'

'Yes … no. Not just because of that. Parveen talked about it before, when she told me I was pregnant. I had to fill in some forms to get permission to have the baby.'

'Why didn't you tell me?'

'I tried not to think about it. And then, Sevlan died and it didn't seem right to talk about it and then,' I made a shuddering sob, 'you said you didn't want the baby and …'

'I never said I didn't want the baby.'

'You said you didn't want it to wear second hand shoes. That's what you said, Robin.'

'Yes but that didn't mean …'

'I'm sorry,' said Frank, 'but I'm going to have to start Robin's session now. Celia, Dot's outside. She'll take you back to the Women's Wing.'

I spent the afternoon with Libby. Gemma and Alice were doing some written assessment tests. Libby told me about her

159

life. I was shocked and fascinated at the same time. As a child, she was removed from her Mother several times. She didn't know who her father was. They put her in a home and she kept running away, back to her Mother. When she was older, they tried to make her train for several different jobs but she could never settle down enough to last through the course. Eventually, she ended up working on landfill excavation which she referred to as treasure hunting.

Libby hated rules. Despite that, she regarded the Assessment Centre as a second home and she'd been through Rehabilitation three times. At the end of each session there, she convinced them that she had reformed but when she went back home, she soon slipped back into her old ways. In other words, she went back to making moonshine. Or poteen. Or happy water. Or the several other names she called it. She told me the main ingredient was potato peelings and she'd developed her own recipe over the years. Sounded disgusting to me but she said it made life bearable.

'Sometimes I think about running off. Finding a way through the checkpoints and settling down somewhere. Somewhere I can be myself.' She sighed loudly. 'But …'

'But what?'

Suddenly, the harsh angles of her face softened, melted down until she seemed as vulnerable as the tiny baby I was carrying inside me.

'I've got a son. Anton. He's nine. They've got him in a home. Won't let me look after him myself; say I'm too much of a risk. They don't understand I wouldn't be a risk if they let me have him with me. But they do let me see him sometimes.'

She rubbed her hands over her face.

'I can't run off and leave him. So I carry on. Slog my guts

out hunting treasure all day, drink my poteen at night and see Anton whenever possible. It's not much of a life but it's all I've got.'

By the time I went to bed I was exhausted, although I hadn't done anything all day except talk. I curled up with my hand on my stomach, holding my baby.

'I won't let anything happen to you. I won't.'

Even though I was so tired, it was difficult to sleep. I went over all the 'what ifs'. What if I hadn't gone to sleep and missed picking Jasmine up? That was only two days before but it seemed like forever. What if Robin's Dad hadn't died, Robin hadn't been ill from work, Agnes hadn't come round that night? What if we lived in a different world where there weren't Guardians?

When I went to sleep, I dreamt I was being chased; my legs churned under the sheets. I ran down a country lane and, suddenly, my unborn baby lay on the ground before me and the air was filled with howling banshees. I bent to pick up the baby but my hands only found emptiness. I surfaced from the dream to find Libby shaking my shoulder.

'Come on,' Libby shouted over the banshee noise that remained from the dream, 'we have to get out.'

'What?'

'We have to go. There's a fire.'

I clambered out of bed, suddenly able to smell the smoke.

The door opened and light flooded in from the corridor, illuminating a grey cloud of smoke. A Guard came in.

'Hands and knees,' she shouted, 'everyone down on hands and knees below the smoke.'

We followed her down the corridor and out into the

stairwell. The smoke was thicker there and I panicked because I couldn't see at all.

'Hold hands in a line and I'll try and guide you to the stairs.'

I took hold of Libby's hand in front and Marie's hand behind.

'Right. Here it is. Hold on to the banister with both hands and walk down sideways. Feel each step with your foot before you stand on it. That way you should be safe.'

That was when the lights went out leaving us in total darkness. The air was so thick I felt I could hold it in my hand. My eyes were streaming; the taste of the smoke filled my mouth and my nose. It was difficult to breathe. I prayed Robin and the children were all right.

The steps went on forever. Left foot out, test for step, left foot down, right foot down. Left foot out, test for step, left foot down, right foot down. I began to feel that I had been doing that for my whole life.

Suddenly the air was thinner and I could see light coming up from below.

The courtyard was full of people milling around. I couldn't see Robin or the children and I panicked. Breathing, already difficult because of the smoke, became harder. My heart hammered inside my chest and my eyes blurred over so that even if they were in front of me I might miss them. Then I heard a harsh cough and I knew it was Sevvy. I followed the noise.

He was perched on one of the stones edging the flower bed near the front door. His arms were hugged to himself and, as I approached him, I realised his coughing was mixed with crying.

'Sevvy,' I shouted.

He looked in my direction but, as I spoke, someone stepped in between us. It was Sally. I pushed her out of the way, hurried over to Sevvy and picked him up.

'Mummy,' he croaked, his voice raw.

'I see you made it,' said Sally.

'Yes, thanks.'

'Born survivor,' she spat and walked away.

'Where's Jas? And Daddy?'

'I don't know. Mummy, I was scared.'

'I know, sweetheart, so was I. Let's go and find the others.'

It was chaos. People wandered round looking dazed. It was hard to tell the officials from the residents because nearly everyone was in night clothes. Suddenly Sevvy wriggled in my arms.

'Daddy, it's Daddy!'

Robin was across the other side of the forecourt, quite near to the entrance. As we pushed through the crowd towards him, someone grabbed my arm. I almost brushed them off but then realised it was Jasmine.

'Are you all right?'

'Yes. What's happened?'

I didn't answer because suddenly there was a whooshing noise behind us and the forecourt was brighter. We reached Robin and, when we'd finished hugging I turned to look. One side of the Assessment Centre was engulfed in flames and the forecourt was filled with dark silhouettes. Someone was pushing us to the perimeter to get as far away from the fire as possible.

There was a siren behind us and a fire engine stopped on the street outside the checkpoint. The Guard lifted the barrier shouting, 'It's this way.' He walked ahead of the engine, pushing aside those who were too confused to move out of the way. We watched their progress and then, for some reason, I looked back. The Guard had left the barrier up. There was only one figure standing nearby.

That was the moment when, for the first time ever, I took charge of my life, our lives. The moment where I spotted an opportunity and grasped it with both hands.

'Robin, look,' I whispered.

'What?'

'The barrier's up and there's no guard. We can get out.'

'But …'

I felt my baby inside me urging me on. It was now or never. Everyone was distracted by the fire and the fire engine. After checking that no one was looking, I pulled Robin and Jasmine towards the unguarded checkpoint. Sevvy was still safe in my arms. Just before we get there, someone touched my shoulder and I almost screamed in frustration. But it was Libby.

'You go, girl,' she said.

Suddenly we were outside, on the street. We weren't in the clear. There was another barrier to get through, the one on the road out of town but again we were lucky. The guard inside was on his phone, talking urgently and waving his arms in the air. For the second time that night I was on my hands and knees, crawling underneath the sight of the window.

'What are we doing?' Sevvy asked in a very loud voice.

'Shhh,' Robin and I said together, probably making more noise than Sevvy did.

Then we were on a quiet empty road surrounded by rustling trees. In the background we could hear the commotion of the Assessment Centre and, in the distance, a large fire flickered.

'So, clever clogs, what do we do now?' Robin asked.

It was a good question. We had nothing with us and only Robin was wearing his day clothes. I had on a pair of striped pyjamas and, on my feet there was a pair of fluffy pink mules. Sevvy was wearing camouflage pyjamas and blue *Sooty* slippers; Jasmine had on the hated green nightie and bare feet.

'This is not good,' I said.

'Maybe we should go back,' Robin suggested.

'They'll take the baby if we go back.'

'We shouldn't go back then. But if we aren't going back, what are we going to do?'

An owl hooted in the distance.

'Perhaps we should ask the owl,' I said, 'they're wise.

Sevvy started to walk away.

'Where do you think you're going, young man?' I called after him.

'I'm going to talk to the owl.'

That made us laugh and my panic level went down.

'We were only joking,' Robin told him.

'Oh,' Sevvy said and then had a bout of coughing that scared me.

'Perhaps we should find some shelter for tonight. Get some rest and work out a plan in the morning.'

We looked round helplessly. We knew nothing about finding shelter and I tried to keep from myself the fact that, if I were honest, we didn't know much about survival at all. At least I didn't.

There was the dark shape of a building at the other side of the field.

'Come on, let's go and see what it is. You never know, we might be lucky.'

There was barbed wire on the fence around the field which made it impossible to get in. Robin took off his trainer and started to prise it apart but it sprang back again. Meanwhile, Jasmine wandered away.

'What are you doing?'

'There's a gap here,' she told us.

She was right. It wasn't very big but Robin removed his other trainer and held the two sides further apart so that first the children and then I could crawl through. When I reached the other side, I took the shoes from him and did the same for him. When he was through I handed him back his shoes.

'I hope it doesn't rain,' he said, pushing his finger through a hole in the side from the barbed wire.

I started to giggle but I was sobered by Jasmine's 'At least you've got shoes.'

Robin picked Jasmine up and I held Sevvy. It took us a while to cover the field, we were all tired and Sevvy was almost asleep which meant he kept flopping over in my arms. Then the coughing would wake him again.

The building was some sort of barn and, although it was locked, Robin managed to force the door open. Inside it was full of sacks of flour. We sat ourselves on the top then the children lay down. They went to sleep almost immediately. Robin put his arm around my shoulders.

'What on earth are we going to do?' I asked.

'I have absolutely no idea,' said Robin, 'let's wait until morning to worry about it.'

'Okay.'

I was glad to have to put it off until the next day. I remembered what Frank had said that morning about focusing on small issues instead of the big ones and I realised he was right. I was desperately worried about how I was going to get something else for my feet instead of those pink slippers but I didn't seem to have the energy to worry about our future and where we were going to live. That was too big to think about.

Part 2

20

Sevvy's coughing woke me several times during the night but he seemed to go straight back to sleep again. I was in a strange state of being half awake and half asleep. I knew where I was, that I was lying on flour sacks in a barn, but people kept coming and going in front of my eyes. Jenny and Dorey sat in front of me and had a long conversation about the feasibility of turning flour into moonshine.

'It would make the sea dusty,' said Libby, who seemed to have joined them without my noticing.

Sevlan, his face now undamaged, sat down beside her.

'I got the sea clean once, I don't know why I shouldn't do it again.'

The sun came in and made my eyelids shine pink so I rolled over to avoid it. I was facing Robin who opened his eyes.

'Hello, sunshine. Welcome to your new life,' he said and I felt a rush of comfort that he was feeling positive about it.

Then he laughed.

'You don't really look like sunshine with that dirty face.'

'You neither.'

His, and the children's, faces were blackened by the smoke from the night before.

'First thing, I'll find us some water so we can at least have a wash. I think I heard a stream last night.'

He began to look round the barn. There was a shelf full of things near the door. He slid down off the sacks.

'There's tons of useful stuff here but I'll just take these for now.'

He held up two measuring jugs and disappeared through the door.

'Where's Daddy going?' Jasmine asked in a sleepy voice.

'Gone for some water so we can have a wash.'

'We need a wash. And I want a drink.'

Jasmine sat up.

'What are we going to do about my feet?'

There were some empty sacks lying underneath the shelf. I picked one up.

'Maybe we can do something with this. All I need is,' I turned to the shelf and found what I was looking for, a pair of scissors.

I cut off some strips and began to bind them around Jasmine's feet.

'They look disgusting.'

'When I was a little girl,' I said, carrying on binding, 'there was a saying, *Beggars can't be choosers*, and do you know what that means?'

'No.'

'It means, put up with it and don't complain because we have no choice.'

Robin returned with the water. I cut off another strip of flour sack and dipped it in one of the jugs, then I started to wipe Jasmine's face.

Robin walked over to Sevvy.

'Come on, sleepyhead, it's time to wake up.'

Sevvy didn't move.

'Hurry up. It's time to wake up and face the day. The sun's shining and everything.'

Sevvy still didn't move. Robin put a hand on his arm and shook him. Nothing.

'Celia, he's burning up.'

I left Jasmine and put a hand to Sevvy's forehead.

'Oh my God, you're right. He's got a fever. Sevvy, Sevvy, talk to me.'

Sevvy forced his eyes open and looked in my direction without focusing.

'Tired,' he said and closed his eyes again.

'What are we going to do?'

The fear was hammering at my body and I couldn't hold a single thought in my mind. We were in a barn with nothing and nobody to help us and Sevvy was ill.

Robin soaked a strip of flour sack in the water and he put it on to Sevvy's hot forehead.

'Maybe, if we can get his temperature down, he'll be OK.'

'But what if we can't? What if we do and he's still not all right?'

My legs shook and I dropped down to the floor beside Sevvy. The weight of my body moved the sacks which disturbed Sevvy's head but he stayed asleep.

All my life there'd been someone to turn to: a parent, a Guardian, a doctor or a nurse but suddenly that had all gone. All I had was Robin and I knew he was as scared and as helpless as I was. I came to a decision.

'There must be a farmhouse around here. We'll go and ask for help.'

'What if they report us? What if we get sent back and you have to have the ...' he looked at Jasmine, 'the, you know?'

It had come to a choice between Sevvy and the child I was carrying. I only hesitated for a second. I realised solid, breathing and in front of me beat the unseen and the unknown any day.

I picked Sevvy up and held him tight against me. We left the barn and looked around. I could see the farmhouse in the distance. I made my way up the field, Sevvy's body feeling hotter against me at each step. The pink mules dragged in the grass and I stepped out of them without stopping. Eventually I reached a gate and swung it open so we could pass through. The path was dusty under my feet and, to my left, two chained dogs barked loudly and threateningly.

'I'm scared of those dogs, Daddy,' I heard Jasmine say behind me.

'Don't worry,' said Robin, 'I won't let them near you.'

At the door, I leant Sevvy against my chest so I could knock. The dogs barked louder. It seemed to take a long time but eventually I heard footsteps and the door opened. It was an older woman who gasped loudly when she saw me.

I spoke without waiting for her to say anything.

'We need help. It's my little boy. He's sick.'

'I can't help you. I daren't risk it. They're strict around here about helping outcasts. We've been in trouble before.'

'But look at him. He's burning up.'

'I'm sorry, I can't ...'

Robin stepped forward.

'If you can't help, do you know anyone who can?'

She had her hand on the door knob to go back inside but she stopped and looked at Sevvy again.

'There is someone but, if anyone asks, don't tell them where you got the information from.'

'We won't,' we said together.

'There's a woman. Hermione. Some call her a healer. The farmers go to her for help sometimes when they can't get a nurse to come out here. The authorities know about her but they turn a blind eye because she's useful – it saves them having to provide a trained nurse for this area.'

'Where can we find her?'

'Best to go through the woods. If you go down this path, it won't take long until you come to the trees. You need to get to the other side of the wood. I've been told that there are markings on the trees to guide you there.'

'Thank you so much,' Robin told her.

I was in too much of a hurry to thank her and I was already halfway towards the gate.

'I hope your little boy's all right,' she shouted after us.

'Thanks,' Robin called over his shoulder.

It wasn't hard to find the woods but when we got there we struggled to find the markings. I sat down with my back against a tree while Robin and Jasmine searched. When I bent over to kiss Sevvy's feverish forehead, he rewarded me by waking and looking straight into my face. But then he spoke.

'I've got monstrouses in my eyes,' he muttered, 'it's scary.'

'I'll get rid of them,' I said and gently wiped the stripy sleeve of my pyjama jacket over his eyelids.

'Thanks, Mummy,' he whispered and went back to sleep.

I held him tight against me. The heat spread through my chest and up to my face. The edges of my vision darkened and I worried that I was becoming ill too.

Robin and Jasmine were working their way through the

trees at the edge of the wood but they didn't seem to be having any success.

'I wish we knew what we were looking for,' Robin said to me as he passed.

I didn't feel to be there. It was like I was on a distant planet staring down at everything and, when I saw a woman approaching, I didn't feel anything: not fear, not surprise, not gratitude. When she saw Robin she stopped and looked set to turn around but then Jasmine appeared out of the woods. The sight of a seven year old girl in a green nightie and flour-sack-shod feet seemed to reassure her that we weren't people to be afraid of.

She sent a smile towards me and then said, 'Hello,' to Jasmine.

'Hello,' said Jasmine, 'we're looking for signs. Can you help us?'

'Are you looking for the signs to Hermione's? That's where I'm going.'

Robin had reached the woman by now and I heard him say, 'Our little boy is ill. We're hoping Hermione can help us.'

'Come on,' the woman replied, 'you can go with me.'

Robin turned towards me and signalled for me to get up. It was a struggle and he came and took Sevvy from me. A breeze cooled the perspiration on my empty arms.

I don't know how long it took to get to Hermione's. I simply put one bare foot in front of the other on the pebble covered floor. I tried to keep my eyes focused downwards because I was afraid that if I tripped over a branch or a stone then I might never get up again.

The woman showed us the signs which pointed the way. We would never have found them without her. They were carved into the trunks of the trees; a tiny *H* with a small arrow beneath. At first glance they seemed to be scars but, once you knew they were there, they were easy to spot.

When we left the darkness of the woods, the sun seemed blinding and it was only when we stopped at the gate that I noticed the cottage. By that stage I wasn't sure whether I was dreaming or if it really was a fairy tale cottage: thatched roof, white painted walls and leaded windows with a garden full of bright flowers.

'Hansel and Gretel,' Jasmine breathed and the woman smiled.

'No, this is Hermione's cottage. She helps people not captures them.'

Suddenly there was a loud ringing in my ears and I realised I couldn't stand up any longer. Then I was on the warm path with dust in my mouth and black spots in my eyes.

21

I woke in a room full of furniture and sunshine. I didn't know where I was and, when I tried to sit up, my head was too heavy for me to support away from the pillow.

'Oh good, you're awake,' a voice said beside me and I carefully looked towards it.

If it wasn't for the white hair and the soft wrinkles on her face, I would have thought she was a child. She was tiny, about as big as Jasmine and her hair hung in long plaits. Her blouse was some sort of linen material and a series of crooked daisies had been embroidered across the front.

'I'm Hermione,' she told me, stroking my forehead. 'How are you feeling?'

'Heavy,' I said, 'everything's heavy. And my tummy aches.'

I suddenly remembered the baby and my hands went down to feel if it was still there.

'The baby's OK. But we have to be careful. I want you to stay in bed until I tell you it's all right to get up.'

I nodded.

'And I want you to drink this all up.'

She held up a cup and I reached out for it.

'Let's get you sat up first.'

She put one hand under my back and the other under my armpit before gently easing me forward while she propped the pillows up behind me.

She picked up the cup again.

'What is it?'

Handing the cup to me, she said, 'It's mainly chamomile with a few other special ingredients from my herb garden. Now take it slowly. You've had a tough couple of days.'

I couldn't remember anything about them but then I remembered something else and started to panic.

'Sevvy. Is he all right?'

'He's fine now. He was rough when you got here and I was really worried but I gave him some Yarrow, Lobelia, things like that and he soon perked up. Young children are like that. Go down heavily but then bounce back before you know it.'

'Can I see him?'

'Yes, but only for a few minutes. I don't want you tiring.'

She went out of the room and I heard her calling for Sevvy. There were heavy footsteps racing up the stairs and then, suddenly, he was by my bedside.

'Mummy, Mummy, are you better? I've been poorly but you've been poorlier.'

'Yes, I'm better now.'

'She's better, Sevvy, but she still needs to rest so you haven't to bother her.'

'I won't.'

He looked at me with worried eyes.

'Is it all right if I tell you things?'

'What sort of things?'

'About here. It's really nice.'

'Tell you what,' said Hermione, 'you talk to Mummy for another minute and then you'll have to go back downstairs. Is that okay?'

'Yes.' He turned back to me and took my hand.

'Hermione's got a great big garden and there's a 'normous field out the back. Me and Jasmine can play out in it as much as we want and Daddy's mended a ball so we can play football and Jasmine's got a doll made of rags, she's called Judy but I didn't want a doll because I'm a boy so I've got a teddy bear only he's not furry because he's a big wooden spoon really but Hermione drew a face on him so he could be a teddy bear and ...'

'I think that's enough, Sevvy,' said Robin who had come into the room unnoticed. 'Why don't you go back downstairs and play.'

'All right,' said Sevvy and rushed from the room again. It was good to see him but I felt exhausted.

'I'll leave you two alone for a minute. Don't wear her out, Robin.'

'I won't.'

He looked down at me.

'How are you doing? Really?'

'I think I'm all right. I'm not sure what happened. I can't remember anything after we came through the gate.'

'You collapsed on the path outside. Hermione's been feeding you herbs and doing other stuff that I don't quite understand. At one point she really thought we were going to lose the baby. Or you. I was so scared, Celia.'

'Are you all right? And Jasmine?'

'We're fine. Jasmine's having the time of her life. She sees herself as some sort of apprentice to Hermione, asking questions and helping with the potions.'

I'd finished my tea and I handed the cup to Robin.

'I'm sorry, Robin, but I think I need to go to sleep again.'

'Don't worry about that. Hermione says you need lots of sleep. She seems to know what she's talking about so I'll go back downstairs and see you later.'

The next time I woke, Jasmine was standing shyly at the bedside with a tray. I struggled to sit up and she slid the tray on to my lap.

'It's a boiled egg. From one of Hermione's hens. I collected it. There were six this morning. This one's a brown one which makes it extra special and it will make you better quicker.'

'Thank you, Jas.'

I slipped the knife through the top of the egg.

'Oh, that looks so good. Look at that golden yolk.'

Jasmine smiled proudly as though she'd laid the egg herself.

'Daddy says you've been helping Hermione.'

Jasmine nodded.

'I'm learning lots of things. I know that Fennel's good for your tummy. Valerian and Chamomile are good for headaches and Echinacea for sore throats.'

'You have been busy.'

'Yes, Hermione's teaching me all the time. I love Hermione, I really do.'

'You're not making a pest of yourself, are you, Jas?'

Jasmine said a scandalised, 'No,' just as Hermione came into the room.

'She's been really helpful. It was a bit busy round here

with two invalids on the go. I couldn't have managed without her.'

'I'm glad about that.'

'Right, Jasmine, let's leave Mummy in peace to eat her egg. We can come up again later.'

When they went downstairs, I realised I was really hungry and I worked my way through the egg and soldiers. The mere act of eating exhausted me and, placing the tray on the bedside cabinet, I slid my way back down under the covers and closed my eyes. I felt warm and safe and I drifted off to sleep against the background noise of my family playing outside.

22

I was in the garden with Hermione. Robin was up a ladder somewhere, Jasmine was sitting on the doorstep talking to her doll and Sevvy was playing Delivery/Collection man. I wondered how long it would take him to forget. His 'teddy bear' was acting as the horse and Hermione had given him her peg bag so he could distribute and collect them on his route.

It was a perfect day. The blue sky was dotted with cotton wool clouds and there was a soft breeze that stroked my face and stopped it being too hot. I was feeling a lot better and was raring to do something more energetic than sit and watch other people working but Hermione wouldn't let me. She said we had to be one hundred percent certain that the baby was safe before I went back into action.

Hermione's hands were busy, even though the rest of her was still. She was knitting a sweater for Jasmine from a cardigan that I had watched her unravel the day before.

I took a sip of the lemonade that Jasmine had helped Hermione make.

'I love your house, Hermione, have you always lived here?'

'No, I've been here about fifteen years.'

'Really? I imagined you'd lived here for ever.'

'No. I lived in London for a long time.'

'What made you move up here? Was it the Upheaval?'

'It was after that. It's a long story and I wouldn't want to bore you.'

I felt like we had all the time in the world and I wanted to hear what had happened.

'I'd like to know. Really.'

'I'd lived in London since I was a child. When the Troubles started, I was working as a doctor as was my husband Doug. We had our own practice. We also had a fancy apartment overlooking the Thames and I thought our life would always be the same. You probably don't remember that time?'

'No, not really, just bits from the television news. They never seemed to explain anything, just talked about attacks on oil wells and chemical factories.'

'There was growing concern about global warming and non-renewable resources while the politicians dragged their feet. That led to various groups taking action. But it all went wrong. No one quite knows how. I'd been involved in politics for a while and I was asked to join an emergency committee. We oversaw groups being sent to deal with the problems, both in this country and world-wide. Doug was in one of them.'

She stopped and took a sip of her lemonade.

'He didn't come back. I gave up our practice and threw myself into full time political work.'

'So how did you end up ...'

There was a crash in the kitchen and a howl from

184

Jasmine. We hurried in to investigate. She was cowering on the worktop and there was a smashed jam jar lying in a clump of jam on the floor.

'I was trying to make a jam sandwich for Judy. I climbed up and the jar slipped. I'm sorry, Hermione, I'm really sorry about the mess.'

'Don't worry about that. Are you all right? Did you cut yourself?'

'I'm not cut or anything.'

She started to climb down.

'Stay where you are till we clean this mess up.'

When the kitchen floor was clean and Jasmine had calmed down, Hermione sent me out to the garden to rest. Jasmine came with me and sat at my feet, asking for a story. Sevvy joined her and I made up a long convoluted tale about a little boy who wouldn't take a bath.

Hermione had a big box of clothes in her attic. Some of them were in the house when she arrived, others she'd collected over the years. She'd already pulled out a few things but one dull morning she decided that we needed to sort through properly to find a good range for ourselves. I'd found several t shirts and pairs of jeans that would do until I was too fat. Then Hermione told me she was planning a dinner party and I needed something more formal.

'A dinner party? Who's going to come?'

'My friends, the ones who live locally.'

Hermione went back to sifting through the clothes.

'What about this blouse?'

She held up a cream, long-sleeved blouse and then hung it on the back of a chair nearby. It looked almost new.

'I'm sure there's a … oh look here it is.'

She placed a long black velvet skirt on the seat of the chair. It looked well with the blouse.

'Come on, Celia, try it on.'

I pulled off the smock-style blouse and floral skirt that both belonged to Hermione. It felt good to take them off, the sleeves of the blouse left marks on my arm and the skirt was so short it was almost indecent. The other clothes she'd given me were on the washing line.

The blouse was soft and slipped softly through my fingers when I picked it up.

'Satin,' said Hermione.

I pulled it on. The buttons were tiny and it took me a while to fasten them all. Hermione said they were mother of pearl. I'd never heard of that before.

Next, I stepped into the skirt and pulled it up to my waist. Hermione fastened the zip and button at the back. It fitted perfectly.

'I think there's a mirror here somewhere.'

She reached behind the wardrobe and pulled out a full length mirror. It had a wooden frame and was on legs. Hermione brushed the dust away with the hem of her skirt and tilted it so it was at the right angle.

As I looked in the mirror, Hermione reached up and held my hair against the back of my head. I twisted from side to side, unable to believe that the woman in the mirror was me. I had never, ever looked so good, not even on my wedding day. I was wearing clothes that weren't new, I was used to that, but this time they looked like they'd been chosen for me and there was a glow in my face, from the sun and from what I could only describe as happiness.

'Were these yours, Hermione?'

'No, they were here when I arrived. The woman who

owned the house, Sarah, enjoyed partying. Before the Upheaval she had a dinner party virtually every week. I came to a couple as I had friends living nearby.'

'Is that how you got the cottage?'

'Sort of. When I became disillusioned with how things were going with the New Way, I escaped up here, where I thought they wouldn't find me. I went to stay with my friends, Gussy and Frederick. Sarah had just died so they moved me in here.'

'Did they find you?'

'They did but it soon became clear they didn't want me back.'

I put my discarded blouse on the arm of a chair and sat down on it. I wanted to know more.

'Why didn't they want you back?'

'I was on the original committee which decided to get rid of money. We'd looked at the communist model but rejected it as we didn't feel it lead to true social equality so we made our own, central distribution of goods according to need not want. I was very firmly behind that principle and I believed that we were moving away from it again. It was all becoming too rigid and uncaring for me and I believe in making my views known.'

Jasmine appeared at the top of the steps.

'Oh, Mummy, you look beautiful.'

I turned to look at her as Hermione said, 'She does, doesn't she?'

'Why are you dressing up?'

'It's for a party,' said Hermione. She obviously saw Jasmine's excited face because she hurriedly added, 'Oh, I'm sorry, sweetheart, it's going to be a grown-up party.'

'Oh,' said Jasmine, putting so much sadness in her voice

that I had to pick her up and hold her. She'd been through so much.

'Careful,' said Hermione.

I put Jasmine back down.

'I've had an idea. Why don't we have a children's party in the afternoon. Some of the people I'm going to invite have children. Then the children could all sleep here, while we have the dinner party. There's an old tent in the shed. It'll be a bit of a squash but it should be fun.'

Jasmine clapped her hands.

'That will be fun. Is there a dress for me?'

There was a dress for Jasmine and an outfit for Sevvy and one for Robin.

We carried on searching and found a motley collection of everyday clothes. We were about to go back downstairs when Jasmine spotted something red, right at the bottom of the box.

'What's this?'

She pulled it out. It was a red coat, probably for a child a couple of years older than her and when she tried it on, the sleeves hung down over her hands and the hem reached almost to her ankles.

'Can I have it? This coat? Can I have it for me?'

'It's a bit big, Jas.'

'She'll grow into it,' Hermione said, 'she's going to need a coat, especially now the rain's arrived.'

I hadn't noticed but rain was pattering against the window and there were big black clouds overhead.

23

'Come on, Celia, you've got to learn.'

Hermione had taken me and Robin to the chicken pen to learn how to kill a chicken. As far as I was concerned, it was a skill I could live without but Hermione insisted that I needed to know. She did the first one. It was, of course, no effort for Hermione. She'd been doing it for years. The problem was that it was the one that Jasmine called Angela in memory of her doll at home. I was worried what Jasmine would say when she found out. Hermione said that we all needed to toughen up if we wanted food on our plates but I wasn't sure we could.

Then it was my turn. Every time I got anywhere near one of the chickens it squawked and ran away.

'Stop dithering, woman.'

'Let me have a go, Hermione. Just this once.'

That was Robin, rescuing me as usual. She gave a disapproving nod and I changed places with Robin. He was more confident than I was and it wasn't long before he had a squawking, struggling hen in his hands.

'Now, Robin, just do what I showed you.'

He twisted the chicken's neck but it didn't work. Not first time anyway. Eventually the chicken flopped lifeless in his hands but, by that time, he was pale and sweating. He caught my eye and shrugged.

'Celia, you can come to the kitchen and help me to pluck and clean these birds ready for tomorrow.'

Sometimes it struck me that Hermione was preparing for us to leave. She seemed keen to teach us everything she knew. She'd even told me her secret recipe for sun screen but she hadn't said why we needed to know all those things when, most of the time, she wanted to do everything herself. It worried me that she might suddenly throw us out.

Most of the time, though, it felt as if she was planning for us to stay. She talked about when the baby was born, telling me that she would deliver it. She was going to teach me to knit baby clothes, despite the fact that there were still five months to go. There were lots of baby knitting patterns up in the attic; left over from the previous occupants she said.

The chickens were for the dinner party. She wanted us to have everything ready in advance, as far as possible, because of the children's party. She had the tent airing out on the lawn and we'd washed six sleeping bags. Sevvy and Timothy, who was Sevvy's age, were going to sleep in the house; so the tent was for Jasmine, Frederick and Gussy's other children and a fifteen year old young man named Luke who was going to take responsibility for the group outside.

It took the rest of the afternoon to pluck and clean the chickens and I didn't ever want to do it again. We stored them in the larder ready for the next day and then began to cook biscuits and cakes.

This was more my territory and Hermione realised that it was safe to leave me alone. As I was taking the second batch of biscuits from the oven, I heard Jasmine talking outside.

'I can't see Angela anywhere. Do you think she's run away?'

'No,' said Robin, who was working nearby, 'she hasn't run away.'

'Well, where is she? Why can't I find her?'

'Why don't we sit down a minute and have a little talk, Jas.'

There was a rustling noise as they sat down.

'You see, it's like this. I don't want you to get upset but we, I mean, I, I mean, we, we've had to kill two chickens for the party tomorrow and Angela was one of them.'

'Oh, okay, that's what they were for anyway, to be eaten. Hermione said so.'

I was dreaming that I was on a ship on a rough sea and, when I opened my eyes, I discovered that it was Jasmine jumping up and down that was causing the feeling.

'It's today, it's today. The party's today.'

By the time I returned from the bathroom, she was back on her own bed with a sulky look on her face.

'Daddy shouted at me. He said it was too much first thing in a morning.'

'He was right.'

Robin looked at me.

'Sick?' he mouthed.

I nodded and climbed back into bed.

'There's lots to do today. Hermione said so yesterday. We should be up and dressed by now.'

'Yes, Jas, we know. Just let Mummy come round a bit. Okay?'

There was a knock on the door and Hermione asked, 'Are the children ready to come and pick tansies with me for the pudding?'

'One minute,' Jasmine shouted, jumping out of bed with a thud.

'I'm coming, I'm coming,' said Sevvy, who I had thought was asleep.

Jasmine dressed herself while Robin helped Sevvy.

'What about washing your face and cleaning your teeth,' I asked, 'and breakfast?'

'When we come back,' Jasmine told me, already on her way out of the door.

I intended to climb out of bed but somehow ended up sinking back against the pillows, eyes closed. Next thing I knew was Richard shaking me awake. He had an oat biscuit in one hand and a cup of tea in the other.

'Have this, then you'll be ready to face the day.'

By the time I managed to dress myself and went downstairs, Hermione and the children were back with a basket full of tansies. The children had a slice of toast and an apple each, then I sent them for a wash and to clean their teeth.

'Right, you two, down to work,' Hermione told them when they'd clattered back downstairs.

She set a bowl in front of them on the table and showed them how to pull the leaves from the tansies.

'What are we making?' asked Sevvy.

'Tansy cakes for you this afternoon and tansy pudding for this evening.' Hermione said, just as there was a knock at the door.

When I opened the door, there was a young man on the doorstep who I hadn't seen before.

'Hello, are you Celia?'

I nodded.

'I'm Luke. From the farm. I've come to put the tent up.'

'Oh, yes, Luke. Hermione said you were coming.'

Hermione welcomed Luke with open arms and insisted he had a drink and a biscuit before going outside. The children seemed a little shy at meeting another stranger and they bent their heads over the tansies. Their bowls were soon full.

'That's really good,' said Hermione, 'now you can go outside and help Luke.'

Shyly, they followed Luke outside but he seemed used to working with children because it wasn't long before I could hear them chattering away to him. Hermione gave me the recipe for Tansy pudding and set me to work. I made breadcrumbs and boiled milk and butter to pour over them. The recipe said to set the mixture aside for thirty minutes and I thought that was a chance to sit down but Hermione had other ideas. There was cleaning the whole house, the tablecloth and serviettes to be ironed, the cutlery and candlesticks to be polished. Robin moved tables and chairs outside for the afternoon and into the dining room for the evening.

By the time three o'clock arrived, I was exhausted. Frederick and Gussy had arrived with their children and Hermione insisted it was fine for me to have a rest. Luke had the children's party totally under control and, although I felt guilty at abandoning everyone, I was ready for a rest.

It was almost six before Robin came to wake me.

'Goodness, I said I'd help with the chicken.'

'Don't worry about it. Everything's done. Hermione's decided to serve the stock as a soup to save time and effort.

I've had a taste, it's delicious. All you have to do is get ready.'

I took a shower and put on my black velvet skirt and cream satin blouse then twisted my hair up like Hermione did for me. I looked like someone else.

Downstairs I went outside to find the children. Sevvy came running towards me, arms outstretched, but his hands looked sticky and I backed away.

'Be careful, don't get my skirt dirty.'

He stopped dead.

'I won't. I'm sorry. Daddy said to be careful but I forgot.'

I patted the top of his head.

'That's all right. Have you had a good time?'

'Yes but Daddy says it's bedtime for me and Timothy.'

I'd totally forgotten about it being bedtime. The children had to be bathed and I'd already put my 'posh' outfit on.

Robin appeared.

'Don't worry. Me and Frederick are going to bathe the little ones and it doesn't matter for the older ones who are staying in the tent. Then it won't take long for me to get ready.'

'But I haven't done anything for tonight.'

'Don't worry. Hermione will find you some finishing touches I'm sure.'

In the kitchen Hermione gave me a long list of instructions and then ran off to get changed. Gussy helped me and together we found flowers for the table, made sure everything was set out, polished the glasses, stirred the soup and mixed honey and cream to go over the tansy pudding.

The first knock at the door was just before seven. To my surprise, it was the woman who turned us away when we asked for help for Sevvy.

As soon as she saw me, she said, 'I'm sorry I couldn't do

anything that day. I knew the Guardian was on her way for a visit and it had just been on the radio that no one should help runaways. I thought someone might have been watching.'

'Well, at least you pointed us in the right direction.'

'I knew you'd be all right with Hermione.'

I smiled and nodded.

'Oh,' she said, 'I'm Laura and this is Pete.'

I put out my hand to take hers.

'I'm Celia and my husband, Robin is somewhere around.'

After I'd shaken Pete's hand, he gave me a basket.

'It's flour for Hermione. We do an exchange for her elderflower wine.'

While Hermione was finishing off the soup, I popped outside to check on the children in the tent. The light was dimming and they were huddled in the tent which was lit by torches. They were telling what they called ghost stories but Luke assured me that they weren't too scary.

Back in the dining room, I took my place at the table. Hermione had put me between Frederick and Pete, Robin was across from me. There were nine of us altogether, including Annie and George who arrived while I was outside. When Hermione had carried in the enormous tureen of soup and placed it in the centre of the table, she took her place at the head. Gussy picked up the ladle and began to dish up the soup.

The dining room looked wonderful and the soup was the best I'd ever tasted. The table cloth looked so white and the soft candlelight caught on the cutlery, reflecting in the windows against the darkness outside.

Everyone had dressed in their best for the occasion and I realised it was the first time I'd ever been to a dinner party.

At the start of the first course, I was worried that it would be too formal and the conversation would be stiff so I kept my head down in case I didn't know how to join in. I soon realised it wasn't like that and it was about the point when Laura spluttered over her soup laughing at Frederick that I lifted my head and felt part of the party. He was telling a story about a sheep strolling into the house and their not being able to get it out. He described how he, Gussy and the five children chased it up and down the stairs and along corridors until they finally cornered it in the kitchen. Then Gussy grabbed it by the scruff of the neck and marched it outside although not before the sheep had made a mess on the kitchen floor.

'Which I, of course, had to clean up,' Gussy added.

Frederick reached over and patted her hand.

'Of course, my dear, and a lovely job you made of it. And of cooking the sheep later.'

Hermione stood up to collect the plates and I helped. I followed her into the kitchen where we put vegetables in tureens and the chickens on two plates. Back in the dining room, everyone was deep in conversation and it took me a while to follow the thread of their discussion.

'Nice couple,' said Laura, 'and the boy was so well behaved. He thought Luke was wonderful, followed him around like a little puppy. Have you heard anything, George?'

'I heard they got to Chester but nothing since.'

'Where were they going?' asked Pete.

'Abertovey. A village in mid-Wales. We sent another couple there a year or so ago and they settled well.'

'I'm sure Rose and Charlie will do just as well,' Hermione said.

I twisted my head towards her.

'Rose and Charlie? Was their little boy called Gareth?'

'Yes he was. Why, do you know them?'

'They were our next door neighbours and Rose was my friend.'

'What a coincidence,' said Laura.

While we ate tansy pudding with honey and cream, I pieced together what happened from what the others said. Rose and Charlie were taken to the Assessment Centre, as we had been, but refused to be separated. Instead, they sat in the reception area and would not agree to anything that the staff asked them to do. Eventually they were escorted from the premises and taken to the edge of town, where they were abandoned and warned never to return. Pete had found them by the roadside when he passed by with his cart. He had taken them back home with him and the family had stayed with them for a while. Then the Guardian turned up unexpectedly but luckily Luke saw her walking towards the house so they were able to smuggle Rose, Gareth and Charlie out the back to George and Annie's. They had helped people to find homes before and they arranged for the family to go down to Wales.

'I'm surprised they let them go from the Assessment Centre,' Robin said.

I nodded; I'd been thinking the same thing.

'They don't waste resources chasing people who don't want to stay. Why should they? If you don't co-operate by following orders, you're no good as a work force or a citizen for them.' George said, 'They don't tell you that though. They'd rather re-educate you ...'

Annie interrupted, 'brainwash you, you mean.'

'Depends how you look at it,' George went on, 'but it all ends up the same. They want you back there, living in their

197

little boxes, following their recipes, recycling all the old stuff till it drops to bits. If you don't want to play their game, then they won't make you but, at the same time, they won't give you anything either. You could drop dead at their feet and they'd step over you and get on with what they were doing.'

'Like Gareth not being able to go to school or have a doctor.'

'Exactly.'

'But you were worried when we went to your door, Laura? If what George is saying is true, what was the problem?'

'The worry wasn't for you, it was for us. They want nothing to do with you and they don't want us to have anything to do with you either. The crime isn't you leaving the Assessment Centre, it's you being helped by one of us.'

'But you're part of that, working for them, doing as they want. Why carry on if you're frightened to do what you want?'

'I suppose we could tell them to stuff it and move away. Start again. But we're happy with our farm; we don't want to be made to leave it. We can put up with their rules and regulations, especially as they can't watch the farms like they can do the people in the towns.'

I felt like a weight had been lifted off my shoulders. I'd been thinking I was a criminal and that, sooner or later, someone would come after us. But they wouldn't. We were safe in that aspect at least. Hermione was safe too, and Frederick and Gussy, and Annie and George, because they were out of the system. It struck me that Laura and Pete were taking risks just being there. I hoped they wouldn't be caught.

But later that evening, Frederick made me realise it wasn't as safe as it had sounded when Pete was talking.

'We might need to be finding a new house,' Frederick told us.

Everyone gasped.

'It's this new building project. They're looking for bricks. They've already knocked down a village to use those bricks and now they're looking for more. I've heard a rumour that they're looking at big old houses like ours.'

'But they can't do that,' I said, 'it's yours. It came from your family.'

'These are people who don't recognise the concept of owning property, remember? I'm hoping we'll be okay, we're off the beaten track and might just get away with it. I've got a spy in the planning office, he'll let me know if it's going to happen and then we'll get moving. I'm sure George here will give us a hand.'

'I certainly will but I hope I don't have to.'

When I looked towards Gussy, I realised she was crying. Frederick put his finger under her chin and tilted her face upwards.

'Don't be upset. It's only things. As long as we're all together, that's all that matters. Bricks and mortar, family portraits and books, we can live without all of those things. Never forget that.'

24

I was cleaning the kitchen while Hermione was out collecting mushrooms. She'd been gone quite a while, but that wasn't unusual. She was a great one for going off visiting friends or getting lost in looking at the view over the hills.

I was feeling good that morning; the sun was shining, the sky was blue and I could hear the children's voices as they played outside. It was so much better than the life we lived before. We were tanned and healthy and there was no Agnes interfering in our lives.

Robin brought in another bucket of water from the well and then watched as I heated it up on the stove.

'I like it here,' he told me.

'Yes, me too.'

He put his hands behind him onto the table and lifted himself up so he could sit on it.

'I've just scrubbed that. It's probably still wet.'

He jumped back down again and rubbed his hands against his bottom.

'Just a bit damp. Soon dry off.'

'Haven't you got anything to do? Fix the gate, clear the shed, feed the chickens, weed the garden?'

'Nope, done all that. The day is mine.'

'Well, what about the children? What are they doing?'

'Jasmine's propped Judy up against a tree and is teaching her about herbs and their medicinal properties. Sevvy's playing a complicated game that involves moving dandelions around on the paving stones. I tried to ask him about it but he said he was too busy to talk.'

'You could get some more water and clean the windows while I mop the kitchen floor. What about that?'

'Did I say I wanted something to do? I'm quite happy doing nothing. It's not a problem you know.'

'I know, but if you wash the windows, then we can do nothing together and that will be more fun, won't it?'

'More fun for you.'

But the windows didn't get washed and the floor didn't get mopped because Hermione returned with a basket full of mushrooms and a serious look on her face.

'I need to talk to you two. Let's make a drink and go into the dining room where the children can't hear us.'

I turned the heat off under the water while Hermione poured three glasses of her home made lemonade. We took them into the dining room and sat down at the table. My heart was beating rapidly because I could tell that Hermione had bad news for us, although I couldn't think what it might be.

Hermione rested her arms on the table and looked at us both before opening her mouth to speak. No words came out. She took a sip of her lemonade and tried again.

'This is hard. I've so enjoyed having the four of you here and I had hoped that you could stay longer, at least until the baby is born. But I've had a message. They're doing a spot check of all the houses in the neighbourhood. Checking that we're not helping fugitives on the run.'

She stopped talking and rubbed her hands over her face. I looked at Robin and saw a well-remembered look of worry spread over his features. I needed to know what this was going to mean for us but I wasn't sure what questions to ask so I settled for asking another one.

'But why should they object to that? You're not taking anything from them.'

'That's true but my friends are. They're looking for an opportunity to link them to a number of people who have run from the Rehabilitation Centre.'

I was shocked into silence.

'Mummy, can I have a drink? I'm thirsty.'

I hadn't noticed Sevvy come in.

'Yes, get yourself one from the kitchen then go back outside.'

'But I wanted Daddy to …'

'Just do as you're told.'

I listened to his feet patter into the kitchen and him pouring himself a drink. Then he left, his steps slower.

'What are we going to do? Could we stay with someone else?'

'I thought about that but it's not going to work. Frederick and Gussy's home is under threat and no one else has room for a family of four. We need you out of here tonight.'

An idea came into my mind and I began to feel excited.

'Would we be able to go to the same place as Rose and Charlie?'

'I don't think so. Sorry. There is a house in Abertovey but it's not fit for occupation and won't be for some time. The community there are working on it but it all takes time, finding the materials and such like.'

This was too much for me and I started to cry. Robin slid his arm around my shoulders and I leant against him.

'Where do you think we can go?' he asked.

'Probably still somewhere in Wales. It's less populated than England. A lot of the people who didn't have their own farms were moved down to Cardiff or Swansea or up into Liverpool. Plus, of course, there are the holiday cottages that are no longer used. That means that there are a lot of empty villages. Problem is that the houses have become dilapidated over the years and need work to make them habitable.'

'How are we going to get there? It's a long way.'

'We can give you some help with that, but you're going to have to do some walking as well. Luckily your pregnancy isn't too far gone. You'll have to take a slowish pace as well because of the children but I would reckon it's going to take a week, possibly longer.'

A week on the road? A week with two young children and another on the way. I burrowed my head harder against Robin's shoulder and said a silent prayer that we'd be all right.

It was about midnight when, through the kitchen window, I saw Pete arrive with his horse and cart. Luke was with him. It was perfect timing: Pete had been asked to take sacks of flour to Altrincham. It wasn't something that happened often but there had been floods and their stocks were low.

As soon as they arrived, they began unloading some of the sacks and Robin went out to help them. Hermione and I were busy packing the rucksacks; we had one each, a smaller one for Jasmine and a tiny one for Sevvy. It was a lot to ask of such small children but we didn't feel we had any choice; Robin would take the main load. He was also carrying the tent that the children had slept in during the party. Hermione was providing us with some dried food and we'd had long lectures on what kinds of things we could, and couldn't, pick up from fields and woodland. She'd included a sheet illustrating poisonous mushrooms and made us promise that we would check it every time. There was a tin plate each, some cutlery and both Robin and I would have a pan hanging from our rucksack.

I'd already packed us some of Hermione's home-made soap and a change of underwear and night clothes but I suspected we were going to be pretty smelly by the time we reached the end of what promised to be a very long journey. Finally, Hermione rolled up two sleeping bags and put a double across the top of Robin's rucksack and a single one, for the children to share, across the top of mine. It wasn't ideal but there was a limit to what we could carry.

Robin had the map safely tucked into his waterproof jacket pocket. It was a strange thing. The landmarks tended to be trees damaged by lightning or old disused warehouses. There weren't many place names marked on it because most town name markers had been removed or fallen over. There were three safe houses shown, places where they would help us. Pete was to take us to the first one that night.

The children were tired; we'd had to take them out of bed to get them ready. Hermione had agreed that they could take the toys she gave them, the rag doll and the wooden spoon 'teddy bear' and they were both clutching on to them like life jackets.

'We're ready,' said Pete, popping his head around the kitchen door.

I turned to Hermione and held out my arms.

'Thank you for everything,' I said, my voice choked with tears.

'I enjoyed every minute,' she told me.

Her face was against my chest but I could hear that she was crying too. Then she stepped back and held me at arm's length.

'Look after yourself, and Robin and the children. And that little baby.'

'I will.'

'Remember, it's not a race. Take your time and you'll all be fine. I wish you didn't have to travel before the baby arrives but if you have to go like this, it's better now than when you get bigger.'

Luke came into the kitchen.

'Dad wants you to hurry up.'

I made one more visit to the bathroom and, by the time I got back downstairs, Robin had loaded himself, the children and the rucksacks on to the cart. They were sitting in the centre and there was a wall of sacks down one side and behind them. I hugged Hermione once more and then, with Pete's help, climbed up into the cart. Robin made the children stand while I settled myself down beside him and then he sat Jasmine on his knee while I took Sevvy.

Pete and Luke began to load the sacks back onto the cart, forming another wall across the bottom and down the other side. I watched as Hermione gradually disappeared. Just before the last sack was put into place, we all waved madly at each other and then she was gone from view although we could still hear as she said, 'Safe journey.'

Virtually straight away we heard Pete say, 'Giddyap, Daisy,' and there was a sudden jerk as we were on our way.

Jasmine started to cry.

'I don't want to leave Hermione.'

'Neither do we,' I said, 'but we have no choice. She'll get into a lot of trouble if they catch us there.'

'But couldn't we go and stay with Freddy and Gussy or Luke or …?'

'No. Luke's parents would be in trouble and it looks like Freddy and Gussy might need to move away too.'

'Why?'

'Because their house could be knocked down. No one can be sure what's happening. That's why we need to get away.'

'It's not fair. We're always losing things, losing people.'

It might have been dark in our flour sack 'cell' but I could tell that she had her sulky face on. Sevvy wasn't sulking, he was fast asleep with his thumb in his mouth, his body warm and heavy against mine. The air around us was powdery and dry although an occasional freshness drifted down from the open air above us. The sky was a deep navy blue and scattered with tiny stars.

'Look,' I said, 'I can see a cat in the stars.'

'Where?' asked Jasmine, interested despite herself.

I pointed upwards, being careful not to disturb Sevvy.

'There. I can see his two ears, his two eyes and then, look, one, two, three whiskers.'

'So can I,' said Robin.

Jasmine moved closer to get a better look. He took her hand and drew the shape of a cat in the air.

'Oh yes,' she said, 'I can see it and, oh look, there's his bowl of milk.'

She settled her head back against Robin and gazed upwards, watching for other shapes. She found a rainbow, a fish and a house before her eyes closed and she went to sleep.

I was watching the sky too but it wasn't shapes I was seeing. It was an unknown future, one without a safety net. There'd always been someone or something keeping an eye out for me. As a child it was Mum and Dad then, when I was older, it was the 'state', in the form of Guardians like Agnes and other professionals like doctors and nurses. After we ran away from the Assessment Centre, there was a brief spell when we had nobody but it only lasted for a few hours until we found Hermione. But even as I was thinking it, I realised that I still had a safety net, that I had Robin and, as long as we were together, we could mesh and face anything that comes along.

I turned my face towards him and whispered, 'Thank you.'

He looked surprised.

'You're welcome. What have I done?'

'You're here. I was feeling scared but then I realised that, when you're with me, I can deal with whatever happens.'

'We'll be fine.'

He took my hand.

'Absolutely nothing to worry about. What's a few miles walk?'

Then he laughed. It was going to be more than a few miles walk. No one had worked it out or, if they had, they hadn't told us. All we'd been told was that it was a long way but other people had done it. I did worry about the baby, taking such a long journey, but at the same time I had a feeling that it was going to be okay; since I had avoided the termination I'd been convinced that, before too long, I'd be holding a happy, healthy baby in my arms. Wherever we were.

Robin pushed himself further towards me, being careful not to wake Jasmine. I rested my head against his shoulder. I felt safe and warm inside our floury room and soon I was asleep, dreaming of finding a house at the end of a rainbow. When I opened the front door, there was a black cat lying in front of an open fire. It turned towards us and said, 'Welcome home'.

Some time later, the cart stopped and I heard voices. Sevvy woke and I held my finger to my lips to warn him to be quiet. He still opened his mouth to speak and I had to put my hand over his mouth to persuade him that I was being serious.

A man's voice asked, 'Where are you going with all these sacks?'

'Down to Altrincham.'

'Have you got a permit? These are government sacks.'

As he spoke, he must have patted the side of a sack as a white puff of flour floated into the air and settled over my face, drifting dry and powdery into my nose and making me want to sneeze. I moved my hand from Sevvy's face to my nose to try to stop it.

There was a rustle of paper from the roadside.

'It all seems in order. You can go on your way. Have a safe journey.'

We heard the horse taking a couple of steps. I could no longer hold the sneeze back even though I held my nose tighter and tighter. A small sputter escaped from my mouth.

'Just a minute,' the man's voice said.

I felt as though I couldn't breathe and my heart was fluttering inside my chest. Beside me, Robin's jaw was clenched and his eyes were narrowed.

'Whoa, Daisy.'

We hear Pete turning around in his seat.

'Yes?'

There was tension in his voice.

'I could use one of those sacks of flour. Get me in good with the wife. We have a big family and they never send us enough flour.'

'Yeah, okay. They won't miss one. I'll come and get it.'

'No, it's right. I'll do it.'

The man pulled a sack one from the middle of the pile, leaving the ones above balanced precariously.

'Right, I'll be off,' said Pete, before shouting, 'Giddyap,' to Daisy and the cart moved off with a jerk.

The disturbed sacks began to move. Robin pushed Jasmine on to my chest, on top of Sevvy and then pressed himself against me, his back towards the falling sacks. I felt the impact through him as one, two, three sacks dropped onto his body.

'Are you all right,' I whispered, a hand over each child's mouth to stop them crying out.

'Yes, think so.'

He twisted himself from side to side to dislodge the sacks and then manoeuvred his body into a sitting position. He flexed his shoulders as Pete halted the cart again.

'Are you okay back there?'

'Yes, fine. No problem.'

'Can you manage to build it back up again or do you want me to come and do it.'

'No, I'll do it.'

Robin stood up and heaved the sacks back into place. He sat down beside me again. The incident had shaken me up and, as we settled ourselves and the children, I could feel a slight tremor in the arm that Robin slid around my shoulders.

As I watched the sky gradually lighten above us, I no longer felt safe. I had no idea where we were and I knew that, if the Guard had discovered us, he would have arrested Pete and left us standing by the roadside. What would we have done? Our map would have been no use to us; it was hand drawn, with starting and finishing points and only the significant details which would help us find our way between them. I wanted to talk through my fears but Robin's head was heavy against me and I realised he was asleep. I sat there feeling alone despite the company of my family and watched the sky turn to a soft pink.

25

The cart stopped and I heard Pete jump down.

'We're here,' he shouted and began pulling sacks down until he made a gap that we could squeeze through.

'Here' turned out to be what I remembered from my childhood as something called a pub. There was a partial name in big gold letters which spelt out *The Go de Hin* . The building looked dilapidated and empty but I was learning not to judge by first impressions. A short plump woman bustled out, closely followed by an even shorter thin man with a big bushy moustache.

'Welcome,' the woman said, 'I'm Pamela but people call me Plum. This is Walter – I call him Weasel.'

I held out my hand, 'Celia', I said, 'this is Robin, Sevvy and Jasmine.'

She smiled down at the children. 'Have you had a good journey?'

'Just one scare, that's all. A Guard stopped Pete,' Robin told her.

Pete smiled.

'Cadged a sack of flour off me.'

'Cheek,' said the woman.

Then she turned towards me.

'I'll make you some breakfast and then you can have a rest before you set out on your journey.'

'I'd better be going,' said Pete.

'No,' said Plum, 'you can't do that. You need a rest, something to eat.'

'Have to. Got to get these dropped off and then I've a field to plough when I get home.'

'Well, then, take something with you to eat.'

She hurried inside.

'We can't thank you enough, Pete,' I said, holding my arms out to hug him.

He stepped awkwardly into my arms and stood unwillingly while I squeezed him tight and stroked his back. Then he moved backwards. Robin held out his hand and Pete took it. Robin patted Pete's shoulder as they shook hands.

'Yes, thanks for your help. I hope you have an easy journey back.'

Pete was more comfortable with the children's hugs and, as he straightened up again, Plum appeared with a doorstep of bread thick with butter and honey.

'You can eat this with one hand, I'm sure.'

We watched and waved as Pete set off again. As he turned the corner at the end of the street, we could see that he was already biting into his bread.

'Poor man, he's going to be exhausted by the end of the day,' Plum said. 'Still, can't be helped. Come on inside, let's sort your breakfast out.'

She led us through the two doors into the pub. In the brief instant between one door closing and the other door opening,

I caught a faint whiff of alcohol, something that I hadn't smelt since I was a child. It reminded me of a wedding we went to, my cousin's wedding. I wondered what had happened to her. I hoped she was happy.

Inside the bar, there was a strong smell of beeswax. Everything was highly polished and the morning sun caught on the brasses on the walls and the table tops. That was how I remembered the bar looking at the wedding except those shelves had been lined with bottles and these shelves were empty. Plum noticed me staring round.

'We kept it the same as when the pub was open. Couldn't see any reason to change it. We stayed open after the Upheaval for a while, serving the drinks for free until the stocks ran out.'

'Kept a bit for ourselves too, but that's gone now,' Weasel added.

'In the Assessment Centre, I met a woman who made her own. Poteen she called it.'

Weasel stroked his moustache.

'I've been known to have a bit of a dabble myself.'

Plum leant towards me confidentially.

'He has a shed. He doesn't tell me what's in it and I don't ask. But I have to say, I've noticed he's a lot happier when he comes out. And his friends too. For myself, I can manage without. Never was a big fan anyway.'

Then she clapped her hands.

'All this talking isn't going to get the baby a new bonnet, is it? You lot sit down at that big table there and I'll go and sort some breakfast out for you.'

She turned away and then shouted over her shoulder, 'Come on, Weasel, you can help too.'

Weasel looked at us and raised his eyebrows upwards then

trotted off behind Plum. We all sat quietly looking round us with interest, until Sevvy interrupted our silence.

'Why's this place?'

'Why's this place what?' I asked.

'Why's it got all these tables and shiny things on the wall?' Jasmine explained.

'People used to come here to drink something called beer.'

'Why?'

'Because they liked it.'

'Why, when they could drink at home.'

'So they could meet people.'

'Why?'

We were rescued by Weasel with a plate full of toast smothered in melting butter and a jar of strawberry jam. He set it in the middle of the table and, as if by magic, produced four plates and knives. Sevvy wanted to put his own jam on but I'd seen his spreading skills and I didn't want to risk it in a strange place.

As we started to eat, I realised how hungry I was. Plum brought in four glasses of apple juice and then a big serving plate covered in eggs, bacon and sausage.

'Help yourselves,' she said, 'I have a few jobs to do in the kitchen and then I'll be back with you.'

Suddenly I felt like I was on holiday; I looked at Robin and smiled.

'What?'

'Do you remember going on holidays when you were a kid?'

'We didn't go on many holidays, didn't have much money and, living at the seaside, Dad thought it was a waste paying money to look at someone else's sea. But we did go up to Scotland a couple of times. Stayed in a small village, can't remember its name. It was so different from Blackpool. The seafront was pretty quiet, a couple of shops and cafés, that was all. The beach was different too, white sand and empty. Went on for miles.'

He stared off into the distance and I knew he was thinking about his father.

'It was the breakfasts I was thinking about.'

'Hmm?'

'The breakfasts. Do you remember? As much as you wanted and no hurry to eat it up. Oh, and the smell when you were coming down the stairs.'

'Oh yes. I do remember now. Great. We lost so much after the Upheaval, didn't we?'

Jasmine shook my arm.

'Mummy, look at Sevvy.'

Having cleared his plate, Sevvy had put his arms on the table and gone to sleep.

'Ah, look at the little sweetheart. Exhausted after his journey.'

It was Plum, back from the kitchen and wiping her hands on a floral apron.

'What about all of you having a rest before you set off? It can't do any harm. You can use one of the bedrooms. We used to do bed and breakfast; it'll be like old times.'

'Oh, thanks, Plum. I think I could do with a sleep,' I told her, 'what about you, Jas?'

'I can try, Mummy, if you want me to.'

'Not me,' said Robin, 'don't think I'll be able to settle. Anyway, I had a good few hours last night.'

'Tell you what, Robin,' Weasel said from the kitchen doorway, 'what about coming rabbitting with me? Have you ever been before?'

'No.'

'Well, it'll be a good skill for when you're on the road.'

'Let's go, then.'

The two men left through the front door. I picked up Sevvy and followed Plum upstairs. Jasmine wandered along beside me, trailing her hand along the raised surface of the wallpaper. There was a window halfway up the stairs; she stopped to stare out.

'Why can't I go rabbitting? I like rabbits.'

'That's why you're not going.'

Plum turned back and took Jasmine's hand.

'Come on, see this pretty bedroom.'

It was a pretty bedroom, although a bit too frilly for me. The walls were decorated in a soft lemon wallpaper covered in gold cursive writing. There were yellow flounced blinds at the three windows; the matching bedspread had a series of white roses embroidered on it. A rag doll wearing a tiara was propped against the pillows between two well worn teddy bears.

'Oh, Mummy, look at the doll and teddy bears.'

'They belonged to my daughter,' said Plum.

She picked up the three toys and sat them on the windowsill.

'Where is she?' asked Jasmine. 'Can I play with her?'

'Oh no, love. She's gone away.'

Plum looked at me and mouthed, 'pneumonia. Twenty years ago.'

Her face was sad for a moment and then she gathered herself together.

'Right. Time for you to rest. Do you need any blankets or anything? I'm afraid the bed isn't actually made up.'

'No, that's fine. It's warm enough for us to lie on top of the bedspread. If you don't mind, that is?'

'I don't mind at all.'

She left the room and I listened to her footsteps on the stairs as I lay Sevvy on the bed. I took my place beside Sevvy and gestured to Jasmine to take her place at the other side.

'Can I hold one of the teddies?'

'I don't think Plum will mind but be careful. They don't look like they'll take much rough stuff.'

She picked up the healthier looking teddy and lay down beside me, resting her head on my breast. It wasn't long before she was breathing at the same, soft, even rate as Sevvy and I knew she was asleep.

I felt relaxed. The holiday mood had stayed with me and I was looking forward to the adventures to come. I knew it wasn't going to be easy but we were on our way to a new life. It had been good living with Hermione but it wasn't fair for us to be putting on her so much. She was entitled to her own life. I knew that sometimes it had been hard for her to have two children running riot in her home.

I woke some time later. I knew I'd been asleep for a while because the patch of sunlight which had been touching the white chest of drawers was at the other end of the room. I gently pulled my arms from under the children's necks and tried to slide from the bed without waking them but I didn't succeed. First Sevvy and then Jasmine opened their eyes.

'Where am I?' asked Sevvy.

'In Plum's little girl's bedroom,' Jasmine told him.

'Oh.'

'Come on, kids, lets go and find Daddy.'

When they climbed down from the bed, I pulled the bedspread straight. Jasmine collected the other teddy bear and the rag doll from the windowsill and propped them up against the pillows again. She stroked the rag doll's hair.

'She's so pretty. Like a fairy queen.'

At the bottom of the stairs, we heard voices coming from the kitchen. Robin muttered something and Weasel replied, 'You've got to be careful not to puncture the stomach.'

When we went in, we found Robin learning to skin a rabbit. Jasmine said, 'yuk,' and went out to sit on the stairs but Sevvy watched with fascination.

'Plum's in the lounge,' Weasel told me, 'through there.'

I went through the door he indicated and found Plum holding something pink and soft looking against her face. When she heard me enter the room, she pushed it into a drawer and turned to face me, brushing the back of her hand against her face.

'I'm sorry, I didn't mean to interrupt you. Weasel told me it was okay to come in. Do you want me to leave you alone?'

'No, don't be silly. I don't know why I hid it really.'

She opened the drawer and took the pink item out again. She unfolded it and then folded it again more neatly. I could see it was a baby blanket.

'It belonged to my little girl,' she told me as she wrapped a piece of tissue paper from the coffee table around the blanket and slid it back in the drawer

'Carrie, that was her name, Carrie had a slight cold, nothing more. Then suddenly it went a lot worse. Weasel went for Maureen, a woman who used to be a nurse, but there was nothing we could do for her. Maureen said, in the old days, they'd have given her antibiotics and she'd be right as rain. But, as things are now …'

The door opened a crack and Jasmine peered in.

'Are we going soon?'

'Don't come in, Jas, we're talking.'

Jasmine looked surprised but turned to leave. Then Plum spoke.

'You don't have to leave the room, sweetheart. It's all right, come on in.'

Jasmine looked at me and I confirmed that it was all right to come in. She walked towards the sofa and sat down, her legs sticking out in front of her.

'Are we going soon?' she repeated.

'As soon as I've made some sandwiches for you to take with you.'

'Oh, Plum, you've done enough for us, there's no need to …'

'I can't send you off without something to take with you, can I?'

We put our rucksacks on our backs and Weasel helped Robin fasten a rabbit to his belt.

'Supper,' Robin said. Then he saw my face. 'Don't worry, I'll skin it.'

We walked through the bar and out onto the street outside.

'Just a minute,' Plum said and ran back into the pub. When she returned, she had two potatoes, two onions and a turnip held against her chest with one hand, and the other behind her back.

'To go with the rabbit,' she told me and pushed the vegetables into the top of Robin's already overflowing rucksack.

Then she moved her other hand forward. She was holding the rag doll and one of the teddy bears.

'For the children.'

Jasmine looked at me for permission to take the doll,

obviously realising what a significant gift it was. I could tell that Plum was making an important gesture towards us and I nodded and smiled, although my eyes were full of tears. Jasmine held out her arms and hugged the doll against her.

'Oh thank you, she's beautiful. I'll look after her for your little girl. I promise.'

Sevvy took hold of the teddy and stroked its threadbare head.

'It's a proper one,' he breathes, 'with fur and everything.'

The farewell was getting as emotional as the parting from Hermione and I needed to be off before I got too upset.

'Thanks so much for everything, Plum. I'll always remember you.'

'And us you. Now be off with you before we all get too silly.'

We set off down the road, off on our adventures.

26

The holiday feeling was back again, the feeling that we were there to enjoy ourselves and take advantage of a break from normality, although I knew there was no normality any more. The sky was a brilliant blue, with the occasional puff of cotton wool cloud. We walked down a country lane which was lined by trees heavy with green leaves and, over to our left, there was the occasional glimpse of a field full of sheep. In front of us, two pheasants pottered along side by side; until Sevvy decided to chase them, that was, and they flapped away into the woods.

'Slow down, Sevvy,' Robin shouted after him, 'we don't want you to tire yourself out too soon.'

'Okay, Daddy,' he told us but it wasn't too long before he was running again.

'Come and hold my hand,' I said loudly, trying to make sure my voice didn't show any sign of concern. George had told us to move at the pace of the 'weakest' which was Sevvy, whose little legs had to take at least two paces to our one. We couldn't afford to have him run out of steam almost before we'd set off.

He stood still and turned to face us.

'Don't want to,' he said sulkily, 'I'm a big boy now.'

'I know you are. That's why I want you to hold my hand, so you can help me. Make sure I don't get lost and tell me when there are stones I might trip over. And you can watch out for interesting things like birds and animals for me. I like looking at birds and animals.'

He pondered that and then wandered slowly towards me to take my hand.

Jasmine was walking close to Robin. There had been a lot of changes for her and, unlike Sevvy, she tended to worry about new things. The trip was very much a venture into the unknown for us all, but particularly for Jasmine who found it so hard to grasp why we had to leave Hermione's.

'Are you all right, Jas?'

'Yes thank you.'

'And what about your new doll? How's she doing?'

'She's a bit scared because she doesn't know where we're going. I've told her I'm going to look after her. I'm holding her tight so she knows she'll be all right.'

'Have you given her a name yet?'

'I've called her Plum. I liked Plum.'

'Me too,' Sevvy says, 'she was nice and she made nice bacon and eggs too.'

'Always thinking of his stomach,' laughed Robin.

We carried on walking. The birds were singing around us and now we could see cows through the gaps in the trees. Eventually our pace slowed and I realised that the path had taken an upward turn. It became harder to walk and Sevvy was dragging on my hand as his pace slowed.

'Do you want to take a break when we reach the top?' Robin asked.

'Yes,' I said and then had a vision of the map and the infinitesimal distance we'd travelled before needing a break. The trip was going to take us forever.

At the top of what seemed to be an enormous hill, we stood still and looked at the landscape below us. In the distance, there was a town surrounded by the usual produce, solar and wind farms. Nearer to us was another produce farm, one that looked as if it wasn't anything to do with the town. It had its own wind turbine and was surrounded by a double layered barbed wire fence, the sight of which brought back another concern. How safe were we out on the road? All the radio reports I had heard about bands of travellers moving around the country stealing from the towns and attacking people came back to my mind. How true were they? George had told us that those stories were greatly exaggerated and that, as long as we kept ourselves to ourselves then we would be perfectly safe. But how did he know that? It would only take one armed person to attack us, steal what we have, kill us even. Robin said I worried too much and that he wouldn't let any harm come to us. I was doing my best to believe him. I didn't have any choice.

Robin took my arm.

'Come on, let's sit down over there.'

The four of us squashed together on a tiny bench that someone had thoughtfully placed overlooking the view. I wished they'd also thought about putting a back on the bench but you can't have everything. Sevvy managed to sit still for five minutes but then he was up and running round the bench.

'Bet you can't catch me, Jasmine.'

She jumped down from the bench and began to chase him. The two ended up rolling in the grass and giggling.

'Come on, sit down and I'll tell you a story.'

The two settled down either side of me and I began a story. It was about a boy and girl going on a journey, 'like me and Jasmine,' said Sevvy. He put his thumb in his mouth and rested his head against my side.

After a while, Robin said, 'I think we'd better be moving on. Do another hour or so and then we'll have lunch.'

'Story's over.'

'Ah, I was enjoying that,' Jasmine moaned.

'Me too,' said Sevvy, although I think he'd actually gone to sleep.

'We'll do some more later. Don't worry.'

We all pulled our rucksacks back on and Robin moved towards the path.

'We can't go yet,' Sevvy told us, 'I want to wee. I'm busting.'

And there was another worry racing into my mind. Toilets, or the lack of them. I couldn't imagine having to go in the bushes. It was something I'd never done and I never wanted to. But I was going to have to.

'Do you want to go, Jasmine?'

She nodded reluctantly.

I took the two children further back into the trees. Sevvy performed almost as soon as we got there but Jasmine stood and looked at me.

'Can I wait till we find a toilet?'

'We're not going to find one, Jas. We have to get used to going like this, in the outside.'

She pulled down her knickers and squatted but nothing happened.

'I can't.'

There was nothing for it but for me to show her it was okay. I squatted too and, after a bit of mental manipulation, managed to urinate. Eventually, Jasmine did too. One more step towards our new life on the road.

We made our final stop of the day at about four pm. In my mind, the journey merged into a collage of silence and sky, talk and trees, walking and wind. When we had stopped at lunchtime, we were grateful for Plum's sandwiches because we hadn't made any plans for that particular meal.

We chose a spot behind a clump of trees so that we couldn't be spotted from the path but, like Robin said, once the fire was lit, we would be easily found if anyone were looking. There was a stream nearby for water. Jasmine helped me choose the toilet place and then Robin sent us off to collect the wood for the fire. While we were gone, he found two branches to support the cooking pot. As soon as we had enough wood, he lit the fire with the flint which Frederick gave us.

As the fire was getting going, he skinned the rabbit and I peeled and chopped the vegetables. After Robin had finished skinning the rabbit, he handed it to me to chop. Finally, I put everything into the cooking pot and added a lot of water from the stream, probably too much but I wanted there to be more than enough to go round. Robin dug the non-forked end of a branch into the ground at the side of the fire. Then he put the other branch into the fork and weighted the end down with stones. I hung the pot over the fire and then looked around to see what the children were doing.

Sevvy had taken off his socks and shoes and was dangling his feet into the stream; a sight which made me resolve to collect drinking water from upstream, although I was aware that there would be other things in the water which I might not want to think about. I knew that we could boil it but that would be so time consuming that I had to hope the clearness of the water meant it was clean.

Jasmine had Plum on her knee and was explaining to her why we were out walking on the road. It seemed that we were looking for a magic bus at the end of the rainbow and we had to be out on the road to find the right rainbow.

Robin was putting tent poles together and I went over to help him. They were made of plastic piping and fastened together with special metal sockets. They fitted into pockets in the tent. For a while, I couldn't believe that it would ever be a tent but, suddenly, there it was.

'All ready for tonight,' Robin said, standing back and looking proudly at our handiwork.

Sevvy came running over and prepared to climb into the tent but I hauled him back.

'Get those feet dry first.'

I pulled the only towel we had out of my rucksack, wiped his feet and legs dry, dragged his socks on and then I lowered him onto all fours and patted his bottom.

'In you go.'

I removed the two sleeping bags from the rucksacks and followed Sevvy inside the tent, kicking my shoes off as I went.

Inside the light had a pink tinge and it felt cosy. I put the two sleeping bags side by side on to the ground sheet and rolled them out. There wasn't much room for anything else.

'Which one's mine?'

'This one. You sleep at one end and Jasmine at the other.'

Jasmine's head popped through the opening.

'Take your shoes off, Jas.'

'Already have done, Mummy.'

'Me and you are going to sleep in this one.'

'We won't fit.'

'One at each end, Jas.'

'If he kicks me in the night, I'll kick him back.'

'I'll kick you again then.'

Jasmine launched herself at Sevvy and, with a look of surprise on his face, he fell over backwards then began kicking out at her.

'Enough, you two. I don't want you wrecking this tent before we've even slept in it. Outside. Now!'

They scampered towards the opening.

'And don't forget to put your shoes back on.'

Outside there was no sign of Robin. I took out the utensils ready for our meal and put the rucksacks inside the tent. Then I looked round for what needed doing next but couldn't find anything. The children were chasing each other but it didn't look like there was any risk of them harming each other because they were both giggling. I stirred the stew then sat on a convenient stone.

It was so relaxing. The pot was making a pleasing bubbling sound and there was the occasional crack from the fire. Above us birds rustled in the trees and off to my left I could hear the stream. It reminded me of Hermione's garden which had a stream running down by the side of it where she got her water. The garden was the most important place for her at her cottage. The only things she'd brought up from London with her had been cuttings from her garden.

She'd told me a little bit more about why she'd left London. She had been talking to one of the doctors who had worked in the same practice as her. He told her that a woman had brought a sick child to him. He'd tried to get the child into hospital but was refused because the mother had been expelled from the town for non-co-operation. She'd found her way back in and made her way to the doctor's home to get help for the child. The Guards came and, once again, took mother and child out of town and abandoned them. Hermione had decided that she didn't want to have anything more to do with what was going on in London.

'No, give it back,' I heard Jasmine say.

My heart began beating fast. Sevvy was nearby but I couldn't see Jasmine anywhere. Robin hadn't returned either. Suddenly, Jasmine and a tall man in guard's uniform appeared from behind a clump of bushes. The man was holding the doll high in the air and Jasmine was jumping up, trying to reach it.

'What are you doing?' I asked, trying to control my voice as I spoke but its tone swooped up and down.

The man stood still for a moment, then lowered his arm and handed Plum back to Jasmine.

'Get away from my daughter,' I heard Robin's voice say from behind me.

The Guard took a couple more steps towards me. I was frightened, really frightened. The Guard held his arms up, in a gesture of surrender.

'I'm sorry,' he said, 'I forgot myself. That's what I do with my sisters. I didn't mean to frighten you. Honestly.'

Robin was suddenly beside me and I was grateful. Jasmine rushed over and stood between us. I had to speak, get the words out.

'You're a stranger. How was she supposed to know you were only playing? How were any of us supposed to know?'

'I can only say again that I'm sorry.'

He held out his hand.

'I'm Gerry by the way. Gerry Austin.'

Robin took his hand and shook it.

'I'm Robin, this is Celia and that's Sevvy over there. Jasmine you've already met.'

'Hi, nice to meet you.'

Sevvy ran over to stand behind me, and then peered out at Gerry.

'Are you going to take us back to that place with bars over the windows?'

Gerry looked at me with a question in his eyes. I hesitated but then decided to go for the truth.

'Assessment Centre. Back in Burnley.'

'I'm not going to take you anywhere.'

'Good,' Jasmine said firmly, 'I never want to go back there.'

Sevvy wasn't so sure.

'It was nice. I liked Leo. He was my friend and I miss him.'

'So what are you doing here?' Robin asked.

'We've heard that a gang of troublemakers might be in the area.'

My heart was off again, hammering against my rib cage and making it hard to breath. Gerry must have noticed my face.

'Oh no, I don't think it's anything for you folks to worry about. This bunch wouldn't bother you. They've got bigger fish to fry. They go for the warehouses on the edge of towns. Steal food, clothing, furniture and then live off the proceeds. Lazy they are, don't want to work. Spend their days idling about and then steal from working communities. Makes me sick.'

'We don't steal,' I hurried to tell him.

'Oh, I can see that. Decent honest folk who hit a bad patch I'd say from looking at you. Is that right?'

'That's right.'

'Well, that's fine with me. I have to warn you that there

are other Guards who don't feel the same way. Guards who will take any opportunity to treat folks badly.'

'But we've been told that the Guards wouldn't do us any harm.'

'They're not supposed to but, you know, there's good and bad in every crowd of people and it's best not to have anything to do with any of us, if you can avoid it.'

I was feeling sick and Robin said, 'So we should avoid all Guards then?'

'Best to avoid everyone if you can. Think about what sort of reasons might cause people to be living out of the towns. They're not all like you. In fact, some of them are downright evil.'

He looked at my face and patted my hand. 'Don't worry about it too much. The odds are you won't come across anyone at all. The roads tend to be pretty empty most of the time.'

'I hope so.'

'I'll keep my fingers crossed for you. Right, well, I'll leave you folks. Have a good evening.'

We all shouted *goodbye* towards his retreating back and watched him as he disappeared off into the trees. I was still feeling shaken; it was beginning to go dark and I felt like we were surrounded by dangerous people. Robin didn't seem worried though.

'Come on, come and look at what I've done before it goes dark.'

He took us over to the stream. He'd put a stick at either side of the water and suspended a string over it, a string that had other strings hanging down into the water.

'It's a fishing rod. Weasel showed me how to do it. Each line has bait on it and, hopefully, we'll have caught some fish by morning.'

'That's brilliant,' I told him, 'absolutely brilliant.'

'Clever Daddy,' said Jasmine.

'Yes,' said Sevvy, nodding decisively, 'clever Daddy.'

We went back to the fire. I stirred the rabbit stew which was bubbling away nicely and then we sat huddled in a group. I tried not to look around for shadows but sometimes I couldn't help myself; we were surrounded by shadows and I didn't know which, if any, I should worry about. Robin started us on a game of *Today the Delivery/Collection Man Brought*.

By the time the stew was ready, I was feeling more relaxed and the children were looking sleepy. They perked up at the prospect of food though and eagerly took their plates from me. As I was about to dish up mine and Robin's, there was a voice that initially made me jump but then I realised it was Gerry.

'Hi, guys. Just thought we'd drop by to say the gang have been caught. You can sleep more secure tonight.'

I rested the spoon on my plate and watched as he walked towards us, changing from a tall dark figure to a moving pattern of light and shade as he neared the fire.

'Oh, thanks so much for telling us. I was worried.'

'That's what I thought.'

There was a minute's silence and then he said, 'That smells good. Rabbit?'

'Yes. Do you want some? There's a bit left over.'

'Only if you have some to spare.'

'There's still some left in the pan. I don't know how we'd keep it until morning. Would your partner like some too?'

Gerry turned round and said, 'Mitch?'

Mitch stepped forward into the light.

'Certainly would.'

I served up mine and Robin's then lifted down the pot, put

it on the floor near Gerry's feet before realising something.

'Oh no, we haven't any extra dishes or spoons.'

'No worry,' said Mitch, 'we're well equipped.

He fished in his rucksack and pulled out two mugs and spoons.

I sat down by Robin and took a taste. It was good. I wasn't sure it would be, being the first time I'd cooked in this way. No one spoke as they ate; being out in the fresh air certainly sharpened the appetite.

When we got to the spoon scraping stage, Robin asked, 'Where are you two stationed?'

'At Styal,' answered Mitch, 'we live in the Barracks there. I'm originally from Manchester and Gerry's from Bradford.'

'What made you want to be guards?' I asked. I wasn't sure it was an appropriate question but it was something I'd often wondered about. Why would anyone choose to do that?

Gerry answered.

'I've always had a very strong sense of wrong and right. I'm from a big family. Eight children. I can remember back before the Upheaval when we didn't have much. There were times when we went hungry. Not very often because Mum was a good manager but Dad was a heavy drinker and that's where the money went. Then, suddenly, life was better. Every day, we were given what we needed. Every day! And Dad wasn't coming home roaring drunk from the pub every night because there wasn't any pub to go to. He had a steady job too; driving the work buses. He was proud of that. I wanted a job which supported this way of life and I thought being a guard would do that.'

'And has it been what you expected?'

'Pretty much. There's times when I'm not too comfortable with what I'm asked to do, such as taking good people like you to the Assessment Centre, but, on the whole I feel like I'm playing an important role.'

'And what about you, Mitch?'

'Oh, it's a different story to Gerry's. I don't even remember the Upheaval, I feel like life has always been like this. I was a bit of a wild lad. Always getting into trouble. Breaking into lockers, stealing extra food even though I didn't need it. Graffiti, vandalising property, stuff like that. Ended up in a Rehabilitation Centre. There was this guy there. Mr Torkington. He was the strictest person I've ever met. At first, I did what he told me because he terrified me but, when I got to know him, I realised it was all a front. At heart, he was a kind man, willing to spend time with me. He made me realise I needed a job with discipline and persuaded me to join the guards. He was right.'

Gerry looked at his watch.

'Speaking of discipline, we'd better be going.'

They both stood.

'Thanks for the food. Much appreciated.'

Mitch opened his backpack and took out a package.

'Here you are. Some sandwiches and a couple of apples. Should help out.'

'Thank you. And thanks for letting us know about those people being caught. I was worried.'

'No need to worry. Keep yourselves to yourselves and have your belongings with you at all times. Always keep in mind, though, that people who are outsiders might be like that for a reason. They're often people who have been expelled because they didn't fit in for one reason or other.'

'Come on, Gerry, let's get back before we're put on a charge. Bye folks.'

'Bye.'

27

We'd been on the road for five hours and I felt as if I'd been walking like that for all of my life. We were on what used to be called a motorway. At first I couldn't remember seeing anything like that before until Robin told me that sometimes they were so full of cars that everyone had to slow down or even stop. I suddenly remembered coming back from a holiday in Wales. It was really hot. The car was stopping and starting, stopping and starting and I began to feel sick but I knew that Dad was already angry at the delay and I daren't say anything until it was too late and I threw up all over myself and the back seat. That made the journey even worse and, by the time we got home, we'd almost forgotten we'd been away. It was as hot as it had been on that journey from Wales but there weren't any cars. It was empty, totally empty.

Sometimes there were big cracks across its surface, often with weeds growing out of them and, if you looked down into the depth of the crack, you could see hundreds of insects crawling about. Sevvy was fascinated, of course, and we had to keep dragging him away.

There was a barrier down the middle of the road and, at first, Jasmine kept hopping over to the other side and pretending to run away. Then she became hot and tired like the rest of us and walked grumpily by my side, her head hanging down and her feet dragging. I couldn't keep looking down because all that grey filled my head and it seemed to make the time go slower.

Robin suddenly stopped.

'What about taking the afternoon off? There's a river down there, we could go and camp beside it.'

I looked over to my left. There was a grass verge which was once fenced but the fence had fallen over. Then there was a drop into a sort of valley and, not too far away, the glint of a stream.

'Sounds like a good idea,' I said, 'we could do with a break.'

'Can we stay there?' Jasmine mumbled, 'Stay there forever then we don't have to walk any more?'

I pulled her to my side and called her a silly sausage before looking around for Sevvy. He was sitting cross-legged by a big crack.

'Come on, Sevvy, let's go.'

He didn't move. I don't think he even heard me. I went over and stood by his side, looking down at what he was doing. He took an ant out of the crack and put it in the palm of his hand. He watched as it scurried around the palm, dropped onto his leg and rushed away to freedom. Then he put his hand back into the crack, presumably to find another one.

'Sevvy,' I insisted, touching him on the shoulder, 'Sevvy, come on, we're going to make our camp now so we can have a rest.'

'Can I stay here?' he asked, 'I'm having fun.'

'No, you can't stay here. You're coming with us.'

He started to wail but when he realised there was the challenge of climbing over the fallen down fence he cheered up. That was the good thing about travelling with Sevvy. He lived for the moment so no journey seemed too long and he didn't look back regretting what we'd had to leave behind. Not like me. Sometimes I lay awake at night thinking about all the things I missed. Like a comfortable bed, clean clothes, putting my feet up, feeling safe in my own, or Hermione's, home. I knew it could be worse. We could be in the Rehabilitation Centre, separated from the children for most of the day, forced to listen to what we should and shouldn't think. But I remembered our little house, the one that I'd made into a home for the four of us. Also Rose, when she was there, then Dorey and then Hermione; women I could talk to. Now I talked to Robin and the children but it wasn't the same.

We made our way towards the river quite quickly with even Jasmine picking up speed. Unfortunately Sevvy went too fast down a steep slope and ended up with his little legs moving so fast he couldn't control them; he fell over and rolled downwards into a clump of long grass. I ran after him but he thrust himself up into the air, laughing, and started back up the slope to try it again.

'Oh no you don't,' I told him and turned him to face the opposite direction.

I was breathless by the time we reached the river but even then I appreciated that it was an ideal place to stop. It was surrounded by trees which could give us shade from the fierce afternoon heat but there was also a fantastic view of open countryside and a huge stretch of grass where the children could play when they'd rested and the afternoon was cooler. I sat down on a rock and thought that I wouldn't move until we had to leave the next day.

Of course, that didn't happen and soon I was up and bustling about. We'd eaten into a lot of the dried supplies that we'd been carrying and I was hoping that we could find something else to eat. Robin had gone to the river and I walked over to him to see what he thought. He was setting up his fishing rod and didn't seem to want to talk. The children had taken off their socks and shoes and were dangling their feet in the river.

I spotted a beech tree and gathered several handfuls of husks. I dropped my collection on the floor next to the pile of rucksacks, took out the plates and tin mugs. I filled the mugs with water from the river and shared out the beech nuts on the plates.

'Lunch is ready,' I announced.

Jasmine pulled her feet from the river and ran over then she stood still with her hands on her hips.

'What on earth is that?'

'You know what it is, it's beech nuts. We went out with Hermione to collect them before. Remember?'

'Yes, but we had other stuff as well. Not just beech nuts for lunch. I want some bread and butter and chicken and things to go with it.'

'Well, you can't have those things. We haven't got those things.'

'But we still have sweets and dried apple and ...'

'Jasmine Travis, are you arguing with your mother?'

'No, I'm not arguing, I'm just saying that I don't want that for lunch.'

'Don't have it then,' I say, 'we need to save those things

for when we can't find anything at all. Now, either eat some of this nice food,' I took a bite of a beech nut, 'or go hungry.'

Jasmine walked away and plonked herself down with her back to us.

Robin sat down beside me and picked up a beech nut.

'Yum,' he said, 'This is good.'

Sevvy had helped himself too and was munching away quite happily. Eventually Jasmine joined us and began eating. When the plate was empty, Jasmine and Sevvy both asked for more nuts and Robin took them to collect some. I wouldn't say that my stomach was full but I was comfortable enough to be able to last for the rest of the afternoon. I wondered if I could have an afternoon nap but it struck me that there was a chance to wash both ourselves and our clothing. It had been four days since we left Plum and Weasel and we hadn't changed an item of clothing. I dragged myself up and began to gather firewood.

'What are you doing?' Robin asked.

'I'm making a fire to heat up some water so we can have a proper wash and change our clothes. Then I'm going to wash the clothes and dry them on that hawthorn bush over there.'

'But I thought we were resting.'

'You can rest if you want to, but I've got things to do.'

I could feel his eyes on my back and I hoped that he'd join in and help; I wasn't sure I could manage by myself. He did help and soon we had enough firewood for a fire. I put the fire together while he built a frame to support the pots for warming the water.

The first two pots we used for washing Sevvy. We undressed him, stood him a rock and tipped the first pot over him. He giggled and wriggled so much that some of the water missed and I shouted at him for wasting water.

'There's lots of water,' he told me, 'lots of water in the river.'

'That's cold water, Sev. Do you want me to wash you in cold water?'

'No.'

'Well, stand still then.'

He stood still while I washed him with my precious bar of soap and didn't even complain when it went in his eyes. Then we rinsed him and put him to stand and air dry on another rock.

Next it was Jasmine's turn. She wasn't happy about being undressed in the open and it took a lot of reassurance before she'd take her clothes off. When the two children were dry and dressed in their clean clothes and it was my turn, I knew exactly how she felt. It was hard to believe that no one was going to wander along and see me perched naked on a rock while my husband poured water on me. But the water felt so good that I soon got over my discomfort and enjoyed it.

'Look at the baby,' Robin said.

I looked down at my stomach. It seemed to have grown a lot over the past few days. Maybe the baby was enjoying the exercise and the fresh air. It certainly couldn't be the food.

After our showers, Robin and I dressed in our underwear and did the washing. We used the shower rock and poured hot water over each item, rubbing the bar of soap over it, then hammering at it with a sock filled with stones to beat the dirt out. When we'd finished, we poured over cold water to rinse then hung the clothes on the hawthorn bush to dry. Finally, we rinsed our legs in the ice cold river to get rid of the dirt from kneeling on the earth to do the washing.

By then my limbs were trembling with exhaustion but it was time to start cooking.

'I thought we were resting this afternoon?'

Robin only laughed. He had caught a fish earlier; he started to clean and gut it. When he'd finished, I put it in a cooking pot to make a sort of fish soup. We'd used the last of our onions so it was going to be a bit tasteless but we were hungry enough for it not to matter.

It was too hot to sit by the fire, although we'd be glad of it later, so we found a dry rock by the river and sat quietly, watching the ripples on the river and listening to the rustling of the leaves.

Robin took hold of my hand and asked, 'Are you happy?'

That surprised me. I hadn't really thought about whether or not I was happy. For me, it was a question of how could I survive the journey.

'I don't know. Are you?'

'Yes, yes I am. I don't know what it is, but I feel like I belong here.'

I thought about that.

'I know what you mean but I'm not sure I feel like that. I think it's because of the baby. I'd like to be properly settled before the baby comes.'

He slid his hand onto my stomach, holding the baby. I rested my head on his shoulder and that was when I realised that I was feeling happy after all.

When we'd eaten and the children were asleep in the tent, we sat by the fireside, watching the sunset and talking about nothing.

Suddenly, Robin pointed and said, 'Look at that.'

Against the pink horizon, a number of shadows moved along the motorway.

'Caravans,' said Robin, 'horse drawn caravans.'

There must have been about thirty of them. They looked very romantic, moving along against the background of the sky but I hoped we didn't bump into them.

28

None of us slept well that night. We were all restless and, about three thirty in the morning, Robin went out and got me a drink of water from the river because I was so thirsty. It was the heat that upset us; it seemed to fill the tent and there was no escape. Eventually we did all settle but then, of course, we slept later than we usually did and so it was a delayed start. We finished off the flapjacks and dried apples for breakfast. Supplies were definitely going down. It would be at least a couple of days before we reached the safe house, but I thought we could manage, as long as we caught some fish and maybe a rabbit.

As we packed our things up ready to leave, the sky filled with thick grey cloud and we heard a distant rumble of thunder, a sound which made Jasmine cower against my side.

We made our way up the field towards the motorway. We had to stop so Jasmine could pick some daisies to put in her hair. No wonder we didn't seem to be getting very far very fast. Then Sevvy picked some grass to put in his hair so he looked like he'd slept in a field, rather than in the tent.

We couldn't find a path that led us directly up to the road so, in the end Robin and I clambered over a fence and then lifted the children over. The effort left damp patches on my shirt.

'Are you all right, Celia?'

'Just feeling a little dizzy, that's all.'

We sat on the hot tarmac until I decided it was better to be walking than have that fierce heat burning into my bottom. It was about half an hour before the rain started; tiny drops at first and then bigger ones that soaked through our clothes. We stopped and fished waterproofs from the rucksacks but all that did was make me feel hotter and as damp on the inside of the coat as on the outside.

Next a wind sprung up, a fierce hot wind that forced the rain against my face and tossed the branches of trees around. Sevvy struggled to maintain his balance against the wind; I grabbed one hand and Robin grabbed the other so that we could both hold onto him. Jasmine pressed her body against mine and buried her face into my side. We had to stop walking and huddle at the side of the road, searching in vain for some form of shelter. Thunder began to rumble again and we saw a brief flash of lightning in the distance.

'Mummy, I'm scared,' Jasmine shouted against the wind.

Sevvy said something I couldn't hear; I just saw his mouth moving.

I think that was the most frightened I'd been in all the time since Agnes came to take us from our home and I found myself longing for the Rehabilitation Centre where at least we would have been safe.

The rain eased for a moment and Robin said something.

'What?'

He pointed off to the left and shouted again. I shook my head and leant further towards him.

'Over there, I think I saw a building. Even if we can't get in, we can shelter against its walls.'

I nodded exaggeratedly so I was sure he'd seen me. Then I knelt beside Sevvy and pulled Jasmine down beside me so that they could hear what I was going to say.

'Listen, we're going to find somewhere we can shelter. We need you to be brave because it's not going to be easy. You need to hold on tight to us and not, I repeat, not run off without us. Understand?'

Both children nodded. I stood and we moved as a group towards the middle of the road. We scrambled over the barrier and then across to the other side. Another fence. This time, Robin climbed over while I hung on to the children. Robin reached over for Sevvy while Jasmine clung on around my waist. Once Sevvy was on the other side, Robin instructed him to hold on to his leg and then he stretched out his arms to pick Jasmine up. Jasmine shook her head. She was afraid to let go of me. The wind was even stronger and a much nearer crash of thunder made her jump and cling even harder. I knew how she felt; given a choice I would be hanging on too. I peeled her fingers open, released her hold from around my waist and pushed her towards Robin's waiting arms. Finally it was my turn and I clambered over the fence, only to realise we'd left the bags on the other side. Robin went to collect them and then we were ready to fight the wind over the field, clinging on to each other, heads down against the stinging rain, hoping we were heading in the right direction.

Sevvy stumbled several times because the going was so rough. I shouted words of encouragement but I didn't think he'd heard because he didn't react at all. Almost simultaneously there was a brilliant flash of lightning above us and a deafening crash of thunder. Jasmine let go of Robin and me, turned and began to run in the opposite direction, her steps speeded by the strong wind. Robin released Sevvy's hand and gave chase. Sevvy staggered but I caught him before he fell. I picked him up and held him tight against me. I could feel his heart pounding against my chest. I watched as Robin caught Jasmine and made his way back towards us.

I turned and looked for the building we were hoping will be our sanctuary. It was much nearer than I expected; I could even read the sign, *Moreton Leisure Centre*.

'Look, Robin, it's there,' I yelled at the top of my voice.

Robin nodded. We huddled together and pressed on, our steps stronger now that our goal was in sight. As we approached, one corner of the sign worked loose. The wind, having got a hold, ripped the sign from its frame and it flew off through the air, landing on the roof.

It looked like the building was once a warehouse but had been converted into a leisure centre. It had obviously been abandoned for a long time, the windows were boarded over and there was greenery growing in some of the cracks. Still, it was quite solid and, if we could get in there, we could certainly shelter from the storm.

Robin said something. Watching his lips, I recognised the word *door* and looked in the same direction as he was. I could see it, but it looked to be well secured with a metal bar and a padlock. Robin handed the children over to me and went over to inspect it. He shook his head and made his way around the building. I watched as he disappeared around the corner and prayed he'd come back.

After about five minutes, he popped his head around the corner and signalled for us to follow him. I picked up the bags, held them against my side with my elbows and ushered the children over to their father.

Robin had found a fire exit and forced it open with a piece of metal that was lying nearby. He pulled the torch from his bag, lit it and pointed it through the doorway. Nervously, we stepped inside and Robin pulled the door closed behind us.

'At least it's dry,' Robin yelled and then laughed, obviously realising there was no need to shout any more, the wind had been reduced to a murmur outside the door.

The air around us was musty and slightly damp but it was cooler than it was outside. Robin swung the torch around. We were in a corridor with several doors on the right side, one double door on the left. Facing me was a notice board. In the middle of notices about football leagues and swimming teams was a notice which said, *This Centre will close for good on 21 September.* No year given.

Robin opened the double door. It led into a big sports hall. It was double height with skylights above so it wasn't totally dark, unlike the corridor. There were two levels of seating down one side. On the floor were white line markings and a scoreboard on the wall. Robin grinned.

'We've picked a good place here.'

I suddenly felt exhausted. I smiled at him as I sat down with my back against the wall. Everything was black around the edges.

'Okay?'

'Will be in a minute.'

Sevvy had discovered there was an echo and was shouting, 'Hello,' at the top of his voice. Jasmine joined him and soon the huge room was filled with the sound of their voices. It grated on my ears and I yelled at them to be quiet then felt guilty at shouting when they'd just been through so much.

'Sorry, Mummy,' Jasmine whispered, her face crinkling ready to cry.

'Just play quietly while Mummy rests for a few minutes.'

The children began to walk along the white lines marked on the floor, arms out as though they were on a tightrope. Robin helped me out of my coat and I was suddenly cooler as the dampness in my t shirt evaporated.

'Better?' Robin asks and I nodded.

He sat down beside me but I could feel that he was restless and I wasn't surprised when he said, 'I'm going to look around.'

As the door banged shut behind him, I was suddenly nervous but realised I was safer in there than I was outside. I called the children over and removed their coats.

'Can we look round too?' Jasmine asked.

'Just in here,' I said and watched through half closed eyes as they raced around, investigating every corner. First they looked around the seating area, pulling the seats down and then laughing as they lifted back up again.

Next they disappeared around the back of the seats and I heard Jasmine say, 'No, Sevvy, you haven't to go out there.'

He stomped back down the aisle and sat down on a step. I thought about saying something to him but couldn't find the energy to do so. Jasmine came down the other aisle and walked around the edge of the hall. She arrived at a door, put her hand on the handle then looked over at me.

'It says *Storage Cupboard*. Can I look?'

'OK, but be careful.'

I heard her oohing and ahhing and eventually Sevvy wandered over to have a look. Together they dragged out a green bundle and rolled it out on the floor. It was some sort of a net, perhaps for tennis. Jasmine told Sevvy it was a ship and soon the two were sailing down a river, spotting things on the shore.

I was feeling better and began to stand up but suddenly the lights came on and the shock sent me back down. Then the door opened and Robin arrived.

'I've found a generator and switched it on.'

'So I see. What else have you found?'

'All sorts of things. Come and look.'

'Kids, can you behave while I have a look round?'

'Can't we look too?' Jasmine asked.

'Maybe later. You stay on your boat.'

'It's a ship.'

'Well, stay on your ship then. We'll be back soon.'

The first thing Robin showed me was the generator but I have to be honest and say that, although I was glad it was there, I wasn't interested in how it worked. Next he showed me the water tank. It was a great big thing. Robin said it was full and, with the generator working, we'd be able to have hot water. Imagine!

Then he took me up the stairs to the section that had been the café. Behind it was a kitchen. Robin had looked through the cupboards. All but one were empty but the one that they seemed to have missed was full of tins of food: ham, tomatoes, peas, beans, rice pudding, pineapple rings and soup. I was fairly sure tinned food didn't go off but decided I'd smell at it before I used any. There were also some biscuits but I wasn't sure they'd be safe. There was an electric cooker in the corner.

Finally, he took me to the changing rooms. The showers in there were dirty and full of spiders but they worked so, if I gave them a clean, we could have a proper shower. Robin went off to sort out the water heater and I returned to the sports hall.

The children were still absorbed in their game and I was suddenly filled with energy. I took our wet coats and hung them on the back of seats. I returned to our rucksacks and emptied them out. Our meagre possessions looked sad lined up against the wall of that big sports hall but at least I had the opportunity to make sure that they were in the best possible condition. I lay the rucksacks out to dry and picked up the tent. I took it over to the seating area and spread it out over a few rows so that it could dry too. Then I did the same with the sleeping bags. They weren't wet but they could do with a good airing.

The children had abandoned their dirty wet shoes. I picked them up and took them into the changing room where I rinsed them under the shower to remove the grass and mud. I left the shower running to clear away the grass and also to get rid of some of the dirt that was in there. Then I turned on the two hand dryers (something I hadn't seen for a very long time) and held one shoe under each to start off the drying process. I did the same with the other pair and then did my own shoes. I also washed my socks through. I left the shoes and socks on the bench to complete their drying and went off to find Robin.

The corridor floor was cool under my bare feet and it felt good even though it was dusty. I heard Robin whistling as I rounded the corner to the room where he was. He jumped down from a ladder when he saw me and rubbed his hands together.

'We'll have hot water before you know it. And I've fixed the bar on the door we came in by so we can get out but no one can get in.'

'Give me your shoes and socks.'

'What?'

'Shoes and socks. Come on, hurry up. I'm busy.'

Grumbling he took off his shoes and socks and handed them over.

It didn't take long before we felt at home in the Leisure Centre. The water heated up nicely and, after I'd given one of the showers a good clean, we each had a *proper* shower. Robin had found some towels in a cupboard, the sort that used to be used for pull down towels in public toilets. We ripped lengths off the big roll so we could dry ourselves properly. Heaven.

Next I made lunch, minestrone soup followed by rice pudding. There was no bread to go with the soup but, after what we'd been living off, it didn't matter. We ate in the café. After we'd eaten, the children begged Robin to make the jukebox work, which he did and then complained loudly about the sort of music it was playing. Jasmine and Sevvy insisted on dancing despite the fact that they'd eaten the biggest meal they'd had in a week. Robin and I put our feet up on chairs and watched them.

'How long do you think this place has been empty?' I asked.

'I don't know. It looks like it's been quite a while; the boards at the windows are pretty weathered.'

'Since the Upheaval?'

'No, after that I think. The juke box has been adapted to work without money. Funny, though, that they left such a lot of stuff.'

'That's what I thought. It's pretty random though.'

'Probably couldn't be bothered.'

'Yeah.'

We didn't talk any more and, before I knew it, my eyes had closed and I was fast asleep. When I woke, Robin had washed the dishes and the café was empty, although I could hear voices. I followed the sound to the sports hall and found the three of them involved in an energetic game of football. Sevvy wanted me to join in but Robin vetoed the idea.

I wandered over to the seating area. The rain was still pounding on the skylights and I could hear the wind howling outside but I felt safe and warm. My thoughts wandered about all over the place: Rose, the house we'd had to leave, the Assessment Centre, our journey so far.

'Mummy, Mummy.'

That was Sevvy, he was shaking my arm.

'I'm tired, can I sit on your knee?'

'Course you can.'

He clambered up onto my knee and looked in my face with a smile.

'I like it here. It feels like home.'

That was when it struck me that I had no regrets. I'd merely been existing before and now I was living, enjoying the ups, struggling with the downs but really living.

'Yes, so do I.'

He rested his head against my breast and closed his eyes. Robin was chasing Jasmine around the court and she was laughing but I could hear another sound. Voices.

'Robin, can you hear that?'

He stopped and listened then nodded.

'I'd better investigate. You stay here with the children.'

He went out and closed the door behind him. The voices seemed louder now the rain and wind had faded into the background and Jasmine was no longer laughing.

'Is everything all right, Mummy? Can those people get in?'

'No, they can't get in. No need to worry.'

Robin came back.

'Come upstairs and have a look. There's tons of people outside.'

'What about the children?'

'Bring them up; they can sit in the café.'

Upstairs, we turned on the lights in the café and settled the children. Then we set off down the corridor to the window which overlooked the car park. I put out a hand to turn the light on but Robin stopped me.

'No need to draw attention to ourselves.'

He was right. There were a lot of people outside in the car park but not only that. There were about fifteen horse drawn caravans too. Dark figures were moving from one caravan to another, carrying boxes, rolls of what looked like material and items of furniture.

'What do you think they're doing?'

'It looks like they're exchanging things. See that man there. He's just swapped two chairs and a box for a table and a roll of material.'

We watched fascinated as this went on for about half an hour and then the caravans started leaving. Soon there were only two caravans left, each with someone in the driving seat. A girl stepped out from one caravan and began speaking to the driver. Suddenly, a man jumped from the back of the other caravan, grabbed the girl and held a knife to her throat. He was shouting at the driver who shook his head but then climbed down from the seat. The man dragged the girl up to the driving seat, still holding the knife at her throat then he threw her roughly to the ground and grabbed the reins before both caravans raced off out of the car park.

The man who had been the driver ran over to the girl and knelt down beside her.

'We have to help,' Robin said and set off for the stairs.

'But what if those men come back?' I shouted after him but I got no answer.

I peered round the café door and told the children to stay where they were then I went after Robin. By the time I reached the bottom of the stairs, he'd opened the door and I heard him shout, 'Are you alright?' and the mutter of a man's voice in response. I reached the open door in time to see the girl stand. Robin and the other man helped her inside and took her past me and into the Sports Hall. She was limping. I made sure the outside door was closed after them.

'Celia, there's a first aid kit behind the reception desk. Can you get it please?'

I found the first aid kit and took it in. They had seated the girl on a bench and Robin was looking her over. She looked to be about fourteen. There was a cut on her forehead and it looked like she might be developing a black eye. The knee of her jeans was ripped and there was a nasty gash underneath.

'Don't think anything's broken,' Robin said, 'but we'd better get some dressings on your knee and head.'

He pulled some scissors out of the first aid kit and began cutting off the lower leg of her jeans.

'No,' she said, grabbing hold of his hand, 'these are my only pair.'

She looked up at the other man.

'Grandpa, don't let him.'

'Sh, Melly, we'll find you some more.'

She sighed but let go of Robin's hand and he finished cutting before dressing the gash.

'I'm Robin, by the way, and this is Celia.'

The man stepped forward toward me and held out his

hand, 'I'm Talbot and we're very grateful for your help.'

Close up, he was older than I'd expected. His hair was white as were the bushy eyebrows above his startling blue eyes.

When Robin had finished, he suggested we go upstairs to the café for a hot drink. No one had really spoken up to then, I couldn't think of what to say and the pair of strangers seemed to be in shock.

I bustled about making a drink while Robin settled them down. As soon as she sat down, Melly began to cry.

'What are we going to do?'

Talbot shook his head.

'I don't know but we'll come up smiling. We always do.'

'Not this time, Grandpa.'

'Did you know those people who robbed you?' Robin asked.

'I'd met one of them before, Griff, at the exchanges. Always thought there was something dishonest about him. But in this game you have to trust the people you're dealing with. It can't work any other way.'

'What happens with the exchanges?'

'There are lots of people, mainly in Wales, but also in other places, who have left the towns and become self-sufficient but no one family can provide for all their needs and there's a law that forbids markets like there used to be a long time ago. So we collect their surplus in exchange for things that they do need. Then we take a cut or they give us something and we take the surplus to exchange it with other families. A lot of us do it. We get together every so often and do exchanges. It's a good system, usually.'

'But something went wrong tonight.'

'It did. That man Griff's a fool though. When word gets

254

round no one's going to trust him again. We didn't have that much to make it worth their while.'

'But they got our caravan and Dobby too.'

Melly had stopped crying but as soon as she said Dobby she began crying again.

'Hush, Melly, don't cry, please.'

Talbot's voice broke as he spoke and he wiped a tear off his cheek.

'But, Grandpa, we have nothing at all, not even a change of clothes.'

She lifted up her leg and surveyed the jeans cut off above the dressing on her knee.

'Maybe I can sew your jeans at least,' I said.

I went downstairs and brought back the cut off piece, the sewing kit that Hermione had insisted we brought and a roll of towelling for her to wrap herself in while I tried to do the repairs. I wished Dorey were there to help.

'I think they're dry,' I said, lifting Melly's jeans from the back of a chair where they'd been drying. She'd taken the needle from me the night before because I'd been making such a mess of mending her jeans for her. She'd done a good job and we decided to wash the blood out of them.

Both Talbot and Melly seemed brighter in the morning. They'd slept on the Sports Hall floor alongside us. Talbot was up before us and had gone out for a walk. He returned with half a dozen eggs. I didn't ask where he'd got them. Robin helped me make breakfast. Melly and Talbot were huddled in a corner talking earnestly.

'Have you folks made any decisions about what you're going to do?' Robin asked when we were seated for breakfast.

'There's a miller down Aberystwyth way who told me he

was looking for help. He's getting older and it's too much for him. I thought we might head that way, see if we can work something out.'

'Is it a long way?' I asked

'Quite a distance on foot but there's no hurry. We'll manage, won't we, Melly?'

'Course we will, Grandpa,' Melly said with a smile.

Her eye was a mess but she seemed really bright. I marvelled at how tough this pair were, to lose everything and still be smiling.

I wanted to help them on their way. I found Sevvy's rucksack and took it to Molly.

'Let's see what there is in the kitchen that you can take with you.

'But you'll want to take it with you.'

'We'll share it out. Let's hope there's two tin openers.'

There were two. The rucksack didn't hold much but there was enough for a couple of meals for them. Talbot insisted that was plenty.

'We're used to surviving. Don't worry.'

Robin took some of the dressings from the first aid kit for Melly and added it to the top of the rucksack. Then we packed our things and put the rest of the tinned goods in Robin's rucksack. We were ready to go.

Outside the sun was shining, the sky was blue and there was a warm breeze blowing. The six of us followed a winding country lane through fields covered in water.

'Can we go swimming,' Jasmine asked.

'No, Jas,' Robin explained, 'that water's too shallow and dirty for us to swim in.'

'Haven't been swimming for ages,' she moaned.

'Tough,' I told her, 'that's the way it is.'

It wasn't long before we reached the motorway again. Talbot and Melly were going in the opposite direction to us. I felt like we were parting from old friends. Melly and Jasmine kept turning round to wave to each other.

We walked for several hours and then we perched on the barrier to eat a lunch of cold beans. A caravan passed and a little girl on the front seat waved to us. We waved back energetically and the driver of the caravan smiled and touched his hat.

29

We carried on down the motorway for another couple of days. We slept in the fields at the side of the road. It was hard going and any thoughts of it being a holiday had dissipated; we'd seen a group of Guards in the distance and the memory of the man with a knife at Melly's throat kept coming back to my mind.

The safe house was near a slip road off the motorway, not far to go; all my hopes were pinned on getting there. Just the thought of having a roof over our head and a chair to sit on, even for five minutes, seemed like heaven to me.

We reached the slip road and then came to the crossroads where the safe house was supposed to be. There was a house there, a big white detached house standing in its own grounds but it was obviously empty. There were boards at the doors and windows and the garden was overgrown. We banged on the boards and shouted but no one came. I sat down on the doorstep, feeling dejected.

'Can we break in?' I asked Robin, 'Stay here for a while.'

'I suppose we could try.'

Robin pushed his fingers around the edge of the board at the door and pulled. The nails gave one by one until the inside of the house was revealed. What a mess. It was dark and smelt of rotten food. There were no floorboards in the hallway and the bottom of the staircase was missing. I could hear the sound of dripping from somewhere deep in the house.

'Do you want to go round the back, see if it's better?'

'No, let's carry on. It's not going to be any better at the back.'

'We could eat lunch in the garden. Have a rest.'

'Good idea. Come on kids.'

I looked round. They weren't there.

My heart started to race.

'Sevvy. Jasmine,' we both shouted.

Nothing.

My heart was thumping. I could see the man with the knife hiding behind every bush, in every shadow.

'You do the garden,' Robin said, 'I'll look outside.'

I looked around the front garden. It wasn't very big and, although the lawn was overgrown, there weren't many places where two children could be. I carried on shouting all the time I was looking.

Satisfied they weren't there, I went round to the back. This was much harder to search. The grass was waist high near the house and even higher towards the back of the vast space. There were bushes and trees against the walls and I despaired of finding the children if they were there but, luckily, I decided to check the back of the house before taking on the mammoth task. There was a boarded up section near the back door; it looked like it led to a cellar. There was a broken off board lying nearby and a corresponding child-sized gap in the boarding.

I peered into the hole. It was dark and smelled slightly off. Surely they hadn't gone in there.

'Sevvy, Jasmine,' I shouted.

I thought I heard a muffled cry but I wasn't sure if my hopes of finding them were tricking me. I shouted again. This time there was a definite noise. Part of me wanted to rip those boards off that instant and find my children but I realised it would be more sensible to get Robin to help.

I soon found him out on the road beating bushes and shouting. He came back with me and together we ripped off the boards and climbed down into a damp, dark cellar. We both shouted the children's names and heard a reassuring cry in the distance. Robin found a door and we followed a maze of passages until we finally reached another cellar. This one was much drier and had a grimy window at one end that let some light in. The children were huddled at one end of the cellar but as soon as they spotted us they ran over for hugs.

I picked Sevvy up and held him tight. After several kisses I felt a wave of anger sweep over me.

'What on earth were you doing? You scared us to death, you naughty, naughty boy.'

I stood him down and turned to Jasmine who was in Robin's arms.

'And you too. You're old enough to have more sense. I thought you didn't like the dark. What made you do this?'

'It was Sevvy's fault, he …'

'That's right, blame your little brother.'

'No,' she said, 'I'm not, I'm not.'

'It was me,' said Sevvy, 'I found a hole and climbed in then I couldn't get out.'

'He was stuck,' Jasmine sobbed, 'so I went in to rescue

him but we couldn't climb out again. We went to see if there was another way out …'

'And we got lost.'

'That's right, we got lost.'

I was feeling bad by then for shouting at them, and I felt even worse when I saw that Jasmine's arm was bleeding.

'Oh, goodness me, look at her arm.'

'Let's get out of here and see if we can get it cleaned up. There's nothing down here to do it with.'

We went out into the corridor again. It was gloomy out there but there was enough light for us to see some steps to our right.

'Might be easier to find our way out up there. I'll go and investigate,' Robin said.

We listened to his footsteps echoing away from us. Sevvy suddenly started crying.

'Is Daddy going away because I've been naughty?'

'No, sweetheart, he's gone to …'

'Come on up, it's all right up here.'

We followed his voice up into a kitchen that, even with dirty windows, seemed bright and airy. Considering the state of the front of the house, it seemed to have survived relatively unscathed. Unbelievably, there was a box on the wall with the words *First Aid* on the front and it was fully stocked with bandages and dressings. Robin turned on the tap. There was a shuddering noise and the whole house seemed to shake before water began to run from the tap; slow and a sludgy brown at first but gradually running faster until it was totally clear.

After we'd cleaned Jasmine up, Robin, being Robin, decided to have a look around. He tried one door but it opened a couple of inches and then stuck. He peered through the gap.

'Leads into the hallway, can't go out there anyway as there's no floorboards.'

Next he found a pantry which, sadly, was empty, as were the cupboards. Finally, he opened another door which led to some steps. Of course he had to go and have a look.

'Be careful, Robin, I don't want you crashing through the ceiling.'

I wiped the table down and set our tin plates on the table, ready for our lunch which was to be tinned tomatoes and ham. Robin was soon back downstairs.

'Not a lot of floor up there either.'

We ate our lunch in almost silence. I don't know what the others were thinking but it was in my mind that, in other times and other circumstances, that was a house I would have loved to live in. I even considered staying but I knew it was totally impractical. After lunch, I rinsed the plates while Robin broke open the back door and then we were off on our travels again.

We never found out why the inhabitants had left that safe house. I only hoped that Hermione and her friends found out soon enough so that no one else would have to feel the disappointment we felt.

30

We were back on the motorway again, on our own unless we could find where the next safe house was. Robin had taken out the map to study it. It said we had to come off the motorway at the point where there were two fallen trees but the bad weather had knocked down so many trees we were unsure where the exact point was. That was worrying until Robin realised something.

'The map says we walk along the canal bank. I can see the canal from here so, however we get down there, it won't make any difference.'

We clambered over a fallen down fence and made our way through an uneven field to the canal bank. Jasmine and Sevvy ran ahead. We had to walk a long way along the bottom of the field until we found a gap in the hedge to let us through onto the towpath.

Once on the path I got the holiday feeling again. It was so different from being on the motorway. The water was very still so that it reflected the blue of the sky. There were bends, curves and the occasional bridge so the view ahead was continually changing. The path was fairly rough and we had to keep our eyes peeled but it made a change from the hard greyness we had been walking on before. Plus there was the odd cottage at the side of the canal; most looked dilapidated and empty but there was one that seemed as though it had been done up and there was a wisp of smoke coming from the chimney. I tried to peer through the window without looking as if I was staring in, but I couldn't see anyone, although I did see a child's rocking horse standing under the living room window and a kitchen windowsill with tomato plants on the inside.

Sevvy had come to walk by my side. He stumbled and I reached out to catch him before he fell on his face.

'He's getting tired.'

Robin said, 'We'll carry on a little longer, then we'll find a place for the night.'

He picked Sevvy up and sat him on his shoulders. Sevvy took hold of Robin's hair and shouted, 'Gee up, Neddy.'

There was a bridge ahead, an ancient stone bridge that looked like it had been there for ever. I was just about to say to Robin how romantic it looked when a little white dog came bounding under the bridge and along the path towards us, yapping loudly.

'Dog,' shouted Sevvy, 'let me down, let me down.'

'Oh, he's lovely,' said Jasmine, rushing towards him.

'Be careful,' I told her but there was no need. The dog stopped at her feet and, when she knelt down beside him, he reached up and gently licked her face. Robin put Sevvy down and he went to stand beside Jasmine. The pair both stroked the dog at once and his tail wagged rapidly.

'Wonder where he's come from,' Robin asked, 'He's obviously not wild.'

'Skipper,' a voice shouted, 'Skipper, where are you?'

A man appeared from under the bridge. He was probably in his sixties, with startling white hair down to his shoulders and wearing a pale blue collarless shirt, red paisley waistcoat and green corduroy trousers. I knew then that we shouldn't trust him but everything seemed out of my control.

At the sound of his name, Skipper dashed towards the man and pranced on his back legs in front of him. He turned, ran back towards Jasmine and Sevvy then stopped, twisting and turning, looking between our children and the man who appeared to be his owner. The man resolved the situation by walking towards us so that Skipper could be with everyone at the same time. He held out his hand towards Robin.

'Hello, my name is Marty. Hope young Skipper here isn't bothering you.'

'No, not at all,' Robin said. 'Nice to meet you. I'm Robin, this is Celia and those two are Jasmine and Sevvy.'

'Haven't seen you around here before.'

'No, we're going to Wales to set up home there. Do you live round here?'

'I have a barge; I travel up and down this stretch of water all the time.'

Sevvy stopped stroking Skipper and moved over to Marty's side.

'Can I see your barge?'

'If it's all right with your Mummy and Daddy here, you can come and have a look right now.'

Sevvy looked up at Robin. 'Can we, Daddy, can we have a look?'

'I don't see why not,' Robin answered.

We followed Marty under the bridge. Ahead of us was a

long barge, painted in red and gold. Standing beside it was a solid looking black and white horse.

'A horse as well,' gasped Sevvy and the two children set off at a run with Skipper barking at their heels.

'She's a beauty,' Robin said, 'Have you had her long?'

'Oh, about twenty years, if not longer.'

We'd reached the barge. It had obviously been well cared for, the paintwork shiny and new looking with the name *Caterina II* painted on the side in gold. Marty rubbed his hand along the stern.

'We spend our time travelling up and down this waterway, the four of us, me, Skipper, Jonty the horse and good old *Caterina* here. Do the odd job, bit of wheeling and dealing, you know the sort of thing. It's a good life and I wouldn't change it for the world. Come and have a look inside.'

Robin went in but I stayed on the path to keep an eye on the children. Not only that, even though I was curious about the inside of this barge, I was remembering Mitch's words about many people being outsiders for a reason. Did this man have a reason?

'Celia, get the children and bring them on board,' Robin called, 'We're going to travel with Marty for a couple of days.'

I didn't feel in a position to argue. It was kind of him to offer us a lift and being pregnant plus having two young children with us wasn't the easiest way to travel. I lifted the children onto the barge and then Marty helped me scramble on myself. I'd rather it had been Robin who took hold of my hand but it wouldn't have been polite to say so.

Inside, the barge was all dark polished wood with brightly flowered utensils and surfaces dotted around. A bit much for me maybe but when it went dark and the rush lights were lit, it felt cosy enough. Marty made us a salad and there was cake for afters. He wouldn't accept any of our food in return.

'No, you'll need that soon enough.'

I did the dishes and, when I returned to the seating area, Sevvy was curled up asleep on the floor.

'I'll show you to the children's bedroom,' Marty said.

He took me through the kitchen to a tiny area that contained two bunk beds and little else. I took off Sevvy's shoes and laid him on the bottom bunk; I had clean clothes for him so I could change him the next day. Marty showed me the bathroom next door and the room down some steps which would be mine and Robin's.

'I'll sleep in the sitting area,' said Marty.

'Oh but we couldn't let you do that.'

'No worries, I'm used to roughing it.'

I gave Jasmine a quick wash, changed her into her pyjamas then settled her into the top bunk. She was quite excited at being up there, once she'd had a practice on the bunk ladder.

Back in the seating area, Robin was deep in conversation with Marty. My eyes were closing and it wasn't long before I made my way down the steps to our bedroom.

31

The next day was the most enjoyable day I'd had since we left Hermione's. We rose early but Marty was up before us, having been out to a cottage nearby where they supplied him with eggs and bread for breakfast. I did the cooking while Marty entertained Sevvy with a story about Jonty rescuing a dog from the middle of the canal. I decided that I had misjudged Marty; he was a loner who had developed his own lifestyle so his manner seemed strange to us but that was nothing to worry about.

After Sevvy had wolfed down his scrambled eggs on toast, he was raring to go. Robin took him for a walk on the canal bank to burn off some of his excess energy. Jasmine wanted to stay by my side. She looked a little pale and I was worried she might be coming down with something but her forehead was cool and she managed to eat all her breakfast.

While I was doing the washing up, Marty harnessed Jonty and we set off down the canal. Jasmine sat at the table, resting her head on her hand and watching through the window.

'Are you all right, Jas?'

'Yes thank you.'

'Do you want anything?'

'No thank you.'

'Why don't you go up on deck with Marty? Watch how he steers the boat.'

'I want to stay here with you.'

We passed Robin and Sevvy on the canal path and stopped so they could get back on. I heard Marty insisting Sevvy put on a life jacket. When all the pots were safely stowed away in the nooks and crannies that passed for cupboards, I went out on deck but I couldn't persuade Jasmine to go with me.

'Where's Jas?' Robin asked.

'Inside,' I told him.

'She should be out here, enjoying the view and fresh air.'

'Well, you tell her then. I've tried.'

Robin went inside and dragged a reluctant Jasmine out. I found a chair and sat down. Jasmine squashed next to me. It was cramped on a seat made for one, especially with her wearing a life jacket, but watching the countryside passing by took my mind off it and Jasmine eventually went to sleep, sucking her thumb.

There were fields all around and I could see a wind farm in the distance. We passed a row of white walled cottages on the canal side; there was a couple sitting outside one of them, each with a child on their knee. The toddler on the man's lap waved at us. We all waved back and the woman took the baby's hand to make him wave too. At the end of the cottages was a garden with what looked like a well stocked greenhouse at the side. There were two people in the greenhouse. One of them pointed to a tomato vine and the other smiled.

Jasmine woke up and wriggled about, as though she was trying to get even closer to me.

'Is there something wrong, baby?'

She looked all around her before whispering, 'No.'

'You'd tell me if there was?'

She hesitated then nodded.

There was a deep-sounding bark from the canal path. A man was walking his dog, a huge German Shepherd. I hadn't had much to do with dogs but it seemed to me that it was a very fierce dog. It strained at the leash towards us as though wanting to attack.

The man said, 'Crusher, heel,' as he pulled back on the leash.

The dog relaxed a little but I didn't feel comforted because the man, dressed all in black with a hood that hung over his face, looked as scary as his dog.

Skipper, yapping, jumped on to the side of the boat. He half crouched, looking ready to jump on to the canal path towards the other dog. Marty shouted, 'Skipper,' and lunged to stop him. He caught hold of Skipper's leg but Skipper jumped, missed the bank and plunged into the water.

'Skipper! Skipper's fallen in the water,' worried Sevvy, 'He's going to drownded.'

'Whoa, Jonty,' shouted Marty

Skipper turned and paddled towards Crusher who was crouching on the canal bank, looking ready to jump in. His owner pulled back on the leash until he was holding it next to the collar then used the rest of the leash to beat the dog about the head.

'I told you to heel, you stupid dog. You've got to learn, dammit, you've got to learn.'

Skipper was scrabbling at the edge of the bank but it was

crumbling under his paws and eventually he gave up and dropped back into the water. The man dragged Crusher away and the pair walked away from us down the path, although Crusher occasionally sneaked a look backwards. Marty gave the tiller to Robin and jumped on to the canal path to haul Skipper out. Then he jumped back on board with Skipper in his arms and put him down. Skipper shook himself and sprayed all of us with icy water, making me gasp and both children giggle with laughter.

'I think old Skipper needs a bath,' said Marty, 'Do you children want to help me?'

Sevvy jumped up and down with excitement and Jasmine managed a nod.

'I'll get some water and old towels.'

He carried a baby bath out on to the deck and lifted Skipper into it. The children took turns at soaping and rinsing him. Skipper wagged his tail and sprayed water over everything again. When Marty lifted him out, the children tried to dry him but Skipper was so excited at all the attention that he couldn't keep still and everyone got even wetter. I took the children in to shower and change. I washed their clothes and hung them out to dry on deck.

That was a good day, travelling and taking it easy at the same time. We stopped for lunch on the canal bank and then Robin and I took the children for a walk in the woods while Marty did some work on the boat. When we brought them back, they had an early tea and were soon fast asleep in their bunks. I offered to make the evening meal and, after checking out Marty's supplies, made a cheese and onion pie, something my mother used to make and an apple crumble for afters. When everyone had scraped their plates, we began to talk.

'So how come you folks are out on the road?'

'We escaped from an Assessment Centre. We stayed with a friend for a while but we had to leave there. We're on our way to Wales. What about you?'

'Someone left the door open in the Rehabilitation Centre in Liverpool and I jumped ship. Met a guy on the road who'd been living in Scotland. His wife had died so he was making his way down to Barrowford where he and his brother had each had a canal barge moored up since the Upheaval. Helped him do up one and he gave me the other in return. Been living on the canal ever since.'

'Sounds like a great life.'

'It is. I travel up and down this stretch of water doing odd jobs, carrying goods between one family and another. Wouldn't give it up for anything.'

'Had you done any sailing or anything before?'

'Yes, used to work in the Merchant Navy. Been all over the world. China, America, Africa, you name it, I've been there.'

'Seems odd that they're no longer there.'

'Ah, but how do we know they aren't? People used to talk about beings living in outer space, we never knew if it was true or not because we didn't hear from them. The same's true nowadays. Why should we think there's only us here? Think about the globes we used to have showing all the places in the world. How likely is it that there was a series of disasters and only us survived? How likely?'

'I never thought of it like that,' I said. He looked to be getting a little agitated and he was worrying me.

'Exactly. People don't think.' He banged his fist on the table. 'They never think.'

I pushed my chair back from the table.

'I'll go and do the washing up.'

'No, Celia,' Robin said, 'You did the cooking.'

'It's all right. It's nice to have a sink and warm water to wash up with. You two just sit there, you've been steering the boat and opening locks all day.'

The washing up calmed me down and I realised that I probably got over anxious about Marty. He was a man with strong opinions, that was all. He was talking to Robin quite calmly and rationally. Through the window, I could see Jonty munching at the grass and the dark shadows of trees swaying in the distance. Two candle flames reflected in the glass and the sight reminded me of the dinner party at Hermione's.

'Going to show Marty the map,' says Robin and hurried past me to our bedroom then back again.

I dried the dishes and put them back where, hopefully, I had found them. The two men were hunched over the map.

'I'm off to bed.'

'Okay,' said Robin, 'I'll be down later.'

'Goodnight.'

32

Next morning I was woken by Jasmine climbing into bed beside me. She was crying.

'What's wrong, sweetheart. Are you feeling ill?'

She shook her head.

'No,' her voice broke, 'nothing wrong,' and then she started to sob.

'Come on, Jas, you wouldn't be crying like that if there was nothing wrong.'

She looked up at me, her face wet with tears.

'That man,' she whispered, 'that man…'

'What man? Marty?'

She nodded her head hard, her lips trembling.

There was a fear deep inside me, down near the baby, and an idea in my head that was too awful to acknowledge.

'What did Marty do? Come on, tell me.'

'He, he, he touched me.'

'Touched you. Where?'

'In bed. In my pyjamas.' She lifted the covers. 'Down there.'

I sat up in bed and shook.

'Robin, Robin, Marty's touched Jasmine. He's, you know, *touched* her.'

Robin was instantly awake. He reached over me, picked up Jasmine and held her in front of him.

'Tell us exactly what happened.'

'He said I hadn't to tell. He said he'd hurt Skipper if I told and I like Skipper.'

'Never mind what he said. You tell me, all right? I won't let him hurt Skipper.'

'He came in this morning and he said I was pretty and that I hadn't to tell and then he put his hand inside my pyjama pants and I didn't like it and I said, 'don't,' and Sevvy woke up a bit and Marty went out and I heard him get off the boat so I came for a cuddle because I was upset.'

'Is that the first time he touched you?'

'Yes but he kissed me goodnight the first night and it wasn't a nice kiss, it was a nasty kiss and he put his tongue in my mouth and I felt sick. He said it was a special secret kiss.'

'Did he kiss Sevvy? Did he touch Sevvy?'

'No, only me.'

'Wait while I get my hands on him, I'll kill him.'

'No, Robin, let's just get out of here while he's gone. I never want to see that slimy toad again.'

We dressed quickly and put all our belongings in the bags. All the while I was thinking that, if we were still at home we could have told Agnes and she would have got the Guards and Marty would have been sent away. But there was no-one to report it to there so we needed to get as far away as we can.

Robin and Jasmine carried the bags outside while I went for Sevvy. He was still fast asleep and I couldn't rouse him enough for him to walk, so I wrapped a blanket round him and carried him.

'Where are you folks going?'

It was Marty. Skipper was by his side on a leash.

'We're getting our children away from you, you dirty bastard,' Robin said, 'I've a good mind to smash your face in after what you did to Jasmine.'

He squared up to Marty, fists clenched.

'No, Robin, don't. Leave him, he's not worth it. Let's go.'

'How dare you make accusations like that? I never touched her.'

'He did, Mummy, he did. I wouldn't lie.'

Marty lunged towards Robin but Robin was ready for him. He swung a fist into Marty's face. Marty staggered backwards, hit his head on the side of the barge and fell onto the path. He lay there, not moving, with blood running down the side of his face. Robin moved toward him, but Skipper growled and wouldn't let him near.

'What have I done?' said Robin, 'What if I've killed him?'

I took Robin's hand and pulled him away. Marty moaned quietly.

'See, he's not dead. Now let's go.'

'What about Skipper?' shouted Jasmine, 'We can't leave Skipper. Marty will hurt him because I told.'

'Skipper will be fine. Marty was just trying to scare you.'

'I'm not leaving Skipper with that nasty man. I'm not.'

Jasmine ran over to Skipper and took hold of his leash.

'Come on, Skipper, you come with us.'

Marty opened his eyes, reached out a hand and grabbed her ankle. She kicked backwards trying to get away but he was holding her too tight. Suddenly, Skipper turned and took Marty's arm in his mouth until he let Jasmine go. Jasmine ran, still holding on to Skipper's leash but Skipper stopped, pulling away until Jasmine was forced to let go. Then Skipper ran back to Marty.

I took Jasmine's hand and dragged her away. Sevvy opened his eyes.

'Hi, Mummy, where's my bunk?'

'We're not staying on the barge anymore.'

'Okay.'

He went back to sleep. Jasmine was crying by my side, muttering, 'He'll hurt him, he'll hurt him,' but then she suddenly went silent and I realised she'd stopped walking. When I turned to look, Skipper was by her side, leash trailing along the ground. He'd made his decision; he was going with us.

Following Robin, I walked briskly for about ten minutes. In the distance, I could see the man with Crusher coming towards us. We turned off the canal path and up through a field. Jasmine and Skipper followed us. By that time I was breathless with the weight of Sevvy and the bag I had on my back. Robin was breathless too, for he was carrying everything else. We stopped at the top of the field and sat down.

Robin covered his face with his hands.

'I should have killed him, while I had the chance. I'm such a bloody coward.'

'No you're not, Robin, you're not. You're a good decent man who protected his child. We had no choice.'

He suddenly lifted his head.

'Jas? Jas? Are you all right.'

Jas was standing off to one side, dragging the leash along the floor while Skipper chased it. Robin stood up and went over to her, arms extended like he wanted to hug her but Skipper growled and looked ready to pounce. Robin backed away and Skipper stopped growling.

'How come that dog's with us? He was with Marty last time I saw him.'

'He came running after us,' I said, 'looks like he wants to be with Jas.'

'Looks like he doesn't like me. Do we really want to have this dog trailing after us? What if he turns on the children?'

'He's not going to do that. He's probably remembering you attacking Marty. That's why he doesn't want you near Jasmine.'

'But I'm not the one who wanted to hurt her. It was Marty. Remember?'

'He doesn't know that, does he? Leave him; it will help Jas forget what happened.'

'One more sign of viciousness and he'll have to go.'

'Okay.'

'Don't know how we'll feed him.

Sevvy was wide awake by now and asking questions.

'Why did we leave that lovely boat?', 'Why did you get me up and not get me dressed?', 'What's Skipper doing here?'

'Never mind all that, get some clothes out of this bag and dress yourself.'

'But what about breakfast?'

'We'll sort something out in a minute.'

I searched through the bag and found a tin of ham. I cut it into fifths and gave them out to everyone, including Skipper. There was something at the back of my mind that was worrying but I couldn't think what it was. It was only when I'd taken the first bite that I realised.

'Robin, did we pack the map?'

His face went white and he dropped his spoon to the ground.

'No, I left it back on Marty's table.'

33

We'd been on the road for two days, walking aimlessly. We couldn't go back to where we'd come from because we didn't know how to and we couldn't get to where we were going because we didn't know where that was either. We thought there might have been a safe house around there but the only houses we had seen had been totally derelict and, although we'd passed one town, we didn't think we'd be welcome there.

It all felt so pointless and I was scared. Scared that we'd never find somewhere to live, scared that our baby would be born out on the road, scared that we wouldn't find enough food to survive and we'd die in some place where our bodies would never be found. Or worse, that Robin and I would die somehow, leaving the children to survive on their own.

Robin kept trying to cheer me up. He made decisions at crossroads, saying, 'I'm sure it's this way,' or 'it was definitely north at this point and north is in that direction.' But I didn't believe him and the children didn't seem to believe him either. Skipper didn't care, trotting alongside Jasmine every step of the way.

We stopped for lunch by the side of a stream. Skipper set off hunting, we never knew what he caught but he didn't bother us for food. Robin set up his fishing lines. We desperately needed food. The supplies we had from the leisure centre were almost gone and we hadn't caught anything for two days. I opened a tin of pineapple rings and handed them out, one each. The children put them on their fingers, like rings and then spun them. Sevvy's flew off in the air and landed in the stream.

'Sevvy, for goodness sake. That was food, not a toy.'

I stood up, took him by the arm and began to smack his bottom hard. Once, twice, three times.

'You're such a naughty, naughty little boy. I wish we hadn't brought you with us.'

He began to howl loudly and then Jasmine started to cry too. Skipper rushed back and licked her face. Robin pulled me away and took Sevvy in his arms to comfort him.

'Don't worry, Sevvy, Mummy lost her temper, that's all.'

'But she said, she said, I was naughty and that she wished she'd left me behind. I didn't mean it, Daddy, I didn't mean it to lose my pineapple thing.'

'I know, Sev. Mummy didn't mean it when she shouted at you like that. Did you, Mummy?'

My anger had popped like a balloon leaving me empty and deflated. I had never smacked either of my children before and I felt devastated that we had come to that point.

'I'm sorry, Sev, I truly am. I should never have talked to you like that. Come here and let's hug better.'

I held out my arms; when my sobbing little boy stepped into them, I closed them tight around him, feeling the depth of the breaths he took as his distress subsided.

'I've got it,' I heard Jasmine say, and we all turned to look at her. She was dripping wet but in her right hand she was holding a pineapple ring. 'I rescued it from the stream.'

Robin and I started to laugh, and the children joined in. The laughter got louder and louder and there were times when I didn't know whether I was laughing or crying but it seemed to serve as a release because, eventually, I began to feel better.

Sevvy took the pineapple ring and started to eat it, nibbling round the edge to make it last.

'Why don't we have the rest of the day off,' Robin said, 'It's not like we're in a hurry to get somewhere, is it?'

We built a fire and, after heating some water, we all had a shower and I did some washing. Then we played a long game of football with the children, using Robin's rolled up sweater as a ball. Skipper played with us but became so excited that he ended up destroying the sweater by taking it in his teeth and shaking it hard. On any other day I'd have been angry but I'd reached a stage where I felt that I just had to accept whatever happened and get on with it.

Robin's fishing lines were very successful and we ate a hearty meal that evening. Afterwards, we put the children to bed and Robin and I sat by the glowing fire, looking at the stars.

'What are we going to do, Robin?'

'Go to bed and have a good night's sleep.'

'Don't be daft, you know what I mean.'

'I don't know, Celia. I was thinking, maybe we should set up permanent camp here.'

'What, live in this little tent forever?'

'No, not forever. Perhaps we could build ourselves a little house. See that tumbling down dry stone wall over there, I was thinking we could use the stone.'

'But what about cement to stick it together? And wood for the floors? And furniture and an oven and …?'

'Look, I haven't thought it through properly yet, but it's not impossible. Other people have done it. Like in the past, before there were all the towns and everything, people would build their own houses. I'm good with my hands, there's running water nearby and it looks like the stream's a good source of fish. It's no good us going on walking forever is it, if we've nowhere to go?'

I nodded. It was certainly something to think about.

'What about when the baby comes? Who's going to deliver it?'

'We'll deliver it ourselves. You've had two babies before.'

'But, what if something goes wrong?'

'We'll just have to pray that it doesn't.'

34

I was cold, wet and miserable. The optimism I had felt as I went to sleep the night before had been washed away by the cold water that lapped around our sleeping bags in the morning. I'd heard the rain hammering at the tent during the night but that had happened before and none had come in. As Hermione had said, the tent was completely waterproof so rain would never drip in on us. It didn't drip in on us that time either. It rolled in from underneath the ground sheet and then up around us. The stream we'd camped by for convenience had broken its banks and flooded out our tent.

We carried the children out as they refused to walk through the cold dirty water. Or in the cold wet shoes that were floating on the surface. Little Skipper held up his head and paddled along behind us. We sat them on the dry stone wall that we had been planning to build a house from the previous night. Skipper scrambled up onto a lower part of the wall. Then we went to inspect the damage.

Half of the field was under water and everything we had was wet: sleeping bags, rucksacks, clothes, food, everything.

We hung what we could from the branches of trees to drain but all the dried food was destroyed. The only food we had left was two tins of tomatoes and a tin of beans. We couldn't make a fire because all the wood was wet. The rain had stopped and the sun had appeared from behind the clouds so it looked like it was going to be a nice day but that wasn't a lot of help.

'Do you remember the drought?' I asked Robin, 'that lovely drought last summer when the water was running out? Why can't there be a drought now?'

'Because we wouldn't have anything to drink, wash or cook with and we couldn't catch fish either.' Robin's face became more worried, 'Fish! I hope my fishing lines are still there.'

He hurried over to the stream. I stayed where I was; I couldn't be bothered to move. I was feeling so helpless I wanted to curl up in a corner and give up.

'They've gone,' he said, 'washed away.'

So that was it. Two tins of tomatoes and a tin of beans between us and starvation. Two kids to feed and another one on the way. What were we going to do? I went over to the children. They were both shivering so I sat between them and hugged them to me, trying to find a little warmth we could share between us.

Robin walked over.

'What are we going to do?' I said, with tears running down my face, 'What are we going to do?'

'Celia,' he warned, 'not here. Not in front of the c-h-i-l-d ...'

'I can spell, Daddy, I know you're spelling children. *I* don't like secrets. Tell me too. I'm a big girl now. Sevvy, you go and stand over there, where you can't hear.'

'No,' said Sevvy, arms folded across his chest, bottom lip sticking out and chin down as far as it could go.

'We can't hide it from the kids,' I said, 'we're in bad shape and we're going to have to pull together to sort things out.'

Robin nodded.

'I think you're right. Let's have a look at our options then.' He counted them off on his fingers. 'We could build a house, like we said last night but …'

'That would take too long and it obviously floods.'

'Exactly. We could hang about here while everything dries, then set off walking again. While we're waiting I could try to catch a rabbit so we can eat.'

'But we can't make a fire with such wet wood.'

'Right. We could go down to the canal bank again and see if we can find those cottages and ask for help.'

'No, Daddy, I'm not going back there, I'm not. That nasty Marty could be there and he might hurt Skipper or me or Sevvy or …'

'All right, all right, that one's out too.'

Sevvy wriggled about excitedly. 'What about the Leisure Centre. I liked it there. There were things to play with. Why don't we go back there?'

'That's a good idea, Sevvy but we don't know where it is. I suppose we could set off in that direction,'

Robin pointed vaguely over somewhere away from the canal.

'If we don't find the Leisure Centre, then we might find somewhere else.'

'Why don't we go back to Hermione's?'

'We can't, Jas, we don't know how to get there.'

'Well, what about where we lived before we went to Hermione's? That was home and we liked it. We should never have left it in the first place.' Jasmine nodded. 'Should never have left there. I had to leave my Angela doll.'

'They wouldn't let us stay.'

'Wait a minute, she might have something there. How's about we find a town, go to the gate and ask if we can live there? Say that we're willing to jump through any hoops they ask us to?'

'But what if they wanted to get rid of the baby, like they did before?'

'I think it's too late for that. They wouldn't abort a baby when you're so far gone.'

Jasmine started to cry.

'They'd get rid of our baby? They can't do that. We love the baby, even though it's in Mummy's tummy. You won't let them, will you?'

'No, we won't let them.'

'All right then, let's go to a high spot to look for a town.'

We had the beans for breakfast, about twenty each. The sun was out properly now and we were all feeling warmer and drier. I made the children put on their wet shoes and we gathered everything together. It's didn't really make sense to put our day clothes on as we would only have to start drying them with body heat all over again. It was unlikely that we'd meet anyone and, even if we did, by wearing our night clothes we'd be signalling that we needed a lot of help.

Robin carried most of the wet stuff and we set off along the road. We could see a hill in the near distance so we headed for that. Pretty soon the road began to lead us upward. Sevvy complained his feet hurt because he had no socks on but Robin told him, 'Everybody's feet hurt so stop complaining. Act like a big boy instead of a baby.'

That, of course, made Sevvy cry but then he gathered himself together and worked hard at keeping up without complaining.

Eventually, when we were all tired and out of breath, we came across a stopping point. It was only about halfway up the hill but it had been set up as a viewpoint and there was a big area covered in cracked tarmac that could have been a car park. The children went over there and began to sing and march across it. I don't know why but, even when they were tired of walking, they still had the energy to play.

It was very warm and my pyjamas were fully dry although my shoes still felt damp and uncomfortable. The packs on our backs were steaming as the sun did its work on them. The countryside was spread out at our feet and, in the distance, we could see a town with all the usual produce and power fields around it.

The Grand Old Duke of York.

Robin pointed, 'That looks like the place to head for.'

'How long before we can get there?'

'Well, without the children we could probably get there by tomorrow but I think we'll have to take an overnight stay. Plus we have to go back down this hill that we've just struggled up.'

And when they were up, they were up.

Robin smiled at the children's words and then pointed off in the distance. 'Look at that.'

It was a collection of houses, probably bungalows, half way between us and the town.

And when they were only half way up,
They were neither up nor down.

'I wonder if there's anywhere there we could live?'

'We could make it there before the day's out and find out. Even if they are totally derelict and we couldn't live there permanently, we could shelter for a while.'

'Sounds good to me.'

'Tell you what, you and the kids have a rest here and I'll see if I can catch a rabbit for later.'

He set off. I noticed a beech tree and called the children over. Together we collected some nuts and then sat down at the viewpoint to eat them

'Where's Daddy gone?'

'He's gone to see if he can catch a rabbit to eat later.'

'Are we going back to the Leisure Centre?' Sevvy asked.

'Don't be silly,' said Jasmine, 'we don't know where it is. We're going to a town, aren't we, Mummy?'

'We're not sure yet. See those houses over there, we're going to have a look at those first. Now, why don't you two eat your nuts and see if you can have a little nap?'

I hung all our clothes, rucksacks and sleeping bags over bushes and trees to dry and I spread the tent out over a patch of grass. Then I sat down beside the children and closed my eyes.

'I've got two!' said Robin, waking the three of us.

'That's great.'

I watch as Robin hung the rabbits from his belt.

'There's some nuts over there if you want some,' I told him but he was obviously keen to be off for he was busy collecting together the almost dry equipment.

'I'll get some for later,' I told him and slid them into my pyjama pockets.

'Can I put my socks on now?' asked Sevvy and I realised that as our clothes were drier we could be dressed properly and be ready to meet the inhabitants of the houses, if there were any.

It was some hours later when we arrived at the collection of houses. They turned out to be seven detached bungalows gathered around a central close. At first glance, it looked as though no one could possibly be living there. Most of the roofs had collapsed inwards, several walls were completely down and there didn't seem to be a pane of glass anywhere. But, when I looked closer, I realised that wasn't true. There was one house with its roof still intact, all the windows either with glass or covered in adobe and a door that wasn't lying flat in the garden.

Once I started to look properly, I saw other things too. All the gardens were well-tended and most of them were filled with vegetables. There were several windmills around the intact house and a solar panel glinting on the roof. The white front door stood slightly ajar.

'There's someone in the garden,' Sevvy said, 'and I'm going to say 'hello'.'

'No, wait,' Robin told him but it was too late, Sevvy had shot away from us and was opening the gate. We had no choice but to follow, Skipper panting along beside us.

By the time we got there he was talking to a slim woman. She looked slightly older than me. Most of her hair was dark but there were two very bright pink streaks in her fringe.

'We're looking for somewhere to live,' said Sevvy, 'can we come and live with you?'

'Sevvy!' Robin and I said together.

The woman laughed.

'I'm not really looking for lodgers just now,' she told Sevvy, turning to face us and holding out her hand.

'Helen Callaghan. Nice to meet you.'

I took her hand. 'Hi. I see you've met, Sevvy, our son. I'm Celia Travis, this is my husband, Robin and our daughter, Jasmine.'

Her smile took in all of us.

Suddenly, Skipper dashed up and licked her hand. She crouched down beside him and stroked his head.

'What a beautiful dog.'

While I was trying to phrase my next question, Sevvy asked, 'What are you doing?'

'That's a good question, Sevvy. I'm making a water feature for my garden. What do you think?'

'It's beautiful,' he whispered.

'Do you want to see it working?'

'Oh, yes please,' both the children said together.

She turned on a small tap and water welled up from the top of the central pipe of the feature. Around the pipe were rows and rows of spoons, small ones at the top and larger ones at the bottom. The water trickled down the handles of the spoons and the bowls filled and overflowed to the next row until the water finally reached the base of the 'fountain' where there were a series of holes in the ground. The sun caught the water at each stage so that it sparkled.

'That's so pretty,' breathed Jasmine.

'The holes lead to pipes which will irrigate the gardens when there's a drought. There's a big water tank in here,' she tapped the wall behind her, 'which drains water from the roof so none of it goes to waste. I've been planning this for ages. It's going to save me hours of going round with hoses and watering cans.'

She looked at the puddles lying on the path, left over from the previous evening. 'Still, I don't need this just now, so I'll turn if off if you don't mind.'

'Ah,' said Sevvy sadly and she laughed at him before turning the tap off.

'Right, that's done. Would you people like to come in for a drink and something to eat? And maybe, if it's not too rude of me to mention it, a shower or a chance to change your clothes?'

'That's really kind of you.'

We trooped in behind her. Here we were going into a stranger's home again, but I felt safe this time.

'Is it okay to bring Skipper in?'

'It certainly is. I love dogs. Sadly, my dog, Baggins, died a few months ago.'

The inside of her house was a shock. In the hallway, there was a sunrise painted on the far wall and, running down the stair wall was a painting of a stream which looked so real I could imagine putting my hands in it. In the corner at the bottom of the stairs was a copper tree with skeletonised leaves attached to the wire branches.

'Are you an artist?'

'Yes, you could say that. I spend my spare time either painting or making things.'

'But where do you get your materials?'

'Some colours I make myself from plants that I find in the woods nearby. Others I've found in the sheds and abandoned houses around here, although that supply has nearly run out now. And the copper tree is made from the copper wire that our neighbour left behind.'

We were in the kitchen, although, looking at the walls, I could almost believe it was a tropical jungle. Sevvy was particularly fascinated by the colourful parrots lined up over the cold box.

'Look at the birds, Mummy, look at the birds.'

'Do you want one?' Helen asked.

Sevvy nodded.

She opened a drawer, took out a parrot and handed it to Sevvy. He held it in his hand and carried it up to his mouth.

'Look, Mummy, the parrot is giving me a kiss.'

'Don't worry,' Helen said, 'it's papier mache and home made paints. There's nothing dangerous there.'

Jasmine looked ready to cry.

'Oh, I'm sorry, Jasmine, I haven't got another one but, what I have got is …' she rummaged through a drawer, 'this!'

Helen held up a purple-haired doll.

'It's an Angela,' sighed Jasmine, 'a proper Angela.'

'Do you want it?'

'I'd love it.'

Jasmine sat at the kitchen table and talked to Angela while Sevvy plonked himself down on the floor and played with the parrot, making it fly around his head and sing *Polly put the kettle on.*

'Nettle tea?'

'Fine.'

'Apple juice for the children?'

'That would be lovely.'

She put the drinks and a plate of biscuits on the table. Sevvy abandoned his parrot and grabbed four biscuits from the plate.

'Sevvy! That's bad manners.'

'I'm hungry. I've only had screech nuts and beans.'

Helen looked at me with a question in her eyes.

'He means beech nuts and beans.'

'Things that bad?'

I nodded. The tears started and, once they'd started, they wouldn't stop.

'That settles it. You folks will stay the night and we'll see what I can do to help.'

'We can contribute some rabbit,' said Robin.

Later the children were put to bed on mattresses on the floor of Helen's spare room. There was a little trouble when Helen insisted that Skipper slept outside in the kennel that, until recently, belonged to her dog, Baggins.

We three adults sat out in her back garden watching the sun go down, Skipper at Helen's feet. Every so often she would bend down and stroke him. She was missing Baggins. We'd eaten a hearty meal of rabbit and salad, followed by strawberries and cream and I found it hard to believe that, earlier that morning, I had been ready to give everything up and go back to live in a town under all those restrictions.

Robin had been telling Helen our story.

'So where were you headed when you set off from Hermione's?'

'We weren't given the name of the place, just a map showing where we had to go. But we left the map behind at Marty's so then we didn't know where we were or where we should be going.'

'I've got some maps, proper maps that used to belong to my mother in the old days. I'm not saying that everything on them will be correct now but at least you could have a look to see if you recognise anything. I'll dig them out later.'

'Thanks for that.'

There was a comfortable silence as we watched the wisps of pink and blue sky turn to night. Then a question came to my mind.

'How did you get to be here, Helen?'

'This was my mother's house and I was brought up here. I went to Liverpool University to do an art degree. After I graduated, I found a job with a Merseyside arts organisation, doing arts projects in schools and in the community. The Upheaval wasn't long after that and the local council made the decision that we no longer needed art in our lives. They set me to work as a painter and decorator in a big city centre restoration project, making big houses into smaller units.

'At first, it didn't seem too bad. I would add extra little touches to my work. Paint a little mouse in the corner of a room, make the ceiling into a night sky for a teenager, paint teddy bears on the walls of children's rooms. But my boss found out and put me on other work for a month. I ended up helping to empty a big DIY warehouse outside the city walls. As the month went on, I became more and more angry at having to do menial work like that when I'd spent all that time studying art. When the warehouse was nearly empty, I told my work mates I was nipping out for some fresh air and simply walked away.

'I made my way back down here to my mother. It was wonderful to see her but so sad to see how she'd aged while I'd been away. This house was still part of the city of Bristol, on the delivery routes and connected to the electricity, water and sewage systems although they gradually cut us off. The neighbours decided to move away but mother and I both wanted to stay, so we did.

'We had sufficient warning before they cut things off that they were going to do so. Two houses had been using solar power so I connected us to their panels. I diverted the stream to make it run nearer to the house so we could use the water and, the thing I'm most proud of, I planted reed beds out the back to act as our sewage system. So we no longer needed anything from the local council, we were totally self-sufficient.'

'Do you provide everything yourself?'

'Most things. I sometimes do a bit of bartering with the travellers who come round here. I grow way too many vegetables and so I can exchange them for anything I need.'

'We met some travellers,' I told her.

'They're mostly good people. Just the odd rogue, but that's to be expected these days.'

We spent the whole evening talking. Helen told us about how her mother died. She'd been ill for a while but, with no access to hospitals, there was no way of diagnosing her or curing her. Helen suspected it was cancer. A local healer, like Hermione, had eased her discomfort and her death had been very peaceful. Helen had buried her in a garden nearby.

Eventually I went up to bed. We were sleeping on mattresses on the floor in Helen's spare bedroom. Robin was still downstairs. Skipper was outside in the kennel. Helen had got her maps out and the pair of them were poring over them, discussing possibilities. I had tried to join in but I'm not really a map person and I was so tired that I had to go to bed.

35

I didn't seem to have been asleep long when Robin shook me awake.

'Look,' he said, pushing a map into my face.

It was dark and I was half asleep so I couldn't see anything.

'Here,' he pointed, 'look at this.'

I still couldn't see and the noise he was making was disturbing the children.

'Can't it wait till morning?'

'No,' he insisted, grabbing my arm and pulling me out of bed.

He dragged me downstairs where a tired looking Helen was tidying away other maps.

I slumped down at the table and said, 'What are you on about?'

He spread the map in front of me and pointed again with a shaking finger.

'Look, that's here, Helen's house, and this place, here is,' he made a dramatic pause, 'Abertovey.'

The name rang a bell in my sleepy brain.

'Abertovey,' I said slowly, 'isn't that where Rose and Charlie went?'

'That's it, I'm sure it is. Abertovey. I can remember Frederick saying it.'

'It is, Abertovey, I remember too.'

I looked at the map again.

'It's not far away, is it? Can we get there, do you think? Can we find it?'

'I'm pretty sure we can.'

'If you two don't mind, I think I'll go to bed.'

'No, that's fine. Goodnight, Helen.'

I was so excited I hardly noticed she was gone.

'But Freddy and the others said there wasn't anywhere ready for us to stay.'

'We can only try, Celia. After the places we've been staying, as long as there's a roof we'll be fine. Or even half a roof. I can fix anything up, you know I can.'

The baby kicked inside me and I lay Robin's hand on my stomach to feel. He smiled.

'See, even the baby thinks it's a good idea.'

We both leant over the map and looked at the journey we had to take. A couple of days at most. The decision had definitely been made.

Robin sat back.

'Right, bed. We need to rest so we can be ready for the journey.'

'I won't sleep, Robin. Not now.'

'I'll help you sleep, love. Don't worry.'

And he did.

Next morning we woke later than we had planned. The children were awake, had had breakfast and were playing outside with Skipper. We'd decided not to tell them where we were going in case something went wrong. They'd had too many upsets.

Helen was busy painting another parrot above the cold box.

'Good morning. Jasmine told me I didn't have a purple parrot so I decided to do one for her before she goes.'

She looked worried.

'You are going, aren't you? It's been nice having you here but I've got used to my solitary life.'

'Oh, yes, we're definitely going.' Robin said. 'You haven't mentioned anything to the children have you?'

'Oh no, that's up to you. Help yourself to breakfast. There's eggs, or porridge or toast. Whatever you want.'

'Porridge? I haven't had porridge since we were at home.'

I could almost taste it.

'Yes, porridge, one of the travellers brought it. I gave some to the children but Jasmine said it tasted like flour and water paste so neither of them would touch it. You'll have to make it yourself though, I'm a bit busy.'

After breakfast, we gathered together our fully dry belongings and said goodbye to Helen. It wasn't easy, even though I felt to have been saying goodbye to people all my life.

'Look after yourselves, won't you? Don't try to do too much in one day, that's when things tend to go wrong.'

Skipper barked and jumped up against her leg. She bent down and stroked him.

'It's been good to meet Skipper. I've been missing Baggins. And if it doesn't work out, you could always come here and we'll find another solution.'

'As long as we don't want to live with you forever?'

'That's it.'

'Will we ever see you again?'

'You never know, Jasmine, you never know.'

There was a flurry of hugs, then we walked down the garden path and closed the gate, leaving Helen standing on the doorstep in her sturdy working boots, ready to go back to work on her irrigation scheme.

So there we were, walking with a purpose and, yet again, a holiday air. The children picked up on our mood and sang as we walked along: *The Sun has Got his Hat on, Ten Green Bottles* and *I Know Where I'm Going;* until our voices were hoarse.

36

We've been in Abertovey for about eighteen months. It's the monthly Social Event tonight. It's held in the Village Hall which we're all in the process of doing up. We haven't finished the toilets yet, nor sorted out the kitchen but it's such a small village that people can always nip home for anything they need.

Abertovey is more of a home than I've ever known. Everyone here has been a friend since that first day when we arrived in the village exhausted. We should have taken Helen's advice and taken our time but the nearer we got, the more Robin and I wanted to know if we really would see Rose and Charlie again and if Abertovey would provide the home that we so badly needed.

Believe it or not, the first person we saw was young Gareth, out playing with a couple of other children. He had kicked a ball that landed right at Jasmine's feet and he came running over. I didn't recognise him at first, he was so tanned and healthy looking but Jasmine knew him immediately.

'Gareth,' she shouted, 'it's Gareth.'

He was confused for a moment and then he too was jumping up and down with excitement. Sevvy didn't speak and, when I bent over him to remind him who Gareth was, I realised that he was burning up. I took him in my arms and Robin and I followed Gareth and Jasmine as they raced towards Rose and Charlie's house.

'Mummy, Mummy, come and look. It's Jasmine.'

Rose hurried out and, her face went through a range of emotions, from shock to excitement.

'How on earth did you get here?' she asked.

'It's a long story,' I told her, 'but can we get Sevvy inside? I think the heat's been too much for him.'

She led us into their cottage. It was quite bare inside but it felt homely. I put Sevvy on the sofa and she brought a damp cloth in from the kitchen to lay across his forehead. Then she looked at me with tears in her eyes.

'Do you remember?'

'That's all behind us now.'

When we'd given Sevvy a drink, he perked up and that was the point when I noticed Rose was pregnant.

'You're having a baby?'

'Due any minute we think.'

'That's brilliant. So am I but it's not coming for a while yet.'

We heard a voice from outside, 'What's going on?' It was Charlie. Gareth had brought him in from the fields where he'd been working.

'It's Celia and Robin and the children.'

None of the houses was fit for us to live in at that point but there was room in one of the barns for us to shelter. We were already used to roughing it after our journey down and a dry barn floor beats a tent in a rainy field any day. Rose and Charlie let us use their bathroom and kitchen until we had our own. We chose a cottage across the road from them and started work straight away. The roof was the first priority as there was a big hole in it. Charlie and a lot of the others helped and it was ready by the time the baby was born. Another little girl. We called her Rosemary Charlotte to show Rose and Charlie how grateful we were for their help. It was a long and difficult birth and at one point we thought we might lose her but Christie, the local nurse, got us through it. Rose's baby was a boy and she called him Kyle John.

So now we have a new life with friends all around us. It's not always easy. Everyone has to work in the fields, even the children, and winter is hard even though we stock up as much food as we can during the rest of the year. When I'm hauling sacks of potatoes into the cellar, I smile at the memory of saving a pinch of flour here and an onion there in our old life.

The children are growing stronger and stronger. It seems like Skipper has always been part of the family. Robin and Charlie make furniture and mend things for the whole village. Rose and I are thinking of setting up a school in the village hall to educate the children; the old library is pretty much intact so there's plenty of books to use.

Life couldn't be better.

My thanks to:

Everyone on the 2006 MMU Arvon week, especially Paul Magrs and David Aermstrong, who made me believe this was a novel worth writing. Shanta Everington who provided non-threatening constructive comments in the early stages. Helen Callaghan who inspired a whole (fictional) chapter. Jane Eagland's Wednesday afternoon writing class who helped me with a difficult scene. The Rosegrove Reading Group, ie. Chereena Brown, Sarah Fanshawe, Nicola Price and Paula Southcott, who thought this was a novel worth publishing. Lindsay Stanberry-Flynn, who pointed me in the right direction. Troubador Publishing who have been both friendly and helpful in making this dream a reality.

And finally, to Jeff and Andrew, who are always there for me.